THE GUARDIANS OF THE HIDDEN SCEPTER

More books by Frank L. Cole

The Adventures of Hashbrown Winters

Hashbrown Winters and the Mashimoto Madness

Hashbrown Winters and the Phantom of Pordunce

THE GUARDIANS OF THE HIDDEN SCEPTER

FRANK L. COLE

BONNEVILLE BOOKS
SPRINGVILLE, UTAH

ISBN 13: 978-1-59955-448-8

Published by Bonneville Books, an imprint of Cedar Fort, Inc., 2373 W. 700 S., Springville, UT 84663
Distributed by Cedar Fort, Inc., www.cedarfort.com

LIBRARY OF CONGRESS CATALOGING-IN-PUBLICATION DATA

   Cole, Frank, 1977-
     The guardians of the hidden scepter / Frank L. Cole.
       p. cm.
     Summary: Fifteen-year-old Amber Rawson, who has a passion for archaeology
   and a talent for deciphering ancient codes, must find the ancient Tebah
   Stick, a biblical artifact capable of global destruction, and save her
   kidnapped archaeology instructor.
     ISBN 978-1-59955-448-8
     1. Archaeologists--Fiction. I. Title.

   PS3603.O4283G83 2010
   813'.6--dc22

       2010019532

Cover design by Danie Romrell
Cover illustration by Mark McKenna
Cover design © 2011 by Lyle Mortimer
Typeset by Heidi Doxey

Printed in the United States of America

10 9 8 7 6 5 4 3 2 1

Printed on acid-free paper

Dedicated to that pretty girl
sitting on the manhole cover

1

Two flashlight beams cut through the darkness of the museum, leaving me no choice but to drop down below the stone sarcophagus.

"Dorothy," I whispered urgently. I watched as Ms. Holcomb's silhouette ducked behind a long glass display case. Crouching low, she hurried over, and the two of us stared at the doorway, holding our breath. Heavy footsteps echoed across the solid marble floor as one of the flashlight beams scanned in our direction. Just two minutes earlier, I had accidentally collided with a brass stanchion surrounding one of the exhibits. I'd sent the whole thing crashing to the floor. Shortly after, we heard the sound of the museum's night security guards charging up the hallway in our direction.

The guards grumbled to each other as they surveyed the room. If their flashlights dropped even a few feet, they would spot us for sure. I reached for Dorothy's hand, but she withdrew, holding her finger to her lips in silence. After taking an extra minute to secure the area, the two guards exited, continuing on to other exhibits in the museum. Dorothy waited a few moments longer before she broke the silence.

"Doesn't that just drive you crazy, Amber?" She peered over the display case and removed some flecks of dirt from the sarcophagus with her shirtsleeve. "Had we really been here to rob the museum, we could've made off with quite a deal of stuff. They seriously hire buffoons for security."

My chest throbbed as I tried to catch my breath. "Do you think they would've arrested us?" I asked.

Dorothy sighed. "Yes . . . probably. Oh, would you look at that?" She leaned in close to the information placard beneath the sarcophagus, unfazed by my question. "They've totally misspelled his name! Very disrespectful if you ask—oh relax, will you? I'm the one that would've taken all the heat. You're just a kid."

"And you're my teacher!"

At fourteen years old and attending the very prestigious Roland and Tesh Private School for the Advanced, where Dorothy instructed my independent archaeology class, I never had many opportunities to enjoy any time off campus. So when Dorothy invited me to accompany her to the museum for some late-night research, I jumped at the chance. It was my fault for assuming the research would be legal.

Dorothy nudged me with her knee. "It wouldn't have been that bad. They know me here. Well, those two morons toting the flashlights don't know me, but the museum curator is a very good friend of mine.

Don't forget, I'm the one that put many of the artifacts in this museum. That has to account for some leniency on breaking and entering."

I could no longer hear the footfalls of the night security. Heaving a sigh of relief, I smiled.

Dorothy's eyes twinkled. "See, I knew you'd have fun!"

It *was* fun—terrifying, but also exhilarating. I wasn't used to activities other than studying or doing home-work. Lately, however, Ms. Holcomb—or Dorothy as she preferred to be called by her students—had taken me along with her on a number of unusual excur-sions. That night's romp through the museum was the crowning jewel. Both of us wore jeans and had our hair pulled back and covered in do-rags. We spent most of the evening stealing down dark, cordoned-off hall-ways and ducking beneath security cameras to examine some of the newly arrived artifacts.

A little over an hour after our near run-in with museum security, the two of us sat on a park bench munching on fast food hamburgers and recounting our adventure.

"You're a good sport, Amber," Dorothy said, her mouth filled with french fries. "Any of my other stu-dents would've bolted for the door the moment the guards entered the room but not you."

"I would have too, but I was too terrified to move," I said.

Dorothy shrugged. "Still, you're definitely a dif-ferent breed. I've been teaching at Roland for almost eleven years now, and you've proven to be one of my best students ever."

I shook my head in embarrassment. "Whatever, I bet you're sick of me always acting like a know-it-all."

"Not true. Not true. In fact . . ." Dorothy wiped her hands with a napkin and reached into her pants pocket. "I have something." She held out a necklace with a long silver chain clasping a light blue stone.

I held the necklace close, examining the stone. "It's beautiful."

"And it's yours," Dorothy said, taking another bite of her hamburger.

"What do you mean it's mine?"

"I want you to have it."

I shook my head and handed the necklace back to her. "Oh no, I can't take this."

"Sure you can," Dorothy said, refusing to take back the gift.

"No, it wouldn't be right. I . . . I don't deserve it."

Dorothy wadded up her sandwich wrapper and dropped it in her sack. She licked the salt off her thumb and pointed at the chain dangling from my fingers. "You haven't even asked about the necklace. I'm almost shocked my top student isn't even slightly interested in an artifact's origin."

"This is an artifact?" My eyes widened with curiosity.

"Yes. Well, kind of."

"Don't tell me. You're going to make me figure it out." I looked sideways at my teacher, and Dorothy grinned as I laid the chain across my lap. "All right, here goes. It's a silver chain, and judging by its weight and lack of sheen, I'm assuming it isn't sterling."

"Good start." She nodded with approval.

"That would at first lead me to believe it was Persian, but it's lacking any sort of design, and that would never fly with Zanjan heirlooms, so I'd say definitely not Persian."

"Oh, you're good."

Nothing gave me greater pride than discovering the true origin of a mysterious item. I nibbled on my fingernail as I rotated the necklace in my lap.

"The stone looks to be turquoise, which was frequently mined by Egyptians in the Sinai Peninsula. So that would make a valid case for the necklace to be of Middle Eastern descent, but something tells me that's just what you want me to think. So I'm going to say it didn't originate in the Middle East."

Dorothy's lips curled up in a smile. "Well, professor, have you come to a conclusion?"

I fell silent for a moment. "It's Asian, and I'd bet it's Chinese."

Dorothy clapped her hands together. "Very good! You were so close."

"What?" I asked, so sure I had chosen correctly.

"It *is* Asian but not Chinese. And it's not turquoise."

"Oh." I looked down again at the necklace.

"But good try, anyway. You got closer than I did when it was first given to me."

I smiled and handed the chain back to her.

"There you go again," Dorothy said, pushing my hand away. "I told you, it's yours." I opened my mouth to protest, but she cut me off. "End of discussion."

I sighed. "Well, thank you. It's really pretty."

"I notice you don't typically wear jewelry, but I was hoping you'd try wearing this. It's kind of important to me."

"Absolutely!" I said. I undid the clasp and draped the necklace around my neck. The stone dropped a few inches below my collar.

"Promise me you won't lose it?" she asked.

"I promise." If my favorite teacher considered this necklace important, then so did I.

"Great. So did you have fun tonight?" Dorothy rose to her feet and carried our trash to a garbage can next to a streetlight.

"Yeah, I had a great time," I said, also standing.

"I'm glad. I felt like I owed this to you since we won't be having class for a couple of weeks."

"Why not?"

"I'm heading off to Syria for a little while. It's somewhat of a special opportunity. I just can't pass this up. I'm sure to have loads of interesting things to show the class when I get back."

Over the past three years, Dorothy had made it a habit of missing classes due to some sort of mysterious work. It was part of the reason her class was so interesting. Ms. Holcomb had troves of ancient relics she had uncovered from all over the globe. My classmates always enjoyed the breaks in our school schedule, but I wished they wouldn't happen so frequently. Either that or I wished I would one day be allowed to tag along.

"Oh, and don't worry, I should be back by the end of the month, which will give me plenty of time to prep you for our final exam. It's going to be a good one."

"When do you leave?" I asked.

"In the morning."

I looked at my watch. "It's morning already." I showed Dorothy the time. *Unbelievable! Still awake and breaking curfew as well. When was the last time I had eaten a hamburger past midnight?*

"So it is," Dorothy said with a shrug.

Two vehicles appeared from around the corner and pulled up to the curb next to where we stood. One was a taxi and the other a dark green van with tinted windows.

"I hope you don't mind, but I called a cab to take you back to campus," she said, bending down to speak with the taxi driver and handing him some money.

"But what about you?" I asked

Dorothy nodded toward the van. "That's my ride. I have to head directly to the airport to catch my flight." The driver of the van stepped out onto the curb. He looked Hispanic with a tall, muscular build and hard eyes. I felt uncomfortable under his gaze.

"Sorry I couldn't drive you myself," Dorothy said, leaning in and embracing me. "I didn't want to have to leave my car at the airport, and I'm in a bit of a hurry."

"Who is that?" I whispered. The man seemed too rough to be one of Dorothy's associates. Plus, what was she talking about? If she had been in that much of a hurry, why had she spent the night snooping around the museum and eating hamburgers up until the last minute?

"Who, Marvin? He's just a good friend of mine. He's actually going with me to Syria to help out with my project." Dorothy walked me over to the taxi and opened the back door.

Something didn't add up. When had Dorothy called the cab? How did Marvin, her driver, know where to pick her up? And why did he look more like a bodyguard than one of her archaeology partners?

"Well, thanks again for letting me come," I said, staring warily over Dorothy's shoulder toward the van. I reached for the necklace around my neck. "And thanks for the gift. I really love it."

Dorothy shot her hand toward mine, stopping me from pulling the necklace out from my shirt. "You're welcome," she said, acting almost embarrassed by her sudden actions. "Sorry, Amber, old habits. It is an artifact after all, and I tend to be a little protective."

"Right," I said. *What's going on? Why is she acting so strange?* Then again, maybe sneaking into a museum, giving away a valuable artifact to a student, and then heading off on a spur-of-the-moment, red-eye flight with a strange and frightening companion fell into the normal category for Dorothy. That didn't seem normal to me, but I wasn't her.

"So, I'll see you in a couple of weeks, but I'll probably send you an update on my progress. Keep an eye out for a letter." She shut the door. I felt anxious as the taxi pulled away from the curb, and I turned around to watch the van through the back window.

Dorothy opened the van's rear door and poked through a black case on the floor. She then closed the case, slammed the rear door, and tucked something down the back of her jeans. It happened so fast, I really didn't get a good view, but it looked small and black.

No, don't be ridiculous! I told myself. *I'm definitely blowing things out of proportion.* Just because she put off her travel planning to the last minute didn't make her trip that suspicious. Lots of people put things off to the last minute.

Still, I wondered what kind of special project Dorothy had to do in Syria. Certainly she wouldn't be breaking the law. Then I thought about our evening together and guessed it wouldn't necessarily be a long shot. But was she really involved in the kind of dangerous work that required rough-looking friends and, though I didn't want to believe it, the use of a gun?

2

Almost a month had passed since my late-night adventure with Dorothy at the museum. Now that it was finals week, I had little time to reflect on anything other than my exams. Adjusting the shoulder strap of my heavy backpack, I crossed the quad and headed toward the cafeteria. Entering the glass doors, I proceeded up the stairs to where hundreds of students sat devouring their meals at cafeteria tables. I grabbed a lunch tray and filed in line. Normally, I would have been a little embarrassed to be standing in line looking like I did—T-shirt and blue jeans with my shoulder-length blonde hair unconditioned and more than slightly frazzled—but at that moment my hunger was in the driver's seat. I could worry about my appearance next week, after finals. After selecting a chicken sandwich, a Caesar salad, and a carton of chocolate milk, I sat down at an empty table to eat. My stomach grumbled as I took a mammoth bite of my sandwich, sighing with satisfaction.

"Since when did you start eating in the cafeteria?" a

boy asked, plopping down in the chair next to me and snatching a crouton from my salad. I looked sideways at the intruder and smiled. Joseph Mitchell grinned at me, looking unperturbed as always. Joseph always breezed through his finals. He didn't get perfect grades by any means, but he just didn't care. He attended Roland and Tesh on a soccer scholarship. His straw-blond hair flopped in his blue eyes as he scooted his chair close to me and nudged my shoulder with his arm. Skinny but athletic with tan skin and perfect teeth, Joseph was much more popular than me, but for some reason he and I had been close friends for almost four years.

Covering my mouth with my hand, I finished chewing my bite of sandwich. I hated eating in front of people, especially Joseph. "A girl's got to eat sometimes," I said, running my tongue across my gums.

"You got something in your teeth." Joseph pointed. Before I could dive into my backpack to fish out my compact mirror, a grin formed on his lips. "Relax, Amber. I was just kidding. How'd your econ final go?"

I glared at him and playfully punched his arm. "I totally failed it."

"No you didn't. You never do." Joseph dug in his pocket and pulled out a folded paper. "Hey, have you checked your mail today?"

"Not yet, why?"

He handed me the paper. "Read it."

I immediately recognized Dorothy's handwriting. I'd been waiting for a letter from her and hoping for a better explanation as to what happened that night a month ago. Joseph was one of my classmates in the independent archaeology class. Ms. Holcomb's class, a one-credit, extracurricular group of about twenty students, met every Tuesday and Thursday from six to eight in the evening. Yet of all my classes, it produced the most homework. I'd spent many weekends rifling through old tomes, dating as far back as the sixteenth century, in search of answers to Dorothy's assignments. Despite losing sleep because of the load, exploration lived in my blood, and I loved every minute of the class.

> *Salutations, my dear students. It is with great regret I must inform you our little extracurricular course will be cancelled for the remainder of the semester. I know this must enrage you, as you've anticipated a fun-filled final two weeks, but there is little I can do. As you know, my first love has always been the field, and I am heavily involved in a special project. It is one that will require my fullest attention and one that will undoubtedly have a very rewarding payout. But enough about me. Let us not focus on trivial matters. There's the dreaded discussion we must entertain involving those two lovely words: Final Exam. Since I'm feeling generous, consider this a gift. There will be no exam. Each of you will receive full credit for your participation in this semester's activities. The knowledge you've learned from our intensive studies will be your reward. Now, I've already sacrificed enough trees in composing this letter, I bid you farewell. Try not to waste the summer. Involve yourself in activities most befitting an archaeologist and gear up for next year.*

> *Yours,*

> *Dr. Holcomb*

"What do you think about her cancelling the class for the rest of the semester?" Joseph asked when I looked up from reading.

I smoothed out the crinkles of the paper and smiled. "I was worried she might do that. But there's something else."

"What's that?"

"This letter is encrypted." Goose bumps rose on my arms. I knew without a doubt in my mind, Dorothy had sent us a hidden message. She had done it before on a few other occasions, and each time I had figured it out. Sure, I earned extra credit, but that didn't matter since I had a perfect score in the class. I did it because I loved coded messages, and Dorothy's were the best.

"Really?" Joseph leaned over my shoulder. He wore too much cologne, but even though it burned my eyes, I couldn't help reveling in the smell up close. "I kind of thought so too, but I wasn't sure. How can you tell?"

"First of all, Dorothy never calls herself Dr. Holcomb." I held up my index finger. "She thinks the title is ridiculous. Second, the letter is too formal. When have we ever known her to write like that? 'Salutations'? 'With great regret'? That's not her style. And third, cancelling the final? That's definitely not something she would do. Cancel class, sure, but she works too hard on those exams to not follow through with them."

"You're right," Joseph said. "Do you remember how two years ago she mailed us our final exams from Kazakhstan?"

"I know." I inspected the letter again. "We've got to have a group meeting tonight."

"Tonight?" Joseph shook his head. "I've got a game in an hour and then I have to study."

Most of the students in Ms. Holcomb's class treated it like any other course. But a small group I had organized took our studies a bit more seriously. Every Friday evening, the four of us would meet on campus to discuss archaeology. With the exception of Joseph, we all got the best grades in the class. But what Joseph lacked in test scores he made up for with enthusiasm.

"Come on, don't you want to get to the bottom of this?" I pressed. "Besides, you know you're not going to study."

"True," he said with a grin. "But I'm really busy right now. Maybe we can meet on Monday."

"I can't wait the whole weekend!"

"Ms. Holcomb does this all the time. It's probably not that big of a deal. Just some sort of assignment we have to figure out that will be on a pop quiz once class starts up again." A couple of boys dribbling a soccer ball in between the cafeteria tables shouted for Joseph to join them. He laughed and held up a finger to them. "Look, Amber, I've got to go."

"But I'll see you tonight?"

He smiled. "Just make sure everyone else comes too. I don't want to be the only one spending my Friday night reading love letters from Dorothy."

Seven hours later, swollen backpack still dangling from my shoulders, I ascended the marble steps to the fourth floor and made a quick pit stop in the restroom to check my appearance in the mirror.

"Oh, Amber," I whispered at my reflection, pulling my hair back into a ponytail and securing it with a rubber band. "You need a makeover."

Our club held all our meetings in the lounge on the fourth floor of the Von Bran Music Building. The lounge had a banquet table, six cushioned chairs, a chalkboard, and a few vending machines. Joseph sat in the room along with Lisa Hardgrave, who was thumbing through a teen magazine when I pushed through the heavy door.

"Hey, hon!" Lisa said with a friendly smile. She brushed a coil of red curls out of her face, revealing heavily freckled cheeks. Lisa should've been a model. Her bright blue eyes caused most of the boys at school to stumble through sentences whenever she batted her lashes. Her parents owned a couple of hotels in New York City, and she always dressed as though she'd just come from some sort of fancy function. Tonight was no exception. Her expensive floral print dress seemed completely out of place next to Joseph's jersey and shorts.

"Yeah, sweets, how's it going?" Joseph said with a smirk.

I gave him a playful shove and plopped down in the chair next to them. Opening my backpack, I pulled out my personal copy of Dorothy Holcomb's letter and spread it out on the table. I had raced over to the mail center after lunch and discovered Dorothy had written me an identical letter; handwritten, exactly like Joseph's.

"Okay, everyone get out your letters and place them on the table." I anxiously scanned the room. "Where's Trendon?"

"Present and accounted for," Trendon said, stumbling through the door with a family-sized bag of potato chips in one hand and his laptop bag in the other. Trendon had black, curly hair in a mess of tangles. He had a round, flushed face, a stout middle, and tree-trunk legs. And he never came to our meetings without some sort of food item in tow.

"You're late," Joseph said, tapping his watch.

"So?" Trendon stuck his chubby fingers into the bag and brought out a handful of chips. "Why did we have to call this meeting during dinner time? It's seafood Friday. They're serving crab cakes in the refectory."

"I think you'll survive one night without fish," I said.

Trendon dropped his bag on the table, sending a smattering of chip crumbs over the letters. "Shows how little you know. Crabs aren't fish."

I ignored what could've turned into an unnecessary argument. "Did you bring your letter?" I wiped some chip crumbs off the letters on the table.

"My what?" Trendon asked, smacking his lips.

Lisa threw her hands up in disgust. "Please tell me you brought Ms. Holcomb's letter."

Trendon smiled. "Oh, that." He fumbled in his pants pocket and produced a wrinkled piece of paper, tattooed with grease stains. Waving his letter like a flag, he returned to his munching. "I got it. Can we make this a short one?" He moved his chair a little ways away from our group and pulled his laptop out from its carrying case.

Joseph grabbed the letter from Trendon's hand and placed it on the table next to the other three. I gave it a quick perusal.

"I think there's definitely a secret message here," I said.

"I agree," Joseph said.

"You guys are dorks," Trendon said. "What makes you think there's a secret message?" He squinted at the arrangement of papers.

"Don't you think it's odd only the four of us received letters telling us there will be no final next week? Marcy and Abigail from class are in my hall, and they didn't get a letter from her," Lisa said.

"That doesn't mean anything." Trendon walked over to the vending machines and paid for a candy bar and a couple cans of soda. When he returned to the table, he began tapping his fingers across his keyboard. The sound of battling video game characters rose from his laptop. "Maybe their letters are on the way and got hung up at the post office, or maybe Ms. H. is short on money and couldn't afford to send everyone mail."

"Okay, Trendon, how do you explain that each letter contains the same message, word for word? Why would she do that?" I asked.

"Why not?" Trendon asked.

"You don't think it's even a tiny bit strange that

each of our letters was handwritten identically? And could you please give us a few more minutes before you start that stupid video game?" I pleaded.

Trendon groaned. "What's the big deal? You wouldn't have even known I was playing if I'd remembered to mute the sound." He shot his hand into his pocket and pulled out a small, plastic inhaler. After rattling the inhaler in his hand, he took a heavy breath of the medicine.

"What are you sucking on?" Joseph asked.

"It's asthma medicine. Duh!"

"You have asthma?" Lisa asked.

Trendon cocked an eyebrow. "No, but it doesn't hurt to be prepared, does it?"

Hypochondria happened to be another one of Trendon's quirks. Whenever someone in one of his classes came down with an illness, Trendon immediately believed he had caught it as well. The flu, shingles, Lyme disease—it didn't matter.

He stood up from behind his laptop and looked at the letters again. "They're not identical."

"Asthma's not identical?" Joseph asked.

"No, dip, the letters . . . they're not identical."

"Yes, they are," I said. "Read them again."

"I can see they have the same words, but look how she's lined up the words on each of the pages." Trendon jabbed his thumb at the first letter and dragged it down the left margin. "See how these words all line up? Now look at this other letter." He pointed to my copy. "They don't line up the same. If she was so concerned about writing us the same letter, why couldn't she line it up the same?"

I concentrated on the words for a few seconds and burst out with excited laughter. On each of the letters Dorothy had made a section where the words lined up differently. "How did you see that?"

Trendon looked at his fingernails arrogantly. "Imagine what I'd be able to do on a stomach full of crab cakes."

"You'd be snoring," Joseph said.

"And loving every minute of it," Trendon retorted.

It took only a minute to jot down all twelve words Dorothy had lined up differently on each page: *salutations, extra, enrage, know, outrageous, undoubtedly, trivial, lovely, exam, knowledge, sacrificed, involved.*

I hoped each of the words could be arranged to create some sort of message, but after ten minutes of positioning the words differently on a piece of paper, none of us could make any sense of it.

"I can't make a single sentence with these words," Joseph said, glancing down at his watch. "It's already after eight, and I'm really exhausted. Let's call it a night."

"We meet until nine," I said.

Lisa stood. "I agree with Joseph. It's not a normal Friday night for me. I've got a lot of studying to do."

"Well, if the princess and the captain of the foosball team are leaving . . ." Trendon said, bundling up his belongings.

"Guys, please! Don't you want to know what she's

getting at?" My voice rose anxiously.

"Not as badly as you do," Trendon said.

We couldn't stop our search after only one hour of trying. "Joseph, can't you wait just fifteen more minutes?" I asked, still clinging to my letter.

Joseph ran his hand through his floppy blond hair and sighed. "We've tried to decode the message, but maybe Lisa's right. I think Ms. Holcomb just lined up the letters differently."

My shoulders dropped, but I hesitated for a moment. "Wait. What did you say?" I asked, my eyes growing wide with a possibility.

"I said I think Lisa's right."

"No, you said she lined up the letters differently." I dropped into my chair and rewrote the twelve words vertically down a piece of paper. "We were worried about the words and what they meant, but look!" I pointed at the column along the edge of the words and felt my stomach clench with excitement. "Just read the first letter of each word."

A silent pause followed as each of my friends examined the arrangement of letters.

Joseph laughed. "Holy cow! It was right there in front of us the whole time!"

The first letter of each word formed the phrase "Seek Out Leksi."

"Ah, I see," Trendon said, rolling his eyes and dropping his hands to his side in disgust. "Now all we have to do is find Leksi. This still doesn't make any sense."

"Yeah, what kind of secret message is that?" Lisa

asked. "Are we going to need a school directory or something?"

I giggled. "Come on, guys. Don't tell me you don't know who Leksi is. It's so simple." I practically hopped out of my chair to gather my belongings.

"You know who she's talking about?" Joseph raised an eyebrow.

"Not who . . . what. Leksi is the name of Dorothy's Ancient Hebrew dictionary she keeps in her top desk drawer."

"Her dictionary?" Trendon snorted. "Why would you know that?"

"Because I pay attention in class," I said. "Don't you remember her little song she sings whenever we have a question about Hebraic word origins?"

Trendon offered me a bored blink.

I exhaled in disappointment. "Let's go ask ole Leksi, Leksi the lexicon!" I sang the words.

"Oh yeah!" Lisa's eyes lit up.

Joseph scratched the back of his neck. "Yep, I remember that obnoxious little tune."

"It's not obnoxious—it's cute!" I said.

"So I guess we're not going home?" Trendon asked, his head drooping.

"Nope, I don't think so." I scanned the eyes of my friends for their approval. "If we hurry, we can make it to Dorothy's classroom before they lock up the building for the evening."

3

Complete silence filled the building when we entered Dorothy's classroom. The only light came from the dim glow outside the windows. We only had about fifteen minutes before the automatic locks engaged on the entry doors. We wouldn't be locked in, but the locks would definitely keep us from leaving without setting off the perimeter alarms. Trendon entered behind me, tripping over the trash can and spilling his bag of candy across the floor.

"Stupid!" he hissed, dropping to his knees to gather up as many candies as he could. "Why don't we turn on the lights, you vampires? I can't see a dang thing!"

I held my finger to my lips and shushed him. "We can't turn on the lights. Everyone on campus will know we're here."

"So what? No one cares if we're here."

"Be quiet!" Lisa ordered in a whisper.

"Why?" Trendon asked, not lowering his voice. "There aren't any security guards in this building. This is the cheapest area of the quad." He pointed to the rows of old-fashioned desks facing the chalkboard, all of which were entirely covered in carvings and graffiti.

"Still, we're not supposed to be in here after ten," I said.

Trendon smirked. "That's not my fault." He popped a candy in his mouth, immediately gagged, and spat it out into the corner of the room. "That's not a Skittle!" he said, sticking his tongue out in disgust.

"You're gross, my friend." Joseph patted Trendon on the back.

I moved over to Ms. Holcomb's desk and began opening drawers. After checking a few without success, I discovered a worn leather dictionary tucked beneath a phone book in the bottom drawer.

"Got it!" I said, placing the book on Dorothy's desk. Lisa looked over my shoulder as I used my pocket flashlight to search each page for any sign of a clue. Releasing a clear sigh of annoyance, Trendon dropped down onto one of the front-row desktops, nearly breaking the wood, and began surfing the net on his iPhone.

Joseph stood by the windows, staring down at the dark quad yard below, seeming to have lost interest in the search. "We'd better wrap things up soon," he said, glancing down at his watch. "I think they're about to arm the building."

"Just a few more minutes," Lisa said. "We're almost to the end of the book."

"Don't tell me. You haven't found anything yet,

have you?" Trendon mumbled.

"Maybe there really is a Leksi on campus," Lisa suggested.

"No, this is it," I said. "It has to be. We're just not seeing it yet." I rifled through to the beginning of the book and started over.

After finishing a second pass with the same result, I closed the dictionary and ran my fingers across the weathered leather cover. It looked as though some air had formed a pocket beneath the inner lining. I pressed on the bubble and heard the sound of air escaping through a hole in the cover. Was that supposed to make a sound? My heart pounded with excitement as I opened the cover and searched for some sort of perforated edge. Seconds later, I pulled open the lining, revealing a folded piece of paper.

"I found something!" I held the paper above my head to grab the group's attention. "Look at this!"

"It's about time," Trendon said.

"Where did you find that?" Lisa asked. "We checked every page."

"It was underneath the cover. She's so sneaky!" I unfolded the paper and started reading.

If you are reading this—and I'm assuming those that are reading this are my trusted students—then I fear I am in great danger. My latest quest has become more than just an ostentatious adventure—I'm afraid it has become a race against evil.

Joseph laughed. "She's so dramatic."

Lisa and Trendon laughed as well.

"I wish I knew what ostentatious meant," Trendon said. "Hey, look it up in the dictionary."

My brow furrowed with worry. "Quiet. I don't know about this. I don't think she's joking." I continued to read.

> You'll have to forgive me for this unusually lengthy explanation. I know it's not my style, but I have much to tell you. I've been taken captive or perhaps worse. In either case, my work is not yet finished, and therefore I need your help. I can grant you only a few particulars because it is better you don't know everything in the beginning. What do I always say? "A blind man will safely cross more roads than those with watchful eyes."
>
> There's an artifact I went to obtain but failed. The problem, however, is that there's also an evil group hunting the same artifact. It's a heated race, and I've passed the baton to you. You must find this valuable object and keep it well hidden. I can't tell you what it is, nor what it does, but it is very dangerous, and if it fell into the wrong hands . . . Oh my. I can't divulge any more than I already have. There are two things you must do to get started. First, I have placed a few essentials in a safe-deposit box in the South Hampshire Credit Union. The box number is 414, and you don't need a key. The bank's manager is a trusted friend of mine. His name is Omar Goff, and he will accept a simple password: Myrus.
>
> Secondly, my good friend, Abraham Kilroy, has

*come into possession of some personal effects of mine.
There's a certain map he has that will be most crucial
to your success. Abraham is a good tree with a few
rotting branches. I'm confident he will help you attain
the necessary items. Once you have them in your possession, you'll know what to do next. I'm counting on
your abilities to investigate, to research, to look beyond
what's in plain view. I must be discreet—otherwise, I
would tell you everything. My dear students, I hope
you know now how much I trust you. There are few
others I can trust, and I advise you to be equally wary
of those you encounter.*

*Now, I'm not asking you to save me; in fact, I
forbid it. All I'm asking is that you do whatever you
can to prevent this artifact from falling into the wrong
hands. I trust you will know what to do. Be vigilant
in all things, beware of False Safety, and don't settle
for the obvious. If you choose not to help, that is fine.
The destruction of mankind will fall on my shoulders.*

Hoping all will be well,

Dorothy

*PS—If you happen to be reading this by mistake
and are not members of my class, consider it a humorous anecdote and leave well enough alone.*

I gaped wide-eyed at the letter. "What?" I whispered, looking up at the others, who each wore a similar expression.

"Is she joking?" Lisa hugged her arms around her
waist.

"I don't think so," I said. "Kidnapped? By whom?" I looked at Joseph. What had started out as a fun little mystery had just turned into something worse. How could Dorothy be in danger? Who would want to harm her? My thoughts swirled in confusion.

"It's got to be something in Syria," Trendon said, scratching his chin. "That's where she went, right?"

"That's right," Lisa agreed. "Do we know why she went?"

They all looked at me, but I didn't know. Dorothy had been very secretive about her trip to Syria. I thought back to that night when she left with Marvin for the airport. "She said it was a great opportunity, but that's all."

"I don't know what she's thinking." Joseph's voice grew louder. "We can't go off on some ridiculous scavenger hunt. It's finals week. I have five soccer games left before the season is over."

"Joseph's right," Lisa chimed in. "It's not our problem, and we've got too much going on right now to get involved."

"You're kidding!" I said, my voice rising. "It sounds like she's out of options! She may even be . . ."

"She's not dead," Trendon said, though his tone didn't sound as confident as usual. "In fact, she's probably been arrested."

"How can you say that?" I balled up my fists, ready to slug him.

Trendon backed a step away from me. "All I'm saying is that she wrote this letter before anything happened. She may not be in as much trouble as we think. Archaeologists are always winding up in jail. It practically comes with the name badge."

I thought about it for a moment but shook my head adamantly. "No, if that was the case, she would've written it in our letters. Why would she go to all this trouble to send us a hidden message? Everything she writes is probably being monitored by whoever's holding her captive."

An uncomfortable silence fell in the room. Lisa squeezed her arms even more tightly. Joseph paced away from the desk toward the window.

"I'm going to help," I announced. "I hope each of you will do the right thing."

"What if that means you get kidnapped too?" Trendon asked.

Lisa glanced up at Trendon and then over to me. "Yeah, what if whatever happened to her happens to us?"

"And are we supposed to go to Syria?" Trendon added. "My parents got ticked off when I snuck along on my brother's Las Vegas trip. I'm sure they'll be hunky-dory about the Middle East."

"I . . . I don't know, guys. I'm just really worried about her. She must be out of options," I said.

Trendon flashed his phone toward me. "It's already past eleven. The perimeter alarms have been set. We need to go home."

"I'm not going anywhere until we decide what we're doing." If Dorothy Holcomb really did need us,

I, for one, was going to help her.

"Are we supposed to just skip our finals then?" Trendon asked. "We all head home in two weeks. We don't have the time. Plus, we don't have a clue where to go."

The glow from the iPhone screen illuminated the concern on Trendon's face. He made sense. I hated when he did that. He hardly ever acted serious, but when he did, it was worth listening to him. I started to think about everything going on in my life. How could I just blow off finals? All my hard work for nothing? But then a memory of Dorothy pushed itself into my mind, occupying all of my attention. We had gone out for ice cream almost two months ago. Dorothy had shown me an ivory flute she'd uncovered in Peru. I remembered how excited Dorothy had been about it and how miraculous it was to find something made of ivory in South America, which should have been impossible. Now Dorothy's life could be in danger. All my other priorities immediately seemed selfish. I pursed my lips together.

"I know where we can go," I said, folding Dorothy's letter and sticking it in my backpack. "We can split up in the morning. Two of us can go to the safe-deposit box, and the other two can go find this Abraham Kilroy. Then we can meet up and decide what we do next. Joseph? How about you?" He had been completely quiet throughout the entire argument. So quiet I had almost forgotten about him.

"I think someone knows we're up here," Joseph

said, his voice hovering just above a whisper.

A sudden jolt of panic struck my throat as the three of us joined him at the window. Together we looked down onto the quad yard, a giant patch of neatly manicured grass with ancient maple trees rising out of it like gnarled towers, that was centered among the six main course buildings.

"Behind that tree," Joseph said, pointing toward the middle of the quad. "Someone keeps poking his head around and looking up at this window."

"We're probably busted," Trendon said. "It's got to be night security."

"Yeah," said Lisa, ducking behind Trendon and looking over his shoulder.

"I don't think so." Joseph shook his head. "If it were night security, they would've come up by now and kicked us out."

I gasped as I caught sight of someone's head peering around the base of the tree trunk. "What's he looking at?"

"Us," Trendon said.

"Are you sure? Maybe it's just our imagination," Lisa said, almost completely hidden behind Trendon's wide shoulders. "We're all really freaked out right now. So maybe it's just . . . Oh my gosh!" She squealed as the man stepped away from the tree in full sight of the window. Dressed in black, the man held something silver in his hand glimmering in the moonlight.

"What's that?" I asked. My heart thudded like a subwoofer.

"It looks like a radio or a walkie-talkie," Joseph whispered. The man brought the object up to his mouth and instantly a static-laced voice echoed down the hall outside Dorothy's classroom. All four of us dropped beneath the windowsill. Someone else was in the building.

4

"Maybe we should just go explain ourselves to whoever it is out there," Lisa whispered. "What if it's really just security?" We stood pressed against the wall next to the door while Joseph tried to catch a glimpse of the hall through a thin crack in the doorway.

"I've got a bad feeling about this," I said. "Something tells me these people are connected to Dorothy's disappearance." I held my backpack in my arms, fingering the zipper pocket where Ms. Holcomb's message lay hidden.

Trendon clicked his tongue. "You're just totally freaked out right now. I'm with Lisa." His arms sagged from the weight of his laptop. "I really want to drop this."

"If they're security, then why is that guy still out there by the tree?" I asked. "Why hasn't he come in with his buddy? Why do they need walkie-talkies?"

"Because they're dorks with no lives," Trendon said. "This type of stuff is fun for them."

"Quiet, you guys," Joseph ordered. He pulled back from the doorway and glanced at me. "I think the guy down below isn't very good with instructions. I don't think they know exactly which room we're in."

"How can you tell?" Trendon asked.

"Because he's currently checking out Mr. Dolfrey's class, three doors down." Joseph bent over to tighten the laces on his sneakers. "He's going to be here any minute. We'll need a distraction." He looked at Trendon expectantly.

"What?" Trendon smirked at us. "What am I supposed to do? Run down the hallway yelling and screaming?" Joseph nodded, which caused Trendon to shift uncomfortably against the wall. "You're crazy! It'll never work."

"Sure it will," said Joseph. "All you have to do is draw him away from here long enough for us to slip out and get to the stairs. Then you duck into Mrs. Wainright's classroom at the end of the hall and lock the door."

"What am I supposed to do then? Wait for first period anatomy on Monday morning?"

"No. Mrs. Wainright's classroom has a fire escape with one of those extendable ladders. We used it when we started that massive water balloon war last year. Just hop down and meet up with us at my dorm room." He gestured to Lisa and me. "You two just have to keep quiet so you don't blow our cover."

Trendon huffed and shook his head. "First of all, I don't run. Second, that's a really long hallway. And third, why do I have to do it?"

"Because you made all the noise earlier," Joseph said. "If you'd been quiet, no one would've known we were here."

"Yeah, but you were the dip standing in front of the window!" Trendon fired back. "If that doesn't scream 'Hey, look at me!' I don't know what does."

Lisa fidgeted with the buttons on her dress. "Like you said, Trendon, it's probably just night security," she stammered. "They won't touch you, especially since you illegally helped them raise their wages last year."

"Okay, you're not supposed to talk about that ever— unless you want to see me in an orange jumpsuit." Trendon glared at Lisa. "Besides, what if it's not security and is in fact some psychopathic killer? Luring him after me wouldn't exactly be a funny mistake, if you know what I'm saying."

"Trendon's right," I said, still hugging my backpack. "It's too risky, and he's too slow. He'll never make it down that hallway in time. No offense."

"None taken, sweetheart." Trendon smiled, relaxing against the wall.

Joseph sighed. "Fine, I'll do it. But you've got to wait until I'm at least four classrooms down and he's tailing me, or you'll get caught on the stairs. Who's going to watch the hall after I go?"

I raised my hand. "I'll do it."

"Good." Joseph leaned forward and stared through the crack in the doorway. "Okay, he just went into Mr. Dudar's class. Remember, wait until he follows me before you make your move." Joseph pushed the door open, and I cringed as the old wood creaked. After taking a few breaths to get ready, he burst out of the door, screaming and smacking the walls as he ran past Mr. Dudar's classroom. I poked my head out and gasped as a black man in a dark leather coat stepped out and started off in pursuit of Joseph. He carried a walkie-talkie in one hand and a silver handgun in the other. I felt on the verge of fainting. How could this be happening?

I grabbed Lisa's elbow. "He's got a gun!"

Lisa's mouth dropped. "Oh no! What do we do now?"

I slipped into the hallway, clasping Lisa's hand. "Go!" I mouthed. Trendon and Lisa tiptoed as quietly as they could down the hall with me bringing up the rear, all the while watching Joseph's escape. He hadn't made it very far, just barely past the center classrooms and the drinking fountains. Why wasn't Joseph running faster? From what I had seen during his soccer games, Joseph ran faster than anyone else on the team. I bumped into Lisa in the doorway of the stairwell. Trendon bounded down the stairs with no thought of the noise he made.

"Hurry!" Lisa whispered. She started down the stairs but stopped to look up at me. "What are you waiting for?"

"I don't think he's gonna make it to Mrs. Wainright's class," I said.

"Sure he will. Joseph's really fast. Come on!"

I watched as the man closed within a few yards of Joseph. If he shot his gun right then, it would be at point-blank range.

"Hey you, moron!" I screamed. I couldn't just stand there and do nothing. Both Joseph and the man stopped dead in their tracks. The man looked up the hallway to where I was jumping up and down and flapping my arms wildly. "Over here!" I looked at Joseph, hoping to give him just enough of a distraction to make it the rest of the way, but he hadn't moved. He had to have seen the gun by now. But for some reason he just stared at me in disbelief.

"Run, Joseph! He's got a gun!" I yelled, finally snapping Joseph out of his bizarre trance. He quickly covered the distance to Mrs. Wainright's classroom and locked the door behind him. Relief swept over me but only for a second. The man now barreled down on me at full speed. In the next instant I was flying down the stairs.

At the bottom, four floors down, I found Trendon practically heaving over in the corner.

"Too many steps!" he groaned.

"Do you still think it's night security?" I asked sarcastically as I frantically searched the room for something to block the door.

"No way!" he sputtered. "They only carry mace."

"Where's Lisa?"

"Right here." Lisa appeared from the doorway of the restroom. "Help me with this!" I joined her at the restroom and helped her push a heavy, steel trash receptacle over to the door. "Trendon, help us wedge it under the door handle."

Trendon gagged. "I'm not touching that! It has toilet paper and other . . . stuff in it. Besides it won't hold."

"We don't need it to hold—just slow him down a bit!" I yelled. Trendon reluctantly lifted the receptacle until the lip wedged under the door handle. "Come on, he's on the stairs, and he's probably already told his buddy outside."

"This way." Lisa pointed to an open classroom. We followed her through the door and over to a window. Trendon lifted it open, and the three of us shimmied out to the ground and found ourselves in between buildings with a full view of the quad. The wind picked up a bit and whipped around the hedges, nipping at our ankles.

We had little time to think of a plan. If we made a wrong choice in the direction we ran, those men would catch us. My eyes darted toward the quad and then back to Trendon and Lisa.

"Let's head to Joseph's dorm room and hope he meets us there," I said, peering over the hedgerow in either direction.

"No way. I'm going to my room and calling the cops. I've had enough adventure for one night." Trendon pushed through the hedges and shook the leaves from his shirt.

"Trendon, it's not safe!" Lisa pleaded. "We can't just go home and pretend nothing's happened. Those men are trying to catch us."

"And Dorothy's been kidnapped," I added. "We can't ignore that."

Trendon grunted in frustration. "Why is Joseph's dorm room the rally point? How do we know he won't be followed there?"

During our escape some of my hair had pulled free from my ponytail, and it now whipped annoyingly across my face as the wind began to blow harder. I reworked my hair and gave my backpack's straps a sharp tug to secure it on my shoulders. "I don't know if it's safe or not," I said. "But that's where he's going, and we can't just leave him. He won't know where we are."

Trendon pulled his iPhone out from his pocket. "I'll text him." He started typing, but I snatched the phone from his fingers. "Hey!"

"Stop it, Trendon!" I hissed. "We're in big trouble, and we've got to think this through."

"We can't stay here," Lisa chimed in.

"Fine, let's go to Joe's," Trendon said, throwing his hands up in defeat. "Now give me back my phone."

A deafening crash erupted inside the building. I guessed the man had kicked through the door, sending the trash receptacle and its contents across the floor. He probably wouldn't think to look in the classroom, but it would only be a matter of moments before he made it outside and charged around the corner.

Trendon started toward the front of the building, but I snagged his arm. "Not that way!" I said. "We can't go through the quad; we'll get spotted by the other guy."

"Then which way?" Trendon asked, annoyed. "Joseph's dorm is clear on the other side of campus."

We needed to stay hidden. If only the buildings didn't operate on a time-lock security system. The course buildings lined up in such a way we could have easily passed through the hallways completely covered, with the exception of the hundred feet or so between structures.

"What about down there?" I asked, pointing to where the grass ended near the rear of the buildings. The ground there made a drastic slope to a drainage ditch, which separated the campus from the surrounding forest. The ditch normally held rainwater and emptied into a main sewer drain a quarter mile to the north near the campus's gated front entry. But it hadn't rained in over a month, and the ditch contained only a shallow trail of murky water. "We could take that all the way to the gate and then work our way back to the dorms."

"Take the sewer?" Trendon asked, a little too loudly. From somewhere just beyond the front of the building, a voice chirped over the walkie-talkie. "The sewer?" he repeated, lowering his voice.

"It's just the drain for rainwater," I reasoned. "It's low enough that we can stay out of sight." I looked at Lisa, who stared down at her beautiful and expensive dress.

"Uh . . . well," Lisa said, her shoulders sagging. She definitely didn't seem too thrilled about the idea. "I'll just buy a replacement." She bent down and removed her sandals.

"Let's go." I pushed Trendon in the back, and he grunted his disapproval.

At two in the morning, the three of us arrived at Joseph's dorm hall. The ditch ended up being filled with more water than a public swimming pool by the time we reached the gated entryway. But the slippery concrete walls made it too difficult for us to climb out before the pool, and with no other option, we waded through the muck.

Trendon stomped brown, muddy footprints across the marble floor of the foyer before he sat down in a pink wing-backed chair next to a pay phone. His layer of mud ended in an almost perfect line across his chest, where he had held his laptop and iPhone above his head.

"I hope Joseph has some hand sanitizer," he grunted, smearing mud from his pants onto the chair arms. "I think I've got mosquito larvae lodged in my underwear." He looked very annoyed at his current situation. Lisa stopped in the public restrooms for a moment and returned with several wads of paper towels that she handed to each of us. After cleaning most of the mud off our skin, we took the elevator to the third floor.

The hall was empty. Since it was a Friday night, I knew most of the boys would still be up watching TV or playing video games in their rooms, but the halls would be virtually vacant aside from an occasional student darting to the restrooms. A strict in-room curfew started at midnight, which meant the resident assistant would soon be around on his patrol. Because none of us had filled out overnight passes, we would certainly receive detention or worse from our own halls for our absences.

"Which room is his?" I asked, staring expectantly at Trendon.

"Oh yeah, I guess you guys wouldn't know that, huh?" he said. "It's just down past the information board."

One of the fluorescent bulbs just overhead flickered, on the verge of sputtering out. Hundreds of announcements and intramural sports sign-up sheets plastered every possible inch of available space on the corkboard.

"Over here," Trendon instructed. He stood in front of room 361 with his hand poised to knock but hesitated.

"What are you waiting for?" Lisa asked. Trendon gave me a confused look and then stared down at the doorknob again. Somebody had already opened the door slightly. He pushed, and it opened all the way, revealing a dark bedroom. The light from the hall illuminated the opening, and the three of us stepped back cautiously from the scene. Joseph's bedroom had been ransacked. Coils and batting poked up from the mattress on his overturned bed. Every drawer in his dresser had been pulled open and their contents—underwear, socks, and blue jeans—were scattered across the gray carpet. Joseph's minifridge and microwave lay busted in mangled heaps of metal and glass. I covered my mouth with my hand.

"I'm thinking your rooms look the same," a voice said from behind us, causing me to jump.

Joseph still wore his soccer uniform, but he had a bath towel draped over his shoulders, which he used to dry his hair. A large bandage was wrapped around the top of his forehead, and the end of a gash, still red with blood, poked out where he hadn't completely covered it.

My hand instinctively shot toward the wound. "What happened?" I gasped.

Joseph flinched, dodging away from my fingers. "Whoa, easy—still a little sore." He forced a smile.

"Did that dude shoot you?" Trendon asked.

"No, I fell from the fire escape and hit my head against a rock. I probably need stitches, but I guess we won't have time for that." Joseph grimaced. "Come on, let's get inside and talk."

He tossed a couple of sweatshirts at Lisa and me and righted his overturned desk chair. "I don't think it'll be long before they come back," he said, pulling a duffle bag from the ruin of his wardrobe. He stuffed some more clothes and a box of wheat crackers in the bag as he talked. "Like I said, I'm almost positive they've been to your rooms as well."

"How could they know where we live?" Lisa asked.

"They found us in Dorothy's classroom pretty easily. These guys are professionals," I said.

Trendon growled. "If they damaged any of my stuff—"

"What were they looking for?" Lisa asked, her voice trembling. She pulled the sweatshirt over her completely soiled dress and stared down at her bare feet. Somewhere in the festering pond of the drainage ditch, she had accidentally let go of her sandals.

"I think it's obvious, don't you?" I waved the letter in front of her. "They probably want whatever it is we'll find out from this Abraham guy." I felt very anxious. We needed to keep moving. Standing in Joseph's ransacked bedroom felt unsafe. We'd only narrowly escaped from Dorothy's classroom. If those guys discovered we were at the dorms, I didn't think we'd get lucky again.

"Maybe we should just give it to them," Lisa whimpered.

I blinked and then looked quickly at the others before blurting, "You're not serious. These criminals have Dorothy! If we give them what she was looking for, they'll probably kill her!"

Lisa's head bowed even lower. "I can't handle this. I'm scared." She buried her face in her hands.

"If I find so much as one broken game cartridge—" Trendon paced back and forth in the room, carelessly trampling Joseph's belongings.

"Cool it, Trendon!" Joseph barked. "We need to plan our next move." He looked to me. "What do you think we should do?"

Joseph's sudden attention caught me off guard. Sure they elected me as their president over our little archaeology organization, but Joseph acted more like a leader than I did. He made it possible for us to escape. I thought back to the hallway and how slowly and almost deliberately he had run away from the man with the gun even though his own life was in danger.

I puffed my cheeks out. "I say we split up like I suggested before. Two of us go to the bank, and the other two find Abraham Kilroy." I glanced down at the letter to confirm I had pronounced his name correctly. "If we're lucky, they won't know where we're going. This letter gives us a head start."

Up to that point, Trendon had been ignoring our conversation, mumbling angrily about his possessions. When I mentioned our game plan, he stopped pacing. "Forget it! I'm not going anywhere but home. I'm going to do an inventory of all my valuables, I'm going to call the police and file a report, and then I'm ordering a giant tub of spicy hot wings, and eating until I throw up!" He exhaled loudly. "I'd love to stay and keep playing with you guys, but I have had it." He started for the door, but I burst in front of him with my fist cocked and ready to fire. "Out of my way, gorgeous!" he said, trying to shoulder past.

"Trendon, think about it," I said. "You're not going to be safe there. Those guys want what we have. They'll stop at nothing until they get it." My hand remained in striking position.

"If you hit me, I'll sue," Trendon said, his eyes glued to my poised fist.

"I'm not going to hit you because you're going to listen to reason. What's gonna happen in the middle of the night when you're all by yourself and that guy with the gun breaks into your room? Huh? Do you think he's gonna just let you go when you say you don't have Dorothy's letter?"

Trendon groaned. "You're impossible!" He glared at me for another minute and then collapsed into Joseph's mangled beanbag chair. "Fine."

Joseph stood and draped the carrying strap of his duffle bag over his shoulders. After checking his watch, he looked up at our group. "It's almost 3:00 a.m. That gives us seven hours until the bank opens. We'll need to take a cab outside of campus so we can be there right when they unlock the doors. Lisa and I will take a quick detour to her dorm to get her some shoes, and then we'll head to the safe-deposit box. You two see what you can find out about this Abraham guy."

"We're starting now?" Trendon asked. "Aren't you forgetting sleep time?"

"I think we need to move right away. Besides, where are we going to sleep?" Joseph asked. "We can't stay here. Who's going to let us bunk this late at night?"

"Could it be possible we're just blowing this way out of proportion?" Trendon looked pleadingly at me. I shook my head slow and deliberately. Trendon frowned. "So that means I miss a good night's rest and I'm stuck with Indiana Jane, huh?"

My eyes narrowed. I agreed that we should get started immediately, but the team assignments disappointed me. I'd hoped Joseph would want to go with me. But not wanting to create an awkward scene, I merely shrugged my shoulders in agreement.

"No one's better at stalking people online than you, Trendon. But if you want to hang out on campus a little while longer while those goons are still here, be my guest," Joseph said.

"I don't want to hang out here either," Lisa muttered. "I don't need shoes."

"We might have to run a lot. You need something," Joseph said.

"Then let's just stop at a department store, and I'll buy new ones." She pulled the gold chain out from around her neck, revealing three plastic credit cards attached at the end.

"Nice accessory." Trendon sounded impressed. "I didn't know Visa was a birthstone."

"Nothing's going to be open this early. You'll have to stop at your room," I said.

"Then it's settled. Let's meet up at 9:00 p.m. in McGregor Park off Landry Avenue. That should give us enough time to get everything we need," Joseph said.

I nodded. "Yes, but don't leave until everyone shows up, just in case we're being followed. Are you ready, partner?" I tilted my head toward Trendon.

Trendon gnawed on his lip. "Oh brother, I'm in for a long night."

5

I rarely left campus during the school year. From time to time, I would join my friends at a pizza parlor a few blocks into town or at McGregor Park to play frisbee, but the school provided everything I needed within its gates. Wandering the poorly lit streets with Trendon providing the directions, I felt out of my element.

The road leading up to the entryway of the school connected with Main Street, which teemed with a variety of fast food restaurants, office buildings, and the occasional outlet store. We stopped twice at twenty-four-hour gas stations to allow Trendon an opportunity to stock up on the essentials: colas, sour gummy candies, and jumbo bags of potato chips. Despite not eating for over twelve hours, I wasn't hungry. Something about being chased by men with guns caused my appetite to vanish.

For the most part we journeyed in silence as Trendon played with his iPhone, searching for any sort of web presence from someone named Abraham

Kilroy. At just after 7:00 a.m., he yawned obnoxiously and pumped his fist in celebration.

"Found the goober!" he said. "We passed his street about four miles back. Oh well." His hand darted out toward me. "I'll take some more Rolos, please," he grunted.

"You're all out," I said, trying to hide my agitation. Since Trendon owned the technology and he was very skilled at using it, I had reluctantly taken on the task of being his personal secretary. His constant barking for more snacks had pushed me to my limit.

"All out?" Trendon looked up from the miniature screen and scratched the puffy circles under his eyes. "Did you eat them all?"

I inwardly counted to ten. "No, I haven't eaten any of your junk, but you've been wolfing it down nonstop for four hours now!"

Trendon examined me with suspicious eyes before waving his hand dismissively. "No worries. My GPS will locate more."

I released an exasperated sigh. "Trendon, no! We're going to Abraham's house right now. I'm tired of walking in circles, watching you eat."

Though he griped each time we passed a service station, Trendon led us straight to Abraham's neighborhood. Tall and skinny with two floors, hardly any yard to speak of, and no garage, the houses in this part of town looked more like apartments than actual homes.

"All right," Trendon said, pointing to the left side

of the road. "Our dude should be in that house there, 114½ Bingham Street."

"Are you sure this is the place?" I asked, stopping on the stoop and pulling my hair back from my eyes.

"Yeah, I guess," Trendon answered, not too convincingly. "From what I found, there happen to be three Abraham Kilroys within a thirty-mile radius of the school. Go figure. I cross-referenced all of them with any hint of a relationship with Dorothy Holcomb, and I found a two-year-old article published in Arch Weekly with his name mentioned as an intern under Ms. H. Fortunately, the article included his middle initial in the byline. It's W, which stands for Winneford—gag me. I was able to search through Roland and Tesh's campus directories and found where he lived last year in a duplex on the other side of town." Trendon rattled off his research like he was reading items on a grocery list. "Turns out, he was evicted in January of the following year and isn't listed in any current directories or even in the online yellow pages. Of course, I have other means of pinpointing people. Our guy has a current eBay account with the handle of CaptainKip226. Three months ago, he included his address on his profile and bingo." Without looking up from his screen, Trendon gestured toward the small apartment.

I laughed. At times, Trendon's brilliance literally dumbfounded me.

Trendon frowned. "But I don't know, maybe he's moved since then. Plus, I always get confused when they throw a fraction on the end of the address. I think that's ridiculous. One-half? Does he live in half a house?" He glanced up for the first time since approaching the humble residence and smirked. "Oh, I guess he does."

I yawned and stumbled, catching my balance against the doorjamb. "What time is it?"

"Almost 8:30." Trendon answered.

"I need a nap," I said, trying to widen my eyes and blink away the fatigue.

"Me too," Trendon agreed. "And some snacks would be swell." As if on cue, his stomach gurgled. "What I wouldn't give for a bag of something munchy and a can of fizz."

I rapped my knuckles hard against the door and moved back a step from the entryway, feeling a tinge of apprehension. What if this wasn't the place? Trendon's exhaustive research would be for nothing.

Several moments went by without any sound of stirring beyond the door. Finally, Trendon nudged me as the deadbolt clicked and the door opened. A man in his early twenties wearing hospital scrubs and several weeks' growth of stubble stood in the entry. He pressed his lips tightly together and seemed annoyed.

"Yes? Can I help you?" he asked, scratching at his left nostril.

"Actually yes, I hope," I said, startled by his sudden appearance. "We're looking for someone and we need your help."

The man waved his hand dismissively. "It's too early in the morning, and I don't donate to charities, so unless you're selling cookies . . ."

"Cookies," Trendon whispered behind me. "Oh, how I wish."

I shook my head. "We're not asking for money."

The man's eyes passed between the two of us. "Sorry, kids, no time." He turned and began to shut the door behind him.

"Are you Abraham Kilroy?" I blurted out. The man paused, leaving the door just inches away from being shut. I leaned forward, trying to see his reaction. He looked over his shoulder and stared suspiciously at me.

"Never heard of him." He slammed the door and quickly locked the deadbolt. It happened so abruptly, I had little time to react.

"Well, there goes that."

"Not quite." Trendon handed me his iPhone with the image of CaptainKip226's profile photo—a dead ringer for the man we'd just talked to.

I scowled and knocked on the door. "Look, we know it's you, Abraham. We just want to talk."

"Go away!" Abraham shouted. "I don't have time to talk with some dumb kids."

"Does the name Dorothy Holcomb mean anything to you?" Trendon asked.

Abraham fell silent for a moment. "I don't know who that is. You've got the wrong house and the wrong Abraham Kilroy, so if you don't mind—"

"Abraham!" I pounded on the door. "Dorothy's in a lot of trouble. She's been taken by some really bad people, and we need your help!" I looked at Trendon, who could only offer an encouraging nod. If Abraham truly interned under Dorothy Holcomb, he would have to respond.

Beyond the door, the deadbolt unlocked, and after some hesitation, the door opened. Abraham's face looked pale. I hadn't noticed during our initial conversation, but the man appeared rather sickly. Dark red circles etched below his sunken, bloodshot eyes.

"What happened to her?" he rasped.

"We think she was kidnapped, and we're not sure what they're planning to do to her."

Abraham considered this information, rubbing his head with his hand and coughing into a handkerchief.

"What's wrong with you, dude?" Trendon asked, taking a precautionary step back to avoid the germs.

"I've got strep throat. I think. Here, come in, and we'll talk." He left the door open and ambled into an adjoining living room.

Trendon leaned in next to me and whispered. "I'm not in the mood for a case of strep throat."

I ignored him and followed Abraham into the small house. Abraham plopped down on a threadbare sofa and motioned toward two blue recliners, also worn and patched. Parts of their wooden frames poked out at the corners. I sat down to the sound of groaning springs. Trendon opted to stand in the corner.

"So what's wrong with Dorothy?" he asked.

"We're not sure, but we think she's still alive," I said.

"It's that bad, huh?" Abraham gnawed on his lip.

"She's always getting in way over her head."

"Yeah, but this is different." I leaned forward in the recliner. "She was able to send a message to us, and she told us to find you. Do you have any idea why?"

"I don't know," he said, averting his eyes from mine.

I could sense he wasn't telling the truth. "She wrote that you have some sort of map, something you took."

Abraham looked up, alarmed. "How could she know that?" He stared down at his upturned palms, deep in thought. "I didn't . . . it wasn't supposed to . . . . How could she know that?" he repeated.

"What is it exactly?" Trendon asked.

"It's supposedly very valuable. Look, I'm not the only guilty one. Dorothy has been on dozens of digs funded by various organizations. Sure she helps them find what they're looking for, but that doesn't stop her from taking something for herself. That map should've been handed over to a museum, but she kept it in the fire safe in her closet."

"You broke into her house?" Trendon asked.

"No," Abraham said, shaking his head. "About a month ago she had to go to Syria for some job interview or something. She was going to be gone for a few weeks, so she gave me a key to her apartment to go water her houseplants while she was gone."

"That was the last time we saw her," I said, looking at Trendon. "She cancelled classes and took a sabbatical. We were supposed to resume classes next week, but then all this happened." I looked down at my hands in my lap and felt my throat tighten.

Abraham had a pained look in his eyes as he stared at me. "You were her archaeology students, huh?" He wiped his nose with the back of his hand. "She's always talking about you guys."

"She's a great teacher and a good friend," I said. I could feel my eyes welling with tears. "That's why we need to know what happened to her. We need to know everything you know."

"But I don't know anything. I was watering those dumb plants one night, and I saw the safe in her bedroom closet. I thought I could open it." Abraham buried his face in his hands. "She's pretty smart when it comes to archaeology, but her combination was easy to guess."

"So you stole her stuff?" I asked.

Abraham looked up at me before bowing his head again in embarrassment. "It was stupid. I needed money and thought maybe she kept some cash stashed in the safe."

"How did you think you'd get away with it, especially if you had a key to her house?" Trendon asked.

"I made it look like a burglary. I tore up some stuff, overturned her bed, and broke a window. I even filed a police report. But she didn't have any money in the safe, just some artifacts, and a map. I took it and a few other things that looked valuable, figuring I could sell them quickly on eBay before she got home."

I stiffened in my chair. "You sold them?"

Abraham slowly shook his head. "I got cold feet. I posted the map for about an hour and then removed it.

I didn't know what I was going to do, but I felt wrong about selling it. Money is easy to replace, I guess."

"Wait a minute," Trendon said, scratching his head. "If Dorothy never returned from Syria, how did she have a clue what you did?"

Abraham considered the question for a moment and then shook his head. "No, she came back about two weeks ago. We were supposed to meet for dinner because she had something to talk to me about, but it fell through."

"Came back?" I asked. "That could mean Syria's not where they're keeping her anymore."

"Well, this just got loads easier," Trendon grumbled.

"Look, Abraham, we're not going to cause you any trouble. We just want your help. Maybe you could lend us this map. We'll return it to you once everything is settled. We won't tell anyone where we got it."

"It's gone!" Abraham shouted. "All of it. My computer's hard drive has been wiped, and all of my personal files are gone."

Trendon and I looked at each other.

"About two weeks ago, I was robbed by two men with guns. I thought they were going to kill me, but for some reason, they let me live. I gave them everything they asked for."

"Guns?" Trendon asked, looking alarmed. "Are you sure about that?"

"I don't know how they knew where I lived," Abraham continued, ignoring Trendon's question. "I seriously had that item posted on eBay for an hour, tops, and that was all it took for them to find me." Abraham buried his face again in his hands, sputtering as his shoulders heaved from a violent cough.

I looked at Trendon. "What do you think about all of this?" I asked.

"Guns!" he mouthed, his eyes wide with worry. "It sounds a lot like the goons that chased us last night. If he's not making the whole thing up, I say we should cut our losses. We had a good run with Ms. H, but I'm not mixing it up with crooks and guns."

I fished Ms. Holcomb's letter from my pants pocket and poured over the words rapidly. These people weren't messing around when it came to that map. I passed over a phrase but went back to it.

"False safety?" I said aloud, confused by a term I had never heard Dorothy use before. In her letter, she warned us to beware of false safety. I glanced up at Abraham massaging the back of his neck. Had Ms. Holcomb wanted us to be wary of him? Was he lying about the map? I studied his face until he noticed me staring. No. Abraham seemed sincere. Then what could "false safety" mean? My eyes widened as I considered a possibility. "Do you still have the key to Dorothy's apartment?" I asked.

Abraham looked up and thought for a moment. "Yeah, why?"

"Trendon and I need to check something out. Will you take us there?"

Trendon chuckled. "I'm not breaking into her house."

"We're not going to break in," I said. "We have a key. So will you take us?"

"I suppose I could, but I don't think you'll find anything," he said.

"This is just . . . silly," Trendon said, rolling his eyes. "We're not detectives!"

"No, we're archaeologists," I said, grinning. "Besides, don't you think Ms. Holcomb's house would be an excellent place to search for clues?"

"Either that, or get shot, Sherlock!" Trendon got to his feet. "Don't you think there's a chance those guys with guns are staking out the place right now, waiting for some idiot with a key—no offense—to go exploring?"

"I don't think they will be," Abraham chimed in. "I've been back twice since I was robbed, and the place seemed to be clear. I think they got what they wanted from me."

Trendon's eyes narrowed as he sized him up. "Why would you go back?"

He swallowed and grimaced, managing a timid smile as he shrugged his shoulders. "I guess I thought the least I could do was water her plants."

6

Abraham unlocked the apartment door and led us into Dorothy Holcomb's living room. He flipped on the light switch, and several warm, glowing lamps dispersed the darkness. "I'm going to take care of her plants first," he said, placing the apartment key on a wooden shelf and heading toward the far end of the living room.

"So this is where Ms. H. calls home, eh?" Trendon scanned the expanse of the living room and scrunched his nose. "I thought she'd have way more junk."

I ran my fingers across a polished oak shelf that was brimming with various framed photographs and paused to pluck up one of the pictures—an image of Dorothy standing next to a large stone tablet depicting the Mayan calendar.

"I didn't know Ms. H. was such a Bible freak," Trendon said, staring across the room and reading one of several cross-stitched scripture verses plastered on the wall.

"1 Kings 18:11," I read. "And now thou sayest, Go, tell thy lord, Behold, Elijah is here."

"Creepy." Trendon paused to read the other passages. "What the heck are they supposed to mean?"

"I like them," I said. "It makes the room feel more . . ."

"Psychotic?" Trendon asked, shaking his head.

"I was going to say secure."

"Well, this is it," Abraham announced. He had finished watering the plants and now rested on the soft, squashy love seat. "Have a look around for a few more minutes if you want, but I should be getting home soon."

I would have loved to spend more time exploring all of Dorothy's treasures, but we had work to do. "Abraham, where exactly is Dorothy's safe?" I asked.

"It's in her bedroom. First door on your right."

I started toward the hall but paused. "Um, do you think you could open it for me?"

"I could try," Abraham said. "But if she really knew what I did, I seriously doubt she kept the same combination. She probably changed it before things, you know, got ugly."

Dorothy's fire safe rested beneath two thick embroidered blankets in the back left corner of the bedroom closet. It stood about two feet off of the floor and had a large black combination dial. Abraham knelt down and began working the knob.

"It took me only three tries to get it right the first time," he said. "Six, twenty-six, fifty-nine—it was the date her father vanished into the Amazon."

"That sounds lovely," Trendon said, giving me a cross-eyed look.

"That was the day she chose her life's path," Abraham said, still operating the safe. "When her father went missing, she spent months searching for him. It was during that time she developed her love of discovery." The dial refused to catch at the completion of the combination. "Sorry. No luck."

"Could you try something else?" I pressed.

Abraham looked over his shoulder, his face frail and his eyes peaked. He looked sicker than ever. "I don't know what else to try," he said, his stomach heaving.

"Maybe another important date—you know, something significant."

"Like the date when her mom was convicted of murder or when her hamster was sucked up by the vacuum cleaner," Trendon said, offering suggestions in his most sarcastic tone.

"Shut up, Trendon," I ordered. "Please, Abraham, I have a feeling there's something in that safe that will help us find Dorothy."

Abraham's head lowered as he focused on the safe again. He attempted three other combinations, his tremulous hands maneuvering over the dial. After his final attempt failed, I groaned with frustration.

"Maybe she used her birth date or someone else's. Do you think that's possible?"

Abraham lost his balance and collapsed into the closet wall. "I don't feel so . . ." His eyes rolled around absently.

Trendon scooped him up under his armpits. "Strep throat, huh?" He helped Abraham up to a sitting position.

"Yeah," Abraham clasped his hand to his forehead. "Yeah, I need my pills." Fishing a child-safety topped bottle out from his robe, he tumbled two bright yellow capsules into his mouth.

"Those look like highlighter eggs," Trendon said. "What's your prescription?" He snatched the brown, opaque bottle from Abraham's hand, and I noticed the missing label.

"It's penicillin, I think." Abraham sputtered into his hand.

"Yeah, I don't think so. Penicillin doesn't look like this." Trendon produced his own brown medicine bottle filled with dull pink caplets. "It looks like this."

I laughed. "Why do you have penicillin?"

"Why don't you? I always keep a supply on hand for precautionary reasons," Trendon said. "I'm certainly going to pop the top after our little encounter with Dr. Death here."

"You're so paranoid!"

"Look, that's not the issue here. The issue is Abraham thinks he's downing penicillin when he's really not. Why doesn't your bottle have a label?"

"It's just what my friend gave me," Abraham answered, his breath escaping his lips in a painful wheeze.

"Your friend?" I grasped for the bottle to examine the strange pills.

"Yeah, he filled my prescription for me. I couldn't go out. I was too sick."

I touched the back of my hand to Abraham's forehead. "You're boiling!"

Trendon drew in close to my ear and whispered. "It looks like someone's trying to poison him."

I felt my pulse quicken. "You don't really think so, do you?"

"What are you guys talking about?" Abraham asked, his eyes squinting with evident pain.

"Nothing. I think we need to get you home," Trendon said, hopping to his feet and reaching down to support Abraham.

"Trendon, we need to open this safe," I said urgently.

"He tried, didn't he? I say we get out of here, talk about it over doughnuts and juice, and try again some other day. I've seen plenty of horror movies, Amber. I'm not waiting for him to start spinning his head around in circles and barfing up pea soup."

"Could you just try one more combination?" I grabbed a sleeve from one of Dorothy's blouses and wiped Abraham's sweaty forehead.

Abraham wheezed. His breathing now sounded like a bubbling cup of club soda. He thought for a moment. "Well, I guess there's one I haven't tried."

"Please, just give it one more try and then we're through."

Abraham leaned over, and with much effort reworked the dial for a fifth time. Slowly he rotated the disk to the numbers: one, eight, and then back to four. Upon the final number, the lock caught and the safe door sprung open. Abraham forced a smile and laughed. "I didn't expect that."

I immediately bent over to examine the contents of the safe. Excitement overwhelmed me, but when I looked, I found nothing more than cool, dark-gray metal lining the inside. The safe was empty. My shoulders sagged as I felt a heavy dose of dejection course down my spine.

"How about that, safe-cracker," Trendon said, patting Abraham on the square of his back. Abraham slumped over limply and began convulsing. His head trembled and saliva poured from his clinched jaws.

"He's having some sort of a seizure!" Trendon shouted.

I threw my arms around Abraham's neck in a vain attempt to prevent him from quaking.

With lightning speed, Trendon dialed 911 on his cell and began barking directions at the dispatcher on the other line. Abraham's body felt dangerously hot, and his irises had disappeared in the back of his head, leaving only the whites showing.

"We have to do something!" I sobbed.

Trendon received some instructions from his phone and raced out of the bedroom. After rummaging around in the kitchen he returned, holding a wooden mixing spoon. "You have to open his mouth," he said. "This might keep him from biting off his tongue." I frantically tried to pry his iron-trapped jaws open, but I didn't have the strength. Trendon pulled me out of the way and handed me the spoon. He managed to open Abraham's mouth, and I jabbed the spoon between his teeth as they clamped down tight. Sixty seconds passed, and Abraham continued to convulse. Suddenly, he lunged forward and gasped. His eyes returned somewhat to normal, and he looked from me to Trendon. "Tell her!" his voice rasped.

I squeezed his hand. "You need to relax, Abraham. Everything's going to be fine." From outside on the ground level, the piercing sound of sirens shrieked into earshot, and red flashing lights cut through the drawn curtains.

"They're here," Trendon said.

"Help is here, Abraham," I echoed.

Abraham blinked, his expression distant and mystified. He looked at me once more. "Tell her I'm sorry!" Then he collapsed face first on the floor, his body still and rigid.

Trendon dropped his phone and grabbed Abraham's throat, frantically searching for a pulse. My lips quivered as I sobbed. Somehow I knew he wouldn't find one.

7

Trendon and I stumbled out of the hospital and onto the sidewalk. Cars whirred in and out of the out-patient parking lot, and several orderlies in sea foam green hospital scrubs crowded around a public ash tray with lit cigarettes dangling from their fingers. It felt much later than seven in the evening. Up to this point, I had lived a pretty fortunate life. Abraham's death would embed itself in my mind for the rest of my existence. I felt an overwhelming pang of guilt.

Blood samples revealed the poison Abraham ingested was an uncommon dosage of thallium, a slow-acting poison resulting in flu-like symptoms during its early stages. With nothing the hospital surgeons could do to revive him, they concluded Abraham had taken the pills for over a week. Still, I inwardly questioned whether or not we could have saved him if I hadn't been so persistent about opening the safe. Why was I so demanding? If we had only called the paramedics sooner. I dabbed at my teary eyes with the back of my sleeve. I needed to sleep, just a quick nap, but I knew this nightmare wasn't over yet.

Trendon and I had just endured three hours of intense questioning from several police officers. One of them had been particularly gruff, but I didn't blame him. Some college kid dies from poisoning, and the only suspects they have are two exhausted kids with a shady story. I'd be suspicious too. I tried to tell Trendon not to go into detail about our run-in with the gunmen at school, but he ignored me. He gave a pathetic recounting of what had happened over the past twenty-four hours, stumbling through the parts about being chased around campus by the two mystery men with guns. I caught one of the officers biting back a smile. I knew they didn't believe us.

Now that we were out of the hospital, I wasn't sure where to go next. Trendon bumped into my arm and mumbled an apology, the heavy effects of our recent events were obviously taking their toll on his ever-readiness to splash a little sarcasm into any situation. His stomach rumbled, and he clutched at his midsection with a fist.

"Look, I don't mean to make light of what just happened, but I—"

"I know," I cut him off before he could finish. "Let's go get you something to eat, but I'm not hungry."

"Thank you."

The two of us walked three blocks to a service station, and Trendon purchased a sack of corn nuts, some beef jerky, and a two-liter bottle of Mountain Dew.

We sat down on the curb in silence. I rested my head on my folded arms as he devoured his meal.

"So what do we do now?" he asked, stifling a belch and wadding up the empty bag of corn nuts. I watched a pill bug meander through a crack in the asphalt but didn't answer immediately. "Hey," Trendon nudged my elbow.

I glanced up. My eyes ached. They felt puffy and swollen. "We go back," I answered, sniffing.

"You mean home?" Trendon's head perked up slightly. "To our dorms?"

"No, I mean back to Dorothy's apartment."

"What? You're joking right?" Trendon shot his wrappers toward the garbage can but missed.

I shook my head as I looked up at him. I could feel the warnings of an excruciating headache approaching.

"Why would we go back to Ms. H's house? There's nothing there."

I stood up from the curb, dusted off my pants, and pulled my school planner out of my backpack.

"Besides," Trendon continued, "how do you propose we get into her apartment? We don't have a key or anything."

I picked a key out from under one of the planner pages and showed it to him.

"You've got to be kidding me!" Trendon said, standing up. "You stole her key from Abraham? When?"

I whimpered as I thought of Abraham lying back at the hospital, covered with a blanket. "As we were leaving the apartment with the paramedics, I remembered he put it on one of the shelves," I said. "I don't know what got into me, but I knew we needed the key."

"Amber, as your friend and someone with a much higher IQ, you have seriously waded out past the buoys, if you know what I mean," Trendon said. "We're in way over our heads."

"I know it seems crazy, but I really do think Dorothy has something she wants us to find back at her apartment."

"What are we going to tell Joseph and Lisa when we meet up with them in less than two hours?" Trendon asked. "Oh hey, guys, how did your day go? Ours? Oh, we just broke into Dorothy's apartment and became accomplices to Abraham's murder. You know, the usual."

"Please stop, I don't want to argue with you right now. We've got nothing else to go on."

"We've got clean criminal records that I'm not eager to taint. Didn't you get enough questioning from Officer Friendly earlier? I bet he'd love to grill us under the heat lamps some more."

"I'm calling a cab. Let me use your phone." Trendon handed it to me and then looked down at the sidewalk, apparently considering his options, while I instructed the operator. When I hung up, I overheard him mumbling to himself.

"Crazy! I know she's crazy, but what am I supposed to do?" He glanced up, and I smiled.

"I'm crazy? Who are you talking to?" I handed his phone back before fishing my wallet out of my backpack and inspecting my wad of cash.

"The only person that's making any sense right now—me!" Trendon bit his lip and turned toward the service station entrance.

"Where are you going?" I asked.

"I'm gonna need more snacks."

⚎

Forty-five minutes later, we stood next to the apartment entrance, staring up at Ms. Holcomb's bedroom window. I felt frightened to go back into that room. Abraham had been murdered by probably the same people who had kidnapped Dorothy. There was no telling what they would do to get their way.

"I don't think you have much time," Trendon whispered.

"What do you mean?"

Trendon flashed his iPhone at me, and a breaking news message showed up on the screen. The headline read: *College Student Poisoned at Local Archaeologist's Apartment.* I swallowed.

"This whole place is going to be crawling with news reporters and whack jobs. You better get going. I'll stand guard."

"What, you're not going with me?" I looked at Trendon, alarmed.

"Sorry, pal, this is your idea. I'll buzz you on the intercom if anything happens down here."

I thought about arguing with Trendon, but judging by his facial expression, the topic wasn't open for debate. I pushed the key into the lock and opened the vestibule door. Glancing back, I watched as he shook his head and ducked down from view.

Every step groaned under my weight, and I found myself continually glancing over my shoulder to search for intruders as I climbed up the five floors. The complex had an elevator at one end of its central hallway, but whenever I could help it, I avoided elevators, especially when by myself.

Outside of Dorothy's apartment, I fumbled the key, dropping it on the floor, when something in the corner of the hall caught my eye. A white and brown cat rubbed its tail nonchalantly against the doorjamb of the apartment across from Dorothy's. I watched it curiously as its tail flicked back and forth. Then the door across the hall opened, and a man wearing a stained white tank top and boxer shorts emerged. He didn't see me crouched across the way as he bent down to pick up his pet. I held my breath, praying he wouldn't notice me.

"What are you doing down there?" the man asked, looking up from the floor. He pulled the cat up by the scruff of its neck and plopped it down in his meaty arms.

"I, um, dropped my key," I said, thinking fast for an excuse.

"You don't live there. Who are you?"

"I'm Dorothy's niece," I lied.

"Who?" the man asked, stroking the back of the cat's head. The cat purred louder and louder.

"The woman that lives here, I'm her niece."

"I don't know her, and I haven't seen her in weeks."

"Yeah, well . . ." I stood and fidgeted with the key. "I better get going. It's late."

The man shrugged, glared at me for a few more moments, and disappeared into his apartment. I felt on the verge of vomiting. I had almost blown everything. How much time had I wasted? More important, how much time did I have before Trendon got spooked and blew our cover?

Inside the dark apartment, the various statues and artifacts cast eerie shadows from the waning glow of the streetlights five floors down. I tiptoed through the living room, leaving the lights off so as not to draw any attention. The safe in Dorothy's closet had closed during the dreaded struggle with Abraham's seizure, and when I tried the handle, it wouldn't budge. I took a deep breath and searched my memory. After a moment's thought, I remembered the successful combination—one, eight, four—and worked the dial to open the safe.

It was still empty, of course, but that didn't matter. I removed Dorothy's letter from my pocket and read over the passage I had noticed earlier. Dorothy had capitalized the words "false safety." If my assumption was correct, this meant the safe was false or something in the safe was false. I felt along the bottom of the safe cabinet, running my fingers along the seams, and my heart leapt as I felt a tiny latch at the back corner of the cabinet. With some effort, I pulled the latch up and the bottom of the safe unhinged.

I discovered several interesting objects hidden within the compartment. First, I pulled out a map drawn on a rolled up piece of hide. The words were illegible, but I recognized the ancient characters. Next, I picked up a small blue stone and, after finding nothing significant about it, placed it on the ground next to the map. Last, I found a knobby stick about a foot in length.

"What does all this stuff mean?" I whispered. I picked up the map and unfolded it. It consisted of two different pictures; one was most certainly the image of a mountain with arrows and inscriptions pointing toward an opening, and I assumed the other was a series of instructions. Next I examined the blue stone, and a thought occurred to me, one that caused my breathing to sharpen. Dorothy had mentioned something in class last year, something that had to do with strange clear stones.

Suddenly, a sharp buzzing sound rang out, and my head jerked toward the hallway door. Trendon had pressed the call button from down on the stoop. Panicked, I gathered up the items in my backpack and, as quietly as I could manage, tiptoed through the apartment, glancing over my shoulder to retrace my steps. Everything seemed in place. Once again my attention was drawn to the Bible verses on the wall. Exodus 9:23,

And Moses stretched forth his rod toward heaven:
and the Lord sent thunder and hail, and the fire ran
along upon the ground.

Trendon was right, I thought. I did find those verses kind of creepy. I grasped the doorknob and was about to turn it when I heard voices coming from the hallway. Frozen with fear, I looked through the peephole. The two men from on campus last night stood across the hall, speaking with the man in the white tank top I had seen earlier.

"Mr. Goodwin, I trust we didn't keep you long?" I heard the black man in the dark trench coat ask.

"Uh . . . yeah, I mean no, you're fine," the man in the tank top answered.

"A girl was it, you said? That went in there?" the black man asked, staring down at his coat pockets. I felt my skin grow cold. *How did they find me?*

Mr. Goodwin's eyes rested on the apartment door, and he nodded. "Yeah. Teenager, really skinny."

"In that apartment directly in front of yours?" the man probed further, keeping his eyes down as he lit a cigarette and pressed the filter to his lips.

"Yeah, that one right there," Mr. Goodwin said, pointing at the door.

The man took a long drag on his cigarette, allowing the smoke to escape his nostrils. He pulled the cigarette from his mouth and for the first time glanced toward the door I hid behind.

"You said you would make it worth my while if I saw anyone go in there," Mr. Goodwin said, taking a step out into the hallway.

That jerk!

The black man smiled. "You're absolutely right."

He snapped his coat open and produced a small brown parcel. "Your payment." He handed the box to Mr. Goodwin's outstretched hand.

"What's this?" Mr. Goodwin smirked down at the package.

"I think you'll find it's exactly what you were hoping for. Now if you don't mind, I strongly encourage you to return to your apartment and forget this entire exchange ever happened."

Before Mr. Goodwin could reply, the two men pushed him rather firmly back in through the doorway. I then watched in horror as they turned and faced Dorothy's apartment.

8

I cowered in Dorothy's bedroom, lying flat beneath the queen bed and wishing my teacher owned a longer bedspread. My backpack, filled with the mysterious wares from Dorothy's safe, rested next to me on the floor. Out in the living room, a door pushed open, and my sense of hearing was enhanced by my horror. Although the men attempted to conceal their entry, I heard every footstep. If only I had taken more time to find a better hiding place. People always looked under the bed first! But with no cell phone to call Trendon or the police, I could only wait and hope they wouldn't find me.

The footsteps grew louder, casting dark silhouettes just beyond the crack in the door. I held my breath, wanting to cry but knowing if I allowed myself to start, I'd soon be sobbing. The shadows passed on, and I heard the guest bedroom door open. Clinging to my backpack, I slid out from beneath the bed. How was this going to work? I could make a run for it, but if they had guns, they could shoot me. Was it better to creep out into the living room or just make a loud, screaming dash for the front door in the hopes that the commotion might surprise them? Was this really happening? I reached for the doorknob just as the dark shadows of someone's feet appeared beneath the door. Unable to move out of the way, I gasped as the doorknob began to rotate.

A sharp buzzing sound rang out through the apartment. Somebody had pressed the call button from down below, and that person was still holding onto it. Trendon had to be responsible. The alarm gave me just what I needed to get my senses back and shift out of the way of the door, tucking myself in the corner between the dresser and the doorstop.

Then the door opened, and from my crouched position I saw one of the men enter, holding a gun. He hadn't noticed me yet, but he looked at the bed as if he thought I was hiding beneath it.

"Malcolm, we've got company!" said a voice from out in the hall. The flashing red and blue lights of police vehicles suddenly cut through the darkness of the apartment. The man standing in the bedroom looked back over his shoulder. "I can hear them coming up the stairs," the voice said, more urgently.

Malcolm then glanced down directly at me. For a moment he seemed stunned to see me sitting there, but that moment wore off fast. Before I could react, he had his gun pointed directly at my chest.

"Stand up," he ordered. My heartbeat drummed in

my ears, and my stomach forced bile into my throat. Trembling, I slid up the wall, my eyes fixed on the barrel of his gun. "You have something for me," he whispered, cocking back the hammer. "I won't ask for it twice." I gasped and unzipped my backpack. "Be quick about it, girl!" he hissed.

"We need to go now!" the man's partner barked.

Malcolm glanced sideways through the door. "Don't worry, Spencer. Mr. Goodwin left his door unlocked. He won't mind if we join him." Their conversation distracted Malcom just long enough for me to make a decision. With hardly any control over my fingers, I removed Dorothy's letter from the backpack. Malcolm snatched it up and gave it a quick look. The gun remained fixed on my chest, his finger on the trigger. I closed my eyes and waited for him to shoot. Tears began to pour from my eyes as I hoped for it to be quick and painless. Instead, Malcolm darted out of the room, leaving me alone. I released an exasperated sob and dropped to my knees. Leaning forward to peer around the opening of the bedroom door, I caught a fleeting glimpse of Malcolm's trench coat slipping out through the apartment door.

A voice shouted from the hallway. The police had arrived. An explosion of gunfire erupted as Malcolm and his buddy opened fire upon the officers. I screamed, covering my ears with my hands to drown out the thunderous sound.

"After them!" one of the officers bellowed. *How did they get away?* The officers had been right on top of them. I had to get out of there fast. Scurrying low across the living room floor, I ducked out of view of the apartment door, which was still standing slightly ajar.

One of the officers squawked into a radio. "Officers down! I repeat we have two officers down. Multiple gunshot wounds. Requesting medical backup immediately!" I could hear the vivid desperation rising in his voice. From the sound of it, the officer stood just outside the apartment. More gunshots rang out from somewhere down below, out on the street. Taking several quick breaths, I chanced looking out into the hallway. Two police officers lay on their backs on the floor, three doors down from Dorothy's entryway. Another officer bent over them, tending to their injuries. His back faced me, and he knelt just far enough out of the way that I believed I could sneak past him across the hall. Malcolm said Mr. Goodwin had left his apartment door unlocked. If I could just get control of my shaking body, maybe I could make it.

"That one almost got past the vest," one of the injured officers whimpered, patting to where a bullet had torn through his uniform and sunk deep within his protective Kevlar. The other officer stirred as well, a good sign for him, but not for me. The more they moved, the faster my window of opportunity closed.

Squatting low to the floor, I darted out of the apartment straight for the door across the hall, refusing to look behind me at the officers and not stopping until Mr. Goodwin's doorknob grazed my head. At any moment, I expected a police officer to reach out and snatch my shoulder, but the snatch never came. With every ounce of my control, I twisted the doorknob, pushed the door open just wide enough for my body to fit, and slipped into the apartment unnoticed.

Standing with my back pressed against the inside of Mr. Goodwin's apartment door, I allowed myself a moment to freak out. My shoulders heaved with almost exaggerated movements. I couldn't breathe. No matter how desperately I tried to take in oxygen, it didn't come fast enough.

"This isn't happening, this isn't happening, this isn't happening!" I repeated over and over in a trembling whisper. Dropping my backpack to the floor next to me, I hugged my arms tightly and slid down until I sat on the floor mat with my knees tucked against my chest.

"Easy, girl. Get a grip," I told myself. I brushed my hair off my forehead and wiped away a mixture of sweat and tears from my face. So much noise still echoed in my eardrums. Just beyond the thin layer of the wooden door, I could hear EMTs tending to the officers and shouting at the other tenants to return to their apartments.

My eyes cinched shut as I tried to rid my thoughts of the man and his gun and replace the images of the horrifying firefight with a more pleasant one. I thought back to the Fourth of July picnic I had spent with my family last summer. The fireworks show had been amazing. My Aunt Shelby had brought potato salad but had forgotten to boil the potatoes. I snorted as I remembered how everyone had forced themselves to swallow the disgusting dish. My breathing slowed. Opening my eyes, I relaxed my shoulders and surveyed my surroundings. An old recliner with smashed beer cans balancing on the armrests sat in front of an ancient television set with aluminum-foil-wrapped rabbit ears. Did people still do that? My eyes traveled toward the kitchen to a plastic bowl on the linoleum floor. *Probably for the cat*, I thought. Once again my pulse quickened, and I rose to my feet.

The apartment seemed too quiet. Where was Mr. Goodwin? I thought back to earlier when I had seen him speaking with Malcolm and his buddy. He blew my cover. I tried to swallow and almost choked on my saliva. Where was he now? Had he gone to sleep? My eyes flashed across the room, finally settling on a closed door that I figured led to Mr. Goodwin's bedroom. *He must be a heavy sleeper*, I thought.

"Trendon!" I whispered suddenly. I had almost forgotten about him. I tiptoed into the kitchen, careful not to create any loud footsteps on the hard kitchen floor, and removed the cordless phone from the wall jack. With my eyes glued on Mr. Goodwin's bedroom door, I punched Trendon's number into the pad and waited for it to ring.

Nothing happened. The phone never connected. I tried again, this time carefully entering each number, and waited. Still no connection. Had someone cut the phone lines? Maybe Mr. Goodwin had just left another phone off the hook. *Great!* I thought. How was I supposed to signal Trendon now? Knowing him, he wouldn't wait forever. The neon numbers of the microwave caught my attention. 9:05 p.m—already late for our meeting with Joseph and Lisa at McGregor Park.

I gnawed my lower lip, scanning the room for another phone, and quietly slid into the living room to search the couch cushions. Plopping my backpack onto the floor next to the recliner, I bent down to peer underneath. No luck.

Something small and black, just barely within my peripheral vision, scurried out from underneath the coffee table and vanished under the bottom of the couch. *Only a mouse*, I thought. Mice didn't really gross me out, at least not as much as insects. If I didn't go near it, the mouse wouldn't bother me.

Sighing in frustration, I slipped into the hallway. *Where is the phone?* I gritted my teeth, sure I already knew the answer. Probably in Mr. Goodwin's bedroom. Part of me wanted to just surrender and wait it out for the hallway to clear of swarming police officers, but that could take forever. Oh how I wished Trendon had come with me. Sure he could be obnoxious, but he also usually thought up clever—albeit unusual—plans. Plus, I could really use a good laugh.

"Okay," I whispered. "You can do this." My hand gripped the cool brass doorknob of the first door. If he had slept through an explosion of gunfire, surely Mr. Goodwin could stay asleep while I crept softly into his room.

Eeerrreeek!

The door groaned from the movement, and I waited for the worst to happen. When nothing did, I inched the door open wider. The moonlight pouring in through the living room windows behind me cast a glow across the end of the bed, and I sighed in relief. Several scattered pillows and a mess of sheets covered the bed, but no one was sleeping under them. As my eyesight began to adjust to the darkness, I took in the layout of the room. The headboard of the bed butted up against the wall directly across from the door. I could make out the brown paper wrapping and the box that Mr. Goodwin had accepted as payment from Malcolm and his partner lying in a heap on top of the messy bedspread. Some sort of cotton stuffing was scattered around the remains of the package. I wondered how much money they paid him. That creep didn't deserve anything.

To the left of the bed was a closet with accordion doors and to the right, a large window with the curtains drawn. A nightstand stood in the corner next to the headboard, and on it was an empty phone cradle with a coiled phone cord stretched taut and dangling down to the floor. I looked back out the bedroom door and into the living room, wondering if there had been some kind of struggle. I shook my head. "It's not important," I whispered. All I needed was that phone.

I took a step forward but jolted back as my foot brushed against something thick and soft lying on the floor. At first, I mistook it for a wadded up sweater, but it had a denser feeling to it, like a stuffed animal. I bent over and covered my mouth with my hand. Lying flat and motionless, Mr. Goodwin's cat seemed unaware of me standing practically on top of it.

My stomach lurched. "Hey there, fella." I whispered. *Cats don't just lie there, do they? Shouldn't it be purring?* I drew closer, extending my hand submissively, hoping to entice the animal with a stroke of my fingers. The cat didn't budge. Its glassy eyes just stared up past me with a vacant, hollow expression. Dead. I felt hot bile rise in my throat, but I choked it back down. *Forget the cat and get going!* I told myself. I didn't want to know what had happened to Mr. Goodwin's cat, but now more than ever I needed Trendon to get me out of this awful apartment.

No longer concerned about staying quiet, I hopped across the floor onto the corner of the bed, keeping my eyes pinned on the dead animal. I reached for the phone, but as my fingers closed around the receiver, they grazed someone's cold hand. Unable to stop myself, I released a high-pitched scream as I looked down at Mr. Goodwin.

9

A soft knock rapped against Mr. Goodwin's apartment door, and I looked out the peephole. The sight of Trendon's wild hair brought me some comfort as I unlatched the door.

It was almost eleven. I had spent the last two hours cowering in the corner while the bodies of Mr. Goodwin and his cat lay dead on the floor in the bedroom. After finding the stiff body, I had mustered enough courage to snatch the phone from his chest and hang it up on the cradle. I waited until I stopped convulsing before calling Trendon from the phone in the kitchen. Then I hid in the living room, waiting for him to arrive.

I hadn't dared to turn on the lights for fear of signaling those criminals again. Instead I had opened my backpack and sat next to the front door, examining Dorothy's mysterious items. The map initially drew my attention; the markings and inscriptions written in some sort of Hebraic dialect. I couldn't read Hebrew, but I did know a few words. One of the words on the page stood out more than the others. Why couldn't I remember what "Tebah" meant? It seemed so familiar.

As I opened the door, I wanted to be furious with Trendon, but logically I knew he'd done exactly what I would have done. He waited until the last of the police officers dispersed, just barely fifteen minutes ago, before attempting to come find me.

"Let me just say this," Trendon said, entering the apartment and closing the door behind him. "That was the longest two hours of my life!"

"Oh really?" I said, my words laced with sarcasm.

"Yeah," Trendon continued, not picking up on my tone. "You can't imagine what I went through down there."

I chewed on the inside of my cheek. "Oh, so you were held at gunpoint by a lunatic and forced to give him Dorothy's letter? You witnessed an awful gunfight from just a few feet away and then had to crawl past injured police officers unnoticed and break into a stranger's apartment only to discover Mr. Goodwin along with his cat had been murdered?" I blurted in one breath. "Does that sound like your night?" My eyes flared with anger.

Trendon swallowed, inching back from my wrath. "No . . . uh . . . not exactly. I hid in the bushes when the gunfire started and then one of those bozo EMTs threw a can of soda over the stoop, and it splashed on my neck." He offered a pathetic smile. "Besides, I thought you were a goner for sure."

"Well, it's nice to know I mean that much to you,"

I hissed. "And that you could suffer just a little while I faced almost certain death."

Trendon rolled his eyes. "Drama," he whispered. "Who's Mr. Goodwin?"

I pointed sharply to the bedroom. "I'm not going in there," I said, looking away from the door.

"What do you mean he was murdered?"

"Both he and his cat are dead. Mr. Goodwin was the one that told those two goons where I was, and I'm pretty sure they poisoned him just like Abraham."

Trendon scrunched his nose. "So let's get out of here then. What are we waiting for?"

"I think we need to call the police," I said. "We at least need to let them know about Mr. Goodwin."

"Not from my phone we aren't." Trendon jabbed his iPhone down into his pocket and backed out of my reach. "I've already placed two emergency calls today from the same location. If that doesn't put me on the most wanted list, then I don't know what would. Besides, if he's dead, what are they going to do for him?"

"Trendon, what if he has family?"

"Yeah, well, what if you left fingerprints all over the place?"

What if I had? Of course I had, but where? I had wandered all over Mr. Goodwin's apartment. It wouldn't take a crack team of CSI specialists to link me to his death. I entered the kitchen, snatched several paper towels, and started wiping down every place I figured my fingers had come in contact with.

"That won't be enough," Trendon said. "You'll never wipe down everything, and those paper towels aren't exactly the right material."

I slammed the roll of towels into Trendon's stomach. "Then help me!" I ordered.

"Okay, okay! Relax. Remember it was your idea to come up here in the first place, and that was obviously a total waste of time."

I growled, grabbed Trendon's wrist, and with all of my strength, started smacking his hand against every surface I could find.

"Hey! What are you doing, psycho?"

"There. Now we're both accomplices to murder," I said, smiling maliciously. "Are you happy?"

"Oh, that's real mature." Trendon snatched back his hand and started wiping down the areas I had forced his fingers to touch.

"And for your information, coming up here wasn't a waste of time." I crossed the room to where my open backpack had toppled over by the front door. "Dorothy wanted us to find these." I showed Trendon the items.

Trendon's lips curled up, and he seemed impressed by my find. Holding the map, he drew his eyes in close, trying to read it. "You found these in her apartment?"

I nodded. "In her safe."

Trendon ran his fingers over the lines on the map. "What do you think this leads to?"

"I don't know. But this has to be our next clue. She said we'll know where to go once we find these."

"When did she say that?"

"In her letter . . ." my voice trailed off. I suddenly felt sick thinking about how I had given Dorothy's letter to that man. What if there were more clues hidden within the text?

"How are these supposed to help? We can't exactly go to a travel agent and say book me a flight to wherever this is. What mountain is this, anyway?"

I licked my lower lip. "Do you think you could find out?"

Trendon glanced up, his eyebrows raised arrogantly. "Could I 'find out'?" he mimicked. "I really could charge top dollar for my investigative Internet abilities."

"Yeah, if they weren't mostly illegal," I said.

"Touché. So what's this other junk for?" He tossed the blue stone and the stick in his hands. "Some kind of ancient Egyptian game? Like jacks?"

I shook my head. "Be careful with those. They're important." My eyes once again fell upon the ominous bedroom door. "We need to get out of here. Do you think Joseph and Lisa will still be waiting for us at the park?"

"Yeah, I called Lisa and told her we were still coming. Her phone was about to go dead, so I didn't get a chance to go into the juicy details of everything, but it sounded like their day went a lot smoother than ours. I think Lisa spent most of the day at the mall shopping for 'supplies,' as she called them. Probably means she bought shoes."

I gathered the items from Trendon and dropped

them in my backpack next to my notebook and wallet. Before zipping the bag closed, I removed the map and stuck it in my pocket, hoping to catch a free moment on the way to the park to take another look at it. Still clutching a paper towel, I picked up the kitchen telephone. "Get ready to go. I'm calling 911 and leaving the phone off the hook."

"Did you cover all your tracks, Bugsy?" Trendon gave another quick rubdown of the kitchen counter with a towel.

"Let's hope."

"Do you really think he was poisoned?" Lisa asked, swiveling on the black vinyl seat of one of the park swings. "Couldn't it have been a mistake? Maybe he took it by accident himself."

Trendon sneered. "Yeah sure, he just happened to take incremental dosages of thallium over the past two weeks. Probably picked it up over the counter at the drugstore. Happens all the time."

"Leave her alone," Joseph said, chucking a rock at Trendon's leg.

After recounting the long list of events that happened over the course of the day, Trendon and I collapsed against the trunk of a large maple tree and rested while Lisa and Joseph soaked in our story on the swings.

"This is not good, guys," Joseph said, shaking his head. "We're in way over our heads."

"Tell me about it," Trendon grunted.

"I just can't believe people are dying because of this. We don't even know the reason," Lisa said.

"Maybe we can get to the bottom of this. What did you guys find?" Joseph looked at me, and I felt a tingling of excitement down my spine. We were getting closer to a very important discovery, I just knew it. Tearing my backpack open, I pulled the blue stone out and held it up for everyone to see.

Joseph's eyes sparkled. "What is that?" he asked, holding out his hand. I passed the stone to him and watched as he inspected it curiously; his interest in my discovery made me even more excited.

"I don't know," I said. "Maybe it's a jewel or some kind of valuable stone."

"Or maybe it's a rock," Trendon mumbled under his breath.

"It's not just some dumb rock, Trendon." I took the stone back from Joseph and held it up close to my eye. "I have my theories on what it is."

"Don't tell me, it's the Eye of the Sphinx. No, better yet, it's one of Ramses' gallstones." Trendon barely ducked as a piece of bark whizzed by his ear. I couldn't keep myself from laughing at Trendon's humor, if only for a moment.

"No, silly, nothing like that," I said. "I just remember hearing Dorothy talk about something in one of our classes. It's going to sound completely crazy, but—"

"You think it's a locator stone, don't you?" Joseph asked.

His question caught me off guard. I had no idea

anyone else in the class had paid much attention to Dorothy's lesson. Joseph barely squeezed a C on his final exams, and now he could recall a term that she briefly mentioned in one class over a year ago? Impressive, to say the least.

"I do. I . . . I think that's exactly what it is. In class, Dorothy said locator stones could be used to pinpoint exact openings into caverns and hidden catacombs." I stood up as my voice rose with excitement. "They're very rare. In fact, no archaeologists in the past century have mentioned using one in any of their studies."

"So why would Ms. H. have one?" Trendon asked, his expression evidently displaying his skepticism. "She has a crappy apartment and drives a 1992 Ford pickup. If these things are so rare, why didn't she just sell it or turn it over to a museum?"

I wanted to slap him. "Trendon—" I started, but Lisa cut me off.

"He's right, you know. You said no archaeologist in the past century ever had one of these . . . stones. That's a pretty big list."

"And how does this stone even work?" Trendon asked, moving carefully away from me to stand next to Lisa. "How can it pinpoint an opening?"

"It's something miraculous, I suppose, something that can't easily be explained by science. Dorothy didn't go into detail during her lesson, probably because no one was paying any attention," I said. Joseph cleared his throat. "Oh, except you and me, of course."

"It's because we could tell it was a crock!" Trendon

shook his fist. "Archaeology is a fun distraction from the real world, but when you start throwing mystical blue stones into the equation, it just turns wacky."

"It's not wacky. It just can't be explained in terms you're comfortable with," I said, waving my finger at him. "If you read the books in class or actually researched the assignments, you would already know that things as mysterious as locator stones are included in manuscripts throughout history."

"There's no such thing as mystical or magical . . . stuff. It doesn't exist. These things are thought up by teachers when they run out of curriculum." Trendon waved his finger back mockingly.

"Trendon, there are artifacts and treasures that haven't even been discovered yet, ones beyond our comprehension." I looked pleadingly over at Joseph and Lisa, who had fallen silent, watching our argument.

"Like what?"

"The Fountain of Youth. The . . . the Holy Grail! Brilliant minds have spent their entire lives searching for these things. They believe they're out there, and not only that, they believe there's power in them."

Trendon glanced around as if indicating I had finally dropped off the deep end. "O . . . kay . . . Let's take a break from crazy talk for a second. Are you telling me this blue piece of glass could lead us to something like the Holy Grail?"

"Maybe."

"Or maybe it's just some marble."

Joseph grabbed one of the swing chains with his

hands. "Let's say you're right, Amber, and what you're holding right now is a locator stone. What do you really think it locates?"

I stared down at the blue stone resting in my palm. "Whether it leads to some treasure or some significant archaeological find, it really doesn't matter. I have a feeling, one way or another, this stone will lead us to Dorothy."

Trendon started laughing. "Can you hear yourself right now, talking all mysterious? Can we just dwell for a second on what happened today? There are people running around killing whoever we come in contact with over these rare discoveries we've supposedly made."

"What's your point?" I asked.

"My point, precious," Trendon puffed out his cheeks, "is that our luck is running out. It's inevitable we're going to get caught, and these are the type of criminals that don't like to leave witnesses if you catch my drift."

"What do you suggest we do then?" I asked. "Give up? Just throw away what we've found and pretend it never happened? Go back to our normal lives and hope these killers just leave us alone?" Trendon started to nod his head enthusiastically, but I continued. "Never mind the fact Dorothy will probably die because of this. Do you want that on your conscience?" He looked up, appearing to contemplate his options.

"These guys won't leave us alone," Lisa said. "They'll keep coming, and like you said, Trendon, it's inevitable we'll get caught."

I looked over at Joseph. "What did you find at the bank?"

Their day had gone without any problems. They entered the South Hampshire Credit Union promptly at ten o'clock; spoke with Ms. Holcomb's contact, Omar Goff; and walked out thirty minutes later with one thousand dollars in cash and several topographical maps of Turkey.

"Turkey? What do you mean Turkey? Like the country?" Trendon blurted out.

"No, like the lunchmeat," Joseph answered, shaking his head. "Of course, the country. That's where I think we're supposed to go, or at least where Dorothy wants us to go."

"No, that can't be it. What the heck's in Turkey?" Trendon asked. "Sand?"

"It has to be some sort of archaeological dig," Lisa started. "I don't know. Syria's fairly close to Turkey, and if that's where Dorothy—"

"Are we sure she didn't just leave those maps in the bank as some light reading material?" Trendon snatched one of the maps and rotated it in his hands, trying to find the right direction.

"I don't think so, Trendon," Joseph said. "They're unopened. It's like she was prepping everything, like she knew something bad was going to happen."

I stayed quiet, listening to their conversation. An important piece of the puzzle now lay in front of us: Turkey. Was that where Dorothy was? My fingers ran along the zipper of my backpack. During all the fuss about the locator stone, I had forgotten to show the group the other items from Dorothy's safe. I still held the map in my pocket. I wanted to pull it out to see if they knew what the word "Tebah" meant.

Opening up my backpack, I could faintly see the end of the stick poking out from beneath my notebook. As I reached for it, I stopped. Something felt wrong. The park no longer seemed safe. Anyone passing by could spot us. My head swiveled rapidly, but before I could react, five heavily armed men appeared out of nowhere and completely surrounded us.

I screamed as one of the men snagged a handful of my hair and forced me down on my knees. Each of my friends received similar treatment.

"Please, don't do this!" Lisa yelled, as one of the men strapped a plastic zip tie around her ankles and fastened it so tightly it cut into her skin. "My parents have money! They'll pay you!" The man in charge of securing her started chuckling.

I frantically searched for help as they strapped my wrists and ankles painfully. How was this possible? It couldn't have been a coincidence; the city was too big with too many places to disappear. How were they always right behind us? Could they have been tracing our cell phone conversations?

Trendon held his wrists up to his mouth, trying to bite the plastic. "You're cutting off my circulation! Can't you loosen it up a bit?" More laughter erupted after his comment, and Trendon's eyes narrowed.

"Laugh it up, you dorks!" One of the men smacked him across the back of his head.

A black SUV zoomed across the park lawn. Its squealing wheels sent a spray of dirt and grass in its wake. Malcolm and his partner, Spencer, stepped down from the vehicle.

"Well, well, well. Congratulations for lasting this long. Now, we really need to be going," Malcolm said.

"You can't leave us alone, can you?" I asked, infuriated by our capture. "Don't you have anything better to do than pick on a bunch of kids?" Malcolm blinked but stood quietly. "You're going to kill us aren't you, just like Abraham and Mr. Goodwin?"

His face remained expressionless. "Kill you? Yes, but maybe not all of you, if you behave."

"Please!" Lisa begged. She writhed on the ground, trying to loosen the zip ties around her ankles. "They're too tight. My hands and feet are numb. Please, just loosen them!"

Malcolm looked down at her with pity in his eyes. "You won't run now, will you, girl?" He slipped his hand around her elbow and helped her to her feet. "That would be a mistake." Whipping out a switchblade from his pocket, he cut the bands free from her ankles and wrists and allowed her a moment to massage them.

"Thank you," she whimpered.

"Do I need to bat my eyes too?" Trendon grumbled. Malcolm ignored him.

"What do you want with us? And what have you done with Dorothy?" I shouted.

"Dorothy? Oh, the spy. I'm afraid I don't really know what's happened to her," Malcolm said.

Spy? What's he talking about? I shot a quick look over to Joseph, who seemed out of it, probably stunned by the whole ordeal.

"We need to see what you've been hiding from us." Malcolm pointed to me. "What do you have in that little knapsack of yours?" He motioned toward Spencer, who unzipped the pack.

Spencer reached down and removed the blue stone. "Bingo," he said, tossing it to Malcolm. I closed my eyes in defeat. We had failed Dorothy. Now we would never be able to help her escape. The thought caused boiling rage to fill my lungs.

"What's so important that you have to ruin the lives of so many people? You're murderers. What are you after?"

Malcolm appeared to consider my question for a moment. "We're after this stone, of course, and thanks to you, we found it. Your friend Dorothy has become quite the pain, and my employer was growing impatient. This stone points the way to something very important. But it doesn't really matter to me, as long as I get paid." Malcolm pushed the stone into his jacket pocket. "What else is in that pack?"

Spencer rummaged around for a second. "Uh, looks like some garbage, a stick, a notebook, and a wallet. You keeping any valuables hidden?" Spencer smirked at me as he slipped his hand deeper into my backpack. "Ooh, it's heavy! Probably filled with—Hey!

Ouch!" He tossed the bag to the ground. "What the? Something just bit me!" He stuck his finger in his mouth and trained his gun on the backpack.

"Something bit you?" Malcolm asked, not too convinced. Everyone, including me and my friends, eyed the bag suspiciously.

Spencer kicked at it, and something black and shiny scampered out. He immediately hopped back. "It's . . . it's . . ."

"It's an Androctonus scorpion," Malcolm said, staring down at the black creature. "It's the same one we gave as payment to Mr. Goodwin back at his apartment. Am I right?" Malcolm looked expectantly at me as I tried to distance myself from the dangerous insect.

"Don't ask me!" I answered.

"Fat-tailed scorpions are deadly poisonous if untreated. Were you laying a trap for us?" He leaned over and smacked me across the mouth. Tears exploded from my eyes as my mouth lit up with pain.

I thought back and remembered seeing what I thought was a mouse in Mr. Goodwin's apartment. The scorpion must have snuck into my backpack while I was hiding out, waiting for Trendon. The insect scuttled across the grass toward Spencer's boot.

"That thing bit me, Malcolm. I need treatment!" Spencer yelped, hurtling over Trendon's shoulders.

"Step on it, already!" Trendon ordered, trying to roll away from the charging scorpion.

Spencer's legs gave out, and it was obvious he was already feeling the effects of the poison. He collapsed onto the ground and groaned. "Antidote . . . please . . ."

Malcolm turned to one of the others. "It's in the case under the driver's seat." The man raced over to the SUV and returned, toting a black, metal case.

While Malcolm prepped a syringe and injected the clear liquid into Spencer's vein, I glanced over and noticed Lisa slyly backing away from the melee. With her wrists and ankles now free from their bonds, she had been able to move a few yards out from the group without anyone noticing. One of the men started backing away from the scorpion, pointing his gun, and I saw an opportunity. Shifting my body sideways, I rolled toward his legs.

The man swore, losing his balance and toppling over onto his back. This brought the attention of the entire group down on me. Lisa saw her opening and broke off in a run. A few moments passed before Malcolm finally took notice.

"Don't let her get away!" he ordered over the cacophony of thundering footsteps.

Lisa headed straight for the road, with one of the men in hot pursuit. The man took aim with his gun, but Malcolm stopped him. "No lethal force! Don't break protocol!"

The man roared with anger, pumping his fists violently as he closed the gap between himself and Lisa. *Run faster!* The man shot his hand out and took hold of her jacket, but she'd already unzipped it and easily shimmied out, sending him toppling over, entangled in the sleek material. She looked back at him scrambling to get to his feet, and I could see her smile triumphantly. Then the footrace ended. I saw it coming just seconds before it happened.

"TRUCK!" I shouted, forcing my diaphragm to belt out the word. Lisa looked back at me in confusion but never slowed her advance. Her feet connected with the asphalt just as a dark red pickup truck came barreling down the road at over forty-five miles an hour. A loud, awful thud rumbled from the road. I wanted to look away, but I couldn't. I watched as the truck made impact and her body crumpled onto the sidewalk.

Desperately I tried to wriggle out from my straps and slammed my head against the hard ground. "Somebody help her! Help her! Lisa! Lisa!" I sobbed. Lisa lay motionless on the ground as the man driving the truck jumped out and raced back to her on foot. She couldn't be dead, she just couldn't be! My eyes shot over to Trendon, who had also started crying. I'd never seen him so determined as he gnashed at the straps with his teeth, almost managing to free one of his hands. He shouted at the goons to call an ambulance, but they just stood and stared at the accident. I looked over to Joseph, hoping he would know what to do. Then my blood froze cold.

Joseph stood next to Malcolm, his hands and feet no longer tethered.

"This was not supposed to happen!" Joseph shouted. "They were not to be hurt." Joseph looked toward Lisa's crumpled body.

"I apologize, Joseph," Malcolm said, looking away

in disappointment. "It was an accident."

"Accident? Accident?" Joseph's voice rose with anger. "I hope for your sake my uncle sees this as an accident."

"Yes, sir," Malcolm said. Did he just call Joseph "sir"? I couldn't believe my ears. Why was Joseph talking to that terrible man? And more importantly, why was Malcolm listening?

"What do we do with the captives?" Malcolm asked.

With regret in his eyes, Joseph took a deep breath and stared out toward the street. I followed his gaze and saw the truck driver trying to administer CPR to Lisa as the sound of sirens rose in the distance. "Not much we can do for her now," he said quietly. "Thanks to your incompetence." He then looked down at me and Trendon. "Take them with us."

"Joseph?" I asked, my voice soft and weak. I didn't know what to say. I looked pleadingly up at my friend, hoping for an answer, but Joseph merely stared down and shook his head.

"Sorry, Amber. I'm afraid this will be hard for you to understand."

10

After three days that passed in a blurry haze, Trendon and I sat with our ankles cuffed to the metal legs of our seats aboard a private jet chartered for Istanbul, Turkey. Several armed guards patrolled the cabin while another guard sat stretched out with an Uzi in his lap and a newspaper in his hands in the seats across the aisle from us. Joseph and Malcolm were somewhere in the front section of the jet, behind a curtain guarded by two more thugs.

Outside the windows, the small, luxurious airplane seemed to be chasing the setting sun on its way to Turkey. Our belongings, including the blue locator stone, the strange stick, and Trendon's collection of electronics had been confiscated. The only bright spot in the whole disaster was that I had managed to keep the map hidden. Because he already thought he had acquired that item from Abraham weeks ago, Malcolm never thought to look for it.

I kept it secret in the bottom of my left shoe. I

wanted more than anything to look at the map and compare it with a map of Turkey. I needed something to drag my thoughts away from Lisa. Each time the image of the car accident crept into my mind, I started crying. I doubted she'd survive the horrific accident. From what I'd overheard before we left, she was in a coma in the ICU, her body broken up badly, and the doctors had only given her a fifty percent chance of pulling through. If the man driving the pickup hadn't called 911 as quickly as he did, she would have died right there in the street. Malcolm saw no need to follow her to the hospital because even if she did wake up, she didn't have enough evidence to incriminate them. He doubted she would even remember the whole event.

I couldn't believe Joseph was a traitor. I didn't want to believe it. He must have been the one giving our location to Malcolm and his goons. Why had he betrayed us? How long had he been involved with these terrible people? Before Dorothy's kidnapping? I never saw it coming, and thinking about it had kept me from sleeping as I tossed and turned for the past three nights.

Since we were kidnapped, Trendon had lost over five pounds and was visibly miffed because of it. Though not as talkative as usual, when he did speak, he laid the sarcasm down pretty thick. It didn't take long before he started annoying the guards.

"Psst! Psst!" Trendon covered a part of his mouth with his cupped hand, obnoxiously trying to get the armed guard's attention. "Hey! Hey, Tuber!" Trendon had given this particular guard the nickname of Tuber because Trendon thought the man's head looked like a large potato. "How about you go rustle me up something to eat, Tuber?"

Tuber's nostrils flared. "Shut up, kid!"

Trendon grinned. "I'm sorry. Could you say that again in my language? I don't understand potato."

Tuber ignored Trendon's comment and flipped the page of his newspaper. This only seemed to egg Trendon on.

"Come on, Tuber! Don't be such a stiff. Go get me one of those fancy meals on a tray. You can ditch the french fries if it makes you feel . . . uncomfortable."

Tuber snatched his newspaper up so harshly from the tray it ripped in half. "I said shut up or I'll—"

"You'll what?" Trendon chimed in. "Shoot me on an airplane? Must I explain to you the physics of what could happen if you did that?" He made a sucking sound with his mouth and imitated someone being yanked back with his hands.

Tuber glared at Trendon for several seconds before pushing up from his seat and moving to the front of the cabin.

"And get us some peanuts and a couple of cans of ginger ale while you're at it!" Trendon ordered. Normally, I would have scolded Trendon, but since his intolerable behavior drove Malcolm's men absolutely crazy, I ignored him. I watched as Tuber grumbled something to one of the men standing by the curtain, and the two of them switched places.

Trendon's eyes lit up when the new guard arrived. "Well, well, long time no see, Pit Stains!" The new guard glanced down at his sweaty armpits and pulled his hand back, ready to slap Trendon.

"Leave him alone, Morens!" Joseph ordered from the opened curtain. The guard looked up at the boy standing at least six inches beneath the chins of the other guards. Joseph wore a Grateful Dead T-shirt and held an open can of Dr Pepper in his hand. Only a kid, just like us. Regardless, the guard clutching an automatic weapon bowed submissively to Joseph. How did he do it? How did Joseph control these hired killers? Last week he had been one of my best friends, someone I trusted. Now he had the authority to have me and Trendon killed? A painful pit surged in my stomach. I wanted to break from my cuffs and strangle Joseph.

"Get them something to eat." Joseph pushed through the curtain. He sauntered over to where we sat glaring at him and dropped into one of the seats across the aisle. For over a minute, no one spoke. Joseph sat stiffly, sipping his soda as if pondering what he would say.

Finally, his shoulders drooped slightly. "I know how you must feel," he said solemnly.

"No you don't! You have no—" I stopped myself, already choking up just looking at this person who was supposed to be one of my friends. Crying would mean a victory for him, and I didn't want that. I gnawed on my lip and looked pleadingly at Trendon.

"So, Judas . . ." Trendon said, glancing sideways at

Joseph. I smiled, trying to find something that would help me control the raging urge to sob. "I believe I left my other bag in the rear cabin. Why don't you be a gem and go fetch it for me?"

Joseph glanced toward the rear of the plane and shook his head. "You don't have another bag, Trendon, and there is no rear cabin."

Trendon's eyes widened. "Really? Well, good. Maybe you'll fall out of the plane and do us all a favor."

Joseph smirked. "Look, you don't understand what's going on here."

"We understand," I said, my lower lip quivering. "You destroyed our friendship! You probably killed Lisa and Dorothy. What else is there to understand?"

"That wasn't supposed to happen to Lisa," Joseph whispered. "Malcolm made a terrible mistake, and he will pay dearly for it. She may pull through—"

"Who are you?" I blurted. "When did you join sides with Malcolm?"

Joseph folded his hands in his lap and tilted his head thoughtfully to one side. "I didn't join sides with Malcolm. He joined sides with us."

My head pushed back against the headrest. This had to be the most confusing turn of events in my life. No one had ever betrayed me so blatantly.

"I . . . I . . . don't get it," I whispered, unable to prevent a large tear from sliding down my cheek. "Who's 'us'?"

Joseph took a deep breath and looked up at the ceiling of the plane. "My uncle is a very powerful and wealthy man by the name of Kendell Jasher. Ever heard of him?"

Trendon shrugged. "Sure." He looked over at me. "Isn't he the one who runs all those sweat shops in Indonesia?"

Joseph's eyes narrowed. "You're wrong. That's not true. The media makes my uncle out to be a cruel man, but that's a lie. He's brilliant."

I wiped my eyes. "What's this have to do with Dorothy? Why did you have her kidnapped?"

Joseph smiled smugly. "I'm afraid your sweet Ms. Holcomb isn't so innocent. She acts the part of the perfect teacher, all the while fooling everyone about what she really is."

"And what's that?" Trendon asked.

"A terrorist."

Trendon and I looked at each other, and then Trendon started to laugh. "Please! You didn't rehearse that well enough before blurting it out. I'd sooner believe Ms. H was a . . . mermaid before I believed she was a terrorist."

I smiled meekly, but I didn't like the direction of this conversation.

"Laugh if you want to, but Dorothy Holcomb is one of the leaders of a terrorist organization. You wouldn't have known because she's so good at concealing her identity. She and her followers steal priceless artifacts and destroy them. And they're not opposed to using violent and deadly means to fulfill their missions." Joseph paused to see our reaction. Although

Trendon still bore a smirk on his face, he didn't seem ready to interrupt. "Ms. Holcomb is particularly nasty with explosives. Do you remember a little ripple of explosions in the Mandara Mountains of Cameroon?"

"Shut up!" Trendon said scathingly.

"That was her handiwork. It's a shame too. Because of her disruption, one of the most important archaeological finds of the twentieth century was botched."

Trendon rolled his eyes. "Can we eat now? I think I'm through with the entertainment portion of tonight's flight." As if summoned by Trendon's request, the guard returned, carrying two plastic trays brimming with food. "Finally," Trendon said. The guard glanced around, looking for a spot to sit.

"You can go sit over there," Joseph said, pointing toward the other guards. "We don't need you right now." The man shrugged and walked away.

I just glanced at the meal in front of me, no longer hungry. "So she's the enemy, huh?" I asked. "How long have you known she was a terrorist? A month?"

"Amber, I'm not a scholar. You've seen my grades. I barely eke by. Before I enrolled at Roland and Tesh there had never been an athletic scholarship. There still isn't, actually. My uncle paid my way into the school. I was planted there to spy on Dorothy from day one," Joseph said, evidently proud of this fact.

"So how come no one knows you're related to this Kendell Jasher? That seems a little far-fetched if you ask me," Trendon mumbled through a mouthful of pot roast.

"That's because our plan worked flawlessly. My parents died when I was eight years old, and my uncle Jasher had the state records altered to show I was placed in foster care and my last name was changed to Mitchell. But I lived with my uncle. When I was twelve, Uncle Jasher made a sizeable donation to the private school from my fabricated foster parents, and the rest is history. Not even the Dean of Students had any clue who I really was. It's amazing what money can buy."

"Yeah." Trendon burped. "Amazing. You're a real loser, you know that? It sounds to me like you're just as much of a pawn in this whole mess as the other idiots sitting on this plane."

"I'm not a pawn!" Joseph sneered.

"Sure you are," Trendon continued, ignoring Joseph's rising temper. "You said yourself Mr. Jasher planted you at the school. That means you're a plant, which is another word for a pawn. He's using you, and you're too dumb to know it."

"No one's using me, and I know what you're doing." Joseph rubbed his chin with his hand and looked impassively down at his fingernails. "You're just trying to make me lose my cool, but it's not going to work."

"Well, at least you know something, Einstein. So tell me, since you've thought of everything, what are you going to do about our parents?"

Joseph popped his knuckles. "Why should I worry about them? If all goes as planned, this excavation will be over soon. School doesn't let out for two more weeks."

"And what about finals? You don't think people will suspect something is out of whack when we don't show up for class?" Trendon folded his arms across his chest.

"Like I said, it's amazing what money will buy. My uncle has already cleared the three of us for a study abroad course. The Dean of Students dismissed the rest of your finals."

Trendon scrunched his nose. "I suppose I should thank you for that."

"So you see, no one suspects anything has gone awry."

My lungs hurt. I hated being this close to Joseph. "None of this changes the fact that you and your evil uncle are criminals!" I shouted. "You'll never convince me otherwise!"

Joseph sighed. "Look, believe what you want, but we had to do what we did to secure the locator stone. We need it for our excavation. I didn't necessarily want you guys to be this involved, but things happen. We're on the verge of discovering something big. Something that could change the world. Dorothy and her friends would've ruined everything."

"If you didn't want us involved, why didn't *you* go to Abraham's apartment instead of us? He was the one that led us to the stone," Trendon pressed.

"I thought that Dorothy would've secured the stone in her safe-deposit box at the bank. It seemed more logical."

"What does the stone lead to?" I asked.

"Why should I tell you?" Joseph asked, looking at me piercingly. For a fleeting moment I wanted so badly to forget everything. Why couldn't things be the way they used to be? I quickly dismissed the idea. Lisa and Dorothy had already paid the price for Joseph's treachery.

"Why *not* tell us? You've told us everything else about your wonderful uncle and your deceitful plan. What's it going to hurt? It's not like you're going to let us live anyway."

"You're still alive because of me." Joseph stood from the chair. "You eat regular meals because of me. You're on this plane right now to Turkey because I convinced my uncle you could be used as leverage . . ." he hesitated, and my pulse quickened. Joseph glared down at me. "Enjoy the rest of your meal. We land in three hours, and if you want me to continue to be nice to you, I suggest you change your attitude." With that, Joseph walked briskly to the front of the plane and disappeared behind the curtain.

11

The jet taxied across the tarmac, settling beneath a private hangar of the Ataturk International Airport. Below the plane, several men with guns paced back and forth. A few held sleek, black Doberman pinschers by metal leashes. I wondered if all the private hangars received this sort of preferential treatment.

A caravan of black Cadillac Escalades transported our group away from the airport. We traveled for more than an hour through bustling roads crowded with people, bicycles, and animals and then surfaced on a highway. The roads seemed less crowded and noisy here, and the drone of the vehicle caused my eyelids to droop. I drearily peered out the window at the enormous mansions towering over neatly manicured lawns. I came from a family with money, but the sheer wealth radiating from these homes amazed me.

We approached a gated entrance secured by two Turkish guards wearing light tan uniforms and armed with machine guns. Malcolm, riding in the back of the Cadillac at the front of the caravan, cracked his window and waved a finger at the guards. The gates opened automatically, and the procession lurched forward. Very few trees grew in this area, but at the end of this gated road was the highest concentration of plant life I'd seen since landing at the airport. Behind the garden, a palace rose up on beautifully sculpted marble columns, its immense sparkling windows reflecting the moonlight like giant flashing mirrors. On top of the roof, spotlights scanned the premises, covering every possible inch of yard in periodic intervals. The driveway circled a giant water fountain with a sculpture of a large bird, probably a condor, appearing to land in the spouting water.

The guards escorted Trendon and I through a rear entrance into the main kitchen. I glanced over at Trendon, who appeared interested in a row of stainless steel subzero freezers spanning the length of the room. Copper kettles, pans, colanders, and large spatulas dangled like well-polished ornaments from an overhead rack. Even at such a late hour, several workers still labored in the kitchen with polish and heavy cloth rags. Beyond the kitchen and through an adjoining hallway, we entered a main foyer where a chandelier the size of a Volkswagen Beetle glittered above a cascading staircase. Everything seemed perfectly in order—not a speck of dust on any surface. Even the artwork on the corniced walls appeared so new and fresh that I wouldn't have been surprised if the pieces had been painted that day.

"Welcome!" a voice echoed from beyond the balustrade of the overlooking floor. I looked up to see a man descending the stairs. His bald head gleamed in the light from the chandelier, and his olive skin could've been made of wax. Wearing a beige polo shirt and neatly pressed slacks, he appeared very casual. "I trust your flight went smoothly?" He extended his hand and clasped Joseph's chin.

"Yes, Uncle Jasher," Joseph said reverently.

I looked at Trendon, who looked utterly confused. That was Kendell Jasher? He looked nothing like his nephew. Mr. Jasher could quite possibly be of Turkish descent.

"Malcolm." Mr. Jasher inclined his head slightly. "I have sufficient security guarding the premises this evening. You and your men are dismissed. We shall discuss matters in the morning." Malcolm bowed and had already moved toward the exit when Mr. Jasher called him back. "Aren't you forgetting something?" Malcolm looked over his shoulder. Kendell gestured toward mine and Trendon's manacles, which were locking our wrists together. "Those won't be necessary here. These children are guests in my home. They won't try to run. Will you?" Mr. Jasher's mesmerizing eyes stared directly at mine. Not knowing exactly how to respond, I shrugged my shoulders.

After Malcolm removed the clamps from our wrists, Mr. Jasher wrapped his arms around our shoulders. "Joseph, your bed has been turned down for the evening. Run along while I show your friends to their quarters." Joseph hesitated, almost appearing ready to protest, but a dangerous gleam in Mr. Jasher's eyes kept him quiet.

Without another word, Joseph hurried down a hallway and vanished from view around the corner. I felt a huge sense of emptiness as I watched him leave. Although I now definitely hated Joseph for what he had done, I didn't want to be alone with Mr. Jasher. He may have appeared casual and friendly, but I knew something evil lurked beneath his expression.

"I apologize for having to bring you here so far from your home. I only hope we can conclude this expedition quickly so you can be reunited with your families." Mr. Jasher's lower lip tucked into a frown. "Times have become dangerous for those of us trying to better society. Thus the ever-growing need for stronger security measures—guns and bombs, cameras and lights, et cetera, et cetera." He held his hand out, motioning to large black cameras with blipping red lights that monitored each corner of the massive foyer. "You're obviously confused by all of this and the drastic means I have undergone to ensure no further disruptions will occur, but I trust that in the upcoming days we will all come to see things the same way."

What was he talking about? I wanted answers but didn't know the right moment to ask for them. Right now I felt physically drained from the flight. I needed time to myself to think, preferably on a soft bed, and then I wanted a free moment to pick Trendon's brain.

Trendon had apparently had enough of the double-talk. "Uh, Mr. Jasher, is it?" he asked, raising his hand like he was in class.

"Yes," Mr. Jasher said.

"What do you got to eat in this joint? Uh . . . sir."

Mr. Jasher looked concerned. "Were you not fed on your flight?"

Trendon shook his head. "Not a bite!" he lied.

"Very well. After you are settled in your rooms, I will have a meal brought up for you. I trust your rooms will be comfortable. I'm afraid you'll be spending the bulk of your stay there. We live in constant threat of attack from our enemies, and that's where you'll be safest."

I wanted to laugh. *That's where we'll be safest? Ha! That's where you can keep a constant eye on us.* At the end of the carpet, the hall forked. Kendell guided us down the left hallway and introduced us to our sleeping quarters. Each room had its own private bathroom, a king-sized four-poster bed, and a window with wrought iron bars overlooking a magnificent terraced landscape that was bordered on one side by the Istanbul Strait. In my room I found an oak desk, a bookcase chock-full of books, and a floor-to-ceiling mirror with an intricately carved golden frame. Trendon's room had wicker furniture, an enormous footlocker that looked like a pirate's treasure chest at the end of the bed, and the mounted head of a strange deerlike animal above the headboard. I stood next to Trendon's bed, watching him eye the eerie animal trophy with evident disgust.

"Your dinner will be up shortly," Mr. Jasher said, standing in the doorway of the room. "You and Trendon may eat together if you'd like. There will be guards posted outside of your room, for your protection, of course, and they will inform you when it is time to retire for the evening. I have a very strict curfew that everyone, including guests, must abide by, so I expect you will comply with it." He turned to leave but paused, glancing back. "Unfortunately, I have many appointments to keep in the morning and throughout this week. I'm a very busy man with little time to treat guests properly. I'm afraid this may be one of the only times we will have the opportunity to speak, so allow me to beg your forgiveness once more for any inconvenience this may have caused you. I sincerely hope that in a week's passing, you'll be on your way home and this entire episode will be nothing more than an inconvenient memory." His lips pulled back in a smile, revealing two rows of perfect teeth. I shuddered. "Good night," he said, and then the mysterious Kendell Jasher exited the room, closing the door behind him.

I immediately looked over at Trendon and opened my mouth to speak, but he held his index finger up to his lips. Cautiously he started moving about the room, scanning behind lamps, furniture, and potted plants, looking for any sort of camera or device that could be spying on us. He bent beneath the desk and ran his fingers under the surface in search of a wire. After a thorough inspection, he returned to the bed.

"I think we're clear," he said quietly. "I'm sure the whole mansion is bugged with wire taps and cameras and that kind of stuff, but I can't find anything in here."

"Do you even know what you're looking for?" I asked.

Trendon frowned. "Not a clue, but what are you gonna do?" He threw his hands up in the air. "Still, we should probably wait until after they bring us our food to start talking about anything. We have to keep as much as we can secret."

Thank goodness for Trendon's skepticism. I would have never thought to check the room for intrusions.

We waited for almost fifteen minutes until a servant rapped softly on the door. He entered, carrying two pewter trays, which he rested on the lid of the footlocker. Trendon rubbed his hands together as he lifted the lid of one of the trays. A delicious aroma wafted out from the steaming bowls of soup and warm loaves of bread. A clear liquid fizzed in a crystal glass. Trendon took a sip and made a face.

"It's like seltzer water or something," he said, resting the glass back on the tray.

The servant politely bowed. "Sorry, but our water may be a tad tainted. Foreigners tend to have stomach aches unless their bodies have adapted. I could bring something else if you'd like?"

"Yeah, how about a couple bottles of soda, or a—" Trendon started, but I interjected.

"We're fine," I said. "Thank you."

"As you wish," the servant said. Then he left the two of us to our meal.

My stomach craved the food. I hadn't eaten anything since before our long flight. The soup tasted wonderful, almost like a hot and sour soup I once tried at a Chinese restaurant, but not exactly the same. Whatever the case, it didn't take me long to slurp my bowl clean. The individual loaves of bread topped the meal off perfectly. They had a chewy crust with a light and fluffy center, and they tasted somewhat like almonds. Even the seltzer water went down my throat just fine after a few sips.

Feeling full and content, and knowing we had limited time to talk, I leaned in close to Trendon and whispered. "We need to discuss what Joseph said on the plane."

Trendon groaned, patting his stomach and releasing a belch that bellowed through the silence. "Yeah, for starters, there's no way he's blood related to Mr. Jasher. They don't look anything alike."

"I agree, but do you think it's all an act? Did Joseph just make it up?"

"Maybe," Trendon answered, swishing some of the seltzer water around in his mouth. "What about the stuff he said about Dorothy? Do you really think she could be a terrorist?"

I scoffed. "No way. You know Dorothy just as well as I do. Terrorist? That doesn't fit. I think she just figured out what was going on, and they put a stop to her."

"Okay, then. How did she get the stone and everything else? These guys are upper-class criminals." Trendon's eyes flashed toward the window as the glass lit up momentarily from the scanning light of the outdoor security spotlights. "Dorothy's smart and all, but it just doesn't make sense that she accidentally got the upper hand on Mr. Jasher."

"Maybe she found them on a dig or something. She's won many awards for her work," I said, not entirely convinced. Trendon had voiced what I inwardly believed myself. Dorothy's involvement in this mystery ran deeper than just a coincidental find during some dig. "Where do you think Mr. Jasher's keeping her?"

Trendon shrugged. "*If* they're still keeping her—" He flinched as I slugged him in the shoulder. "Ouch! All I meant was maybe they don't need her anymore now that they have us. Maybe they let her go."

"That's not what you meant, Trendon," I said, scowling at him. "Why would they need us anyway?"

"You heard Joseph, for 'leverage.'" Trendon tried imitating Joseph's voice, but it sounded more like a whiny kid.

I cautiously looked around the room. "Do you really think we're secure right now?"

"There's no way to know for sure, but Jasher couldn't have known we were coming until just recently."

Reaching down, I slid Dorothy's map out from within my shoe. Keeping my eye on the bedroom door, I unfolded the map. "What do you think this leads to, now that you know it's in Turkey?" I whispered even lower than before.

Trendon wiggled his fingers, asking for the map. He examined it for a moment before surrendering it back to me. "I can't read that gibberish. It looks like a mountain, but maybe that's because we're looking at it wrong. For all I know, the map is upside down."

I flipped it over and shook my head. "No, these are definitely Hebraic characters." I straightened the material, and my eyes fell once again on the word that had stood out before: *Tebah*. I jabbed at the word with my thumb. "I know this word," I said. "Why can't I remember it?"

"Tei . . . bah?" Trendon tried pronouncing it. "Tebah, Tebah . . ." he repeated it several times until I grew wary and shushed him.

"Be quiet! What if someone hears you?"

"They'll think I'm wigging out on seltzer water. Don't worry."

"Can you remember Dorothy talking about that word?"

Trendon chuckled. "Don't look at me. You're the pro at this stuff. No pressure or anything, but we need answers—fast. The sooner we figure out what's going on, the better. Somehow we need to get the word out to the authorities about what's going on here. The only problem is, people like Jasher usually own the police."

"What about Joseph?" I asked.

"What about him? He's a moron, and if I had actually stayed in karate when I was younger, I would've

Kung Powed his butt by now!"

In spite of everything, I had to smile. I wanted to tousle Trendon's black curly hair. "Do you think he really believes his uncle is doing the right thing?"

"What does it matter?"

I looked down at my lap. "Trendon, I really hate him right now just as much as you, but maybe there's still a chance he could change. We went through so much together over the years. That has to count for something. Maybe he's just been brainwashed." I folded the map and returned it to my shoe.

"Brain wiped," Trendon said, snatching a few crumbs from his plate.

Trendon had never been really close to Joseph. They had always been friends, but more like pals. I believed Joseph felt more for me, or had that all been part of his act?

The door opened, and a man wearing one of the khaki uniforms stepped through. He had a head-set radio and a black handgun strapped to his belt. "Bedtime, kiddies," he mumbled with an accented voice and a smirk on his lips.

Two hours later, unable to sleep, I tugged the chain on the desk lamp in my room. Casting a weary look toward the barred window, I spread the map out on the wooden surface of the desk. The light from the hall still crept under my door, and occasionally I saw someone's shadow pass by. Figuring I probably didn't

have long before someone got curious, I started searching my memory for answers.

Several minutes passed, but nothing came to me. I
rummaged in the top desk drawer and found a couple
of sharpened pencils. *What's here in Turkey?* I thought
back to my studies and tried to piece together some
sort of direction. What items of importance had been
discovered in the past century? Archaeologists found
the House of David Inscription in Israel, the Amulet
Scroll near Jerusalem, and of course the Dead Sea
Scrolls. But those had already been discovered. What
were people still looking for? Better yet, what were
they looking for in Turkey? As far as I could recall,
only burial sites and ancient temples still remained in
this region. Important? Sure. But worthy of changing
the world? Not likely.

I tried a new approach. Had there been something
in Dorothy's apartment that could answer my question?
I remembered the knickknacks, the small trinkets, and
the statues resting on most of the mantle space. Then
I remembered the cross-stitched Bible verses on the
walls of Dorothy's apartment. Those verses just seemed
to stand out awkwardly in her apartment's decor.

A chilling ripple traveled up my spine. Time to put
my photographic memory to work. Storing images in
my mind for long periods of time happened to be one
of my best qualities. Pressing my eyelids shut, I searched
my memory and, within a few seconds, remembered
one of them: 1 Kings 18:3. It had been something about
Elijah, but I couldn't exactly recall all of the words.

What was the other one about? I thought harder, pulling my eyelids shut even tighter. Exodus 9:23.

Without a doubt, that one had been about Moses. I sighed in frustration. I needed to know what the verses meant. Maybe they didn't have anything to do with Jasher and Dorothy, but the memory of them gnawed at my brain.

My focus fell on the bookshelf across the room. Walking over to the shelves, I started hunting through the titles. Some I remembered from school, like *Great Expectations* and *Moby Dick*, but others I couldn't even read, written in some foreign tongue.

I continued searching until the end of the row. If Mr. Jasher kept titles like the literary classics in his library, maybe . . . just maybe . . .

After reading through several more titles, I found a King James Bible resting on the third shelf, tucked between a copy of Homer's *Iliad* and a weathered volume of Edgar Allen Poe's poetry. Pumping my fist, I snatched the Bible from its spot and quickly thumbed to the verses I'd recalled only moments before.

And Moses stretched forth his rod toward heaven:
and the Lord sent thunder and hail, and the fire ran
along upon the ground.

I contemplated this passage for a moment before determining it didn't help. Moses came from Egypt, and from what I remembered from Bible school, the children of Israel didn't make any detours into Turkey. I thumbed to the other verse.

And now thou sayest, Go, tell thy lord, Behold, Elijah is here.

More goose bumps rose on my flesh but only because this passage creeped me out. The story of Elijah had always troubled me as a younger girl. Strange whirlwinds. Fire from heaven. Not quite the normal phenomena that would follow in the wake of a simple man. But Elijah came from Gilead, which was somewhere in Jordan. No good.

Neither of those verses explained our current predicament in Turkey. I almost tossed the Bible aside and admitted defeat, but something nagged at me to keep looking. Maybe another verse would answer it. I rifled through the pages of the Old Testament, looking for anything to trigger a memory.

Another shadow passed beneath the door, and I could hear the voices of the guards just beyond the wall. I had a few minutes left, maybe less, before they burst in and forced me to follow Mr. Jasher's curfew.

"Why can't I figure this out?" I pleaded out loud. This puzzle felt like a safe that was impossible to crack. I dithered between chapters, and my fingers hesitated on one of the thin pages. The thought of cracking a safe caused me to think of something else. Dorothy's safe. She had only recently changed the combination to something new, one that even surprised Abraham.

One, eight, four.

Maybe that combination didn't describe an important date in Dorothy's past. Maybe they corresponded to another code. I flipped to Genesis (the first book in the Bible), chapter eight, verse four.

Staring down at the page, my whole body filled with a tingling sensation. The recollection of Dorothy's class discussion a couple years ago came surging back into my mind. I knew what the word *Tebah* meant.

> *And the ark rested in the seventh month, on the seventeenth day of the month, upon the mountains of Ararat.*

The mountain depicted on the map was Mt. Ararat. And that meant Dorothy was trying to stop Kendell Jasher from finding Noah's ark.

12

I saw very little of Mr. Jasher's mansion over the next three days while I was imprisoned in my bedroom. My meals came like clockwork. Breakfast arrived at 7:00 a.m., they served me lunch promptly at noon, and they delivered dinner just after 6 in the evening. Though the food was delicious and plentiful, I would've willingly gone without it if I could've gotten out and talked with Trendon. I hoped he was faring better than me, but with his attitude, I doubted it.

To pass the time, I studied the map, searched for any clues in the Bible, and showered. I must have taken at least half a dozen showers daily. The air pumping through the air conditioning vents felt cool but dusty. And with no clean clothes to change into, I always felt grimy and gross. Kendell Jasher's initial façade as a gracious host proved to be a load of bunk. He had probably already forgotten we were sleeping in the same house.

I found creative ways to do research on Mt. Ararat,

the supposed dwelling place of Noah's ark. For starters, the mountain itself was somewhere in the land of
Armenia, directly east over the border. I discovered
that in one of the ancient maps included in the back of
the Bible. Most kids my age would have been confused
by the fact Mr. Ararat couldn't be found within the
borders of Turkey, but not me. I figured it probably just
recently became incorporated in present-day Turkey.
Stuff like that always happened to nations sharing their
borders with other countries, especially when those
countries have unstable governments.

As I sat cross-legged on the floor with my back
stiffly up against the bed, reading the first chapter of
Shakespeare's *King Lear*, I glanced up at the wall clock.
Five minutes until six and time for another slight break
from the monotony of solitude. As usual, the guard
gave a warning knock on my door before entering, just
in case I happened to be in the process of changing
into a pair of pajamas I didn't have.

But this time instead of balancing a tray of food on
his hand, the guard brought in a navy blue garment
bag and laid it on the bed. "Mr. Jasher would like you
to join him for dinner this evening in the main dining
hall," the guard said. "You have fifteen minutes to get
dressed. Be ready when I return."

I stared dumbfounded at the back of the guard's
head as he exited. Cautiously, I unzipped the garment
bag, half-expecting some sort of floral gown waiting for me. Wasn't that what happened in the movies
whenever a girl was being held captive in some evil

overlord's palace? *Yuck!* Instead I discovered a pair of blue jeans, a yellow v-neck top, and a change of clean underwear and socks. Embarrassed by the undergarments, I snatched it all up and quickly dressed. With only a few minutes before my escort returned, I flipped to the back of the book I had been reading and tore out one of the blank pages. I doubted Trendon and I would be given a moment to talk in private, and I needed to send him a message. Snatching one of the pencils from the desk drawer, I scribbled two sentences on the paper.

> *Jasher is searching for Noah's ark in Mt. Ararat.*
> *We need to get working on a plan to get us out of here.*

The warning knock struck, and I frantically folded the message into a tiny square and wedged it behind the beltline of my blue jeans, just as the door opened.

Mr. Jasher sat in an ornate, high-backed chair at one end of a long dining room table with an enormous centerpiece of fresh cut flowers and five place settings. Joseph sat next to him but didn't make eye contact with me. Instead he stared down at his empty soup bowl. Malcolm sat kitty-corner from Mr. Jasher, watching me as I entered. Oh, how I hated all of them; the loathsome feelings undoubtedly radiated through my body language. Two other place settings for me and Trendon completed the table, but Trendon hadn't arrived yet. As I sat, I couldn't help but stare at the empty chair where he should've been seated.

"Ah, I'm afraid your friend is not feeling well and will not be joining us this evening," Mr. Jasher said, answering my question. I shot an alarmed look at Joseph, who had glanced up from his bowl. What did Mr. Jasher mean when he said Trendon wasn't feeling well? If anything happened to him—

"Relax, Amber. He's all right," Joseph said softly, as if sensing my alarm. "He has an upset stomach, that's all."

My eyes narrowed, and I looked away from the traitor. This would be a pointless meal after all, now that Trendon wouldn't be there. I had no desire to carry on casual dinner conversation with this evil group.

"It was the same for Joseph when he came here a couple of years ago," Mr. Jasher said with a smile. "He spent more time in the restroom than any other room in the mansion." Mr. Jasher chuckled, and Malcolm smirked, but no one else at the table stirred. I saw no need to humor him and felt anxious to get the meal over with.

I glanced toward the exits, noticing two guards posted at either door. No escape. Even if I did miraculously get past the guards, I had no idea where to find the main entryway in the enormous mansion. My shoulders drooped, and I slouched in my chair as they served the first course.

Everyone ate in silence, the only sounds coming from the clinking silverware. I nibbled at my Chicken Kiev and hardly touched any of the vegetables or salad.

I wasn't hungry, and from what I could see, neither was Joseph. His plate went almost entirely untouched.

As the servants served the final course—a raspberry sorbet with mango slices, garnished with a sprig of spearmint—Mr. Jasher finally spoke. "So Joseph tells me you are quite the up-and-coming archaeologist. Is that true?" In no mood to make small talk, I kept my eyes fixed on the crystal dish and swirled the sorbet with my spoon until it turned into a gooey glop of red slush. "You get top marks on all your assignments and have a natural knack for solving puzzles. That is quite impressive." Mr. Jasher gave his nephew a sideways glance. "Unfortunately, Joseph never acquired our love of discovery, did you, Joseph?" My eyes fluttered up from my glass, focusing on Joseph for a second. Joseph bowed his hand and seemed embarrassed. "But no matter," Mr. Jasher continued, waving one hand dismissively while he sipped his drink with the other. "He has a bright future in . . . soccer." He looked at me and rolled his eyes.

What a jerk! I thought. *He's your nephew.* I felt sorry for Joseph for a few seconds until I remembered he deserved this sort of treatment. What did I care?

"May I be excused, Uncle?" Joseph asked.

Mr. Jasher's smile widened. "Of course you can, nephew. Run along and practice your, what do you call it . . . dribbling?"

Joseph stood and offered me a passing look before leaving the dining area. Why did I suddenly feel sad about his leaving? Trendon and I might never see our families again, and he could freely do whatever he wanted.

Mr. Jasher's glass clinked against his plate. "My apologies for that little family drama. Joseph has trouble taking a joke."

I could see nothing playful about Mr. Jasher's comments. Finally finding the ability to speak, I cleared my throat. "I thought you said you were going to be too busy to meet with us."

"Yes, I did, but I was able to rearrange a few appointments to squeeze this dinner in. Amber, I know how you must feel being locked up here all day."

No he didn't. How could he even say that? I dropped my hands into my lap and fidgeted with my napkin. When would this meal be over?

"I feel horrible, simply horrible, about everything, and I wanted to make it up to you somehow." I wouldn't look up from my lap. "So I have arranged a meeting for you with Dorothy."

What? Was this just another one of his cruel humorless antics? My eyes shot up to view his expression. Mr. Jasher seemed genuine. A flood of emotions filled my chest. Dorothy was alive! This would prove it. I wouldn't have to keep doubting or fearing the worst. Maybe I would find a way to help her. And if anyone knew how to get out of a jam, Dorothy did. I almost couldn't keep myself from smiling, but I didn't want to reveal my excitement.

"When do I get to see her?" I asked, covering my mouth with my hand to conceal a smile.

"We shall leave after you've finished your sorbet. The drive takes about an hour, and it is a bit of a bumpy ride." Mr. Jasher smiled. I gnawed on my lip to keep from bursting into a huge grin, and Mr. Jasher started laughing. "You see, I'm not all that bad, am I?" he asked, twirling his fork around in his fingers. "I'm just someone trying to survive and leave as little destruction in my wake as possible. I'm no different than any other entrepreneur." He glanced over at Malcolm, and I noticed the conniving grin they shared, like they both knew the punch line of some inside joke. A lump formed in my throat. *Don't be a fool, Amber!* I told myself. These men wouldn't do anything for me unless it played into their plans.

I shook off my excitement. "Why?" I asked coldly.

"I'm sorry, what's that?" Mr. Jasher asked.

"Why do I get to see her?" I hid my emotions as best I could. "What's the point?"

He shook his head in confusion. "Don't you want to talk with her? Make sure she's well?" He looked baffled, as if wondering how I could ever doubt his legitimate kindness. "I thought that would make you feel a little more at ease while you stay here, but if not, then . . ."

"No, I do want to see her," I interjected. "I'm just trying to figure out your motive."

Mr. Jasher looked hurt by my words. "There's no motive, I assure you. You have the wrong idea about me, my dear. I'm a man of few motives, but when I have one, I don't hide it. Dorothy is no friend of mine, that's for certain, but I'm sure she's just misunderstood. I hate seeing her shackled like a dangerous animal, but I can't let her run around, continuing to destroy my work and endangering my employees and my own life. That's just not practical. This meeting is an opportunity for me to show her a little kindness as well. I know she's dying to speak with you. If there is any motive it is only that perhaps you could talk some sense into the poor woman so that I can send her back to her family along with you and Trendon. That's all."

I studied his face for several moments before nodding my consent. I didn't really believe him, but I didn't want to ruin my chances of meeting with Dorothy. Whatever the reason for this change in plans, I believed Kendell needed some information. Maybe he thought Dorothy would slip and reveal something important about their hunt to me. I couldn't let that happen. I stood from my chair.

"But, dear, you haven't finished your dessert. It is quite lovely," he said, craning his neck to look at my place setting.

"I really can't eat right now," I said, dropping my napkin across the table.

"Well then, I shall have my servants bring you up a bowl later this evening when we return."

"What about Trendon? He wants to talk to her too." I gestured toward the empty place setting.

"I'm afraid that's impossible." Mr. Jasher apologized. "He will be more comfortable resting tonight. Where we're going there aren't proper facilities for him to use."

"Can I see him before we go?" I asked.

Mr. Jasher and Malcolm stood. "Amber, he really is sick, but I swear to you he's safe in his room. Don't trouble yourself about his well-being." He snapped his fingers, and several servants began clearing the dining table.

"Please. I just want to know if there's anything he wants to ask her. It would only take me a minute, and then we can go."

Mr. Jasher looked at Malcolm, considering this request. "All right," he answered. "Malcolm will take you there, but be quick. It is already very late, and we really need to get going."

Trendon lay curled in the fetal position on his bed with a damp towel wrapped around his head. Even though he looked miserable, I couldn't help but smile with relief at the sight of him.

"No more crackers and Sprite for crying out loud!" he bellowed, curling his hand into a fist and slugging himself in the stomach.

Malcolm stood in the doorway as I crouched next to the bed and nudged Trendon's arm.

"Trendon, it's me, Amber," I whispered.

The towel fell off Trendon's face, and he glowered at me. "What do you want?" he grunted.

"I'm glad to see you too," I answered.

Trendon groaned in response. "It feels like I swallowed a bucket of Pop Rocks and a helium balloon keeps blowing up in my stomach!" As if on cue, a loud grumbling ignited in his belly, and he buckled over in pain. "You'll have to forgive me if I don't jump up and river dance with joy!"

"What did you eat?" I asked, patting my friend on the shoulder.

"Argh, I don't know. Everything!"

I shook my head in sympathy as Trendon writhed and his stomach continued to produce noises like a garbage disposal. "I wanted you to know I'm going to go see Dorothy now."

Trendon scrunched up his face. "What is that? Some sort of quote from *The Wizard of Oz*? Is this a dream?"

"Dorothy Holcomb, remember? Our teacher?"

More groaning. "Oh sure, you mean the person responsible for this horrible field trip."

"Yeah, that one. They're going to let me go talk to her tonight for a little while."

"Oh." Trendon started to roll over. "Well, have fun."

"Don't you want me to ask her anything?" I asked, growing annoyed with the big baby. This could be our first real opportunity to find answers, and Trendon only cared about wallowing in his bed.

"No!" Trendon snapped. "Ask me tomorrow and maybe I'll think of something. But right now I want to crawl up into some hole and die."

I looked toward the doorway, and Malcolm tapped his watch, so I stood up from the floor. "I hope you feel better, buddy," I said, reaching over and lifting up Trendon's shirt to pat his bare, bubbling stomach.

Trendon flinched, covering his belly with his hands and glaring up at me irritably. "What do you think you're doing? There's no baby in there!"

"I'm just worried, that's all. Chill out!" I returned the glare and raised my eyebrows. Trendon just frowned. "Well, you don't just pat a person's stomach. That's not cool. Now leave me alone." With another grumble from his midsection, Trendon rolled over and slammed his pillow over his head.

I threw my hands up in defeat and left with Malcolm. As we walked through the halls in silence, heading toward Mr. Jasher and one of his many vehicles, I stole a quick look down at where my folded message had once hidden beneath my jeans. I could only hope Trendon noticed the tiny slip of paper stuck just above his sweaty belly button.

13

I sat alone in the backseat of the SUV as it rumbled up an old, unpaved road. We had been driving for over an hour, mostly through quiet, unpopulated areas. I stared down at the handcuffs shackling my wrists to a metal rod that was bolted into the vehicle's floor. A precaution, Mr. Jasher assured me, taken with my utmost safety in mind. Why didn't he just admit his real intentions and be done with it? Why did he have to carry on the ridiculous charade of some innocent businessman? His act didn't fool anyone, especially not me.

The vehicle slowed as we approached a wrought iron gate, guarded by an elderly man in a light blue parka. The man beamed his flashlight at the windshield and ducked down to peer through the driver's side window. He muttered something in Turkish in an annoyed voice and then hopped back obediently once he recognized Mr. Jasher riding in the passenger seat.

"My apologies," he whimpered, scuttling over to

the control box and pressing a button. The gate opened with the clamor of whirring gears and grinding metal, sounding as though it hadn't been oiled in many years. I glanced out my window at the entrance sign printed in Turkish in big bold letters. In parentheses beneath it I read the title in English: Yedikule Fortress. The headlights of our vehicle gave me a clear view of the massive stone castle with several towers rising up above the keep and a forest of countless, sinewy trees with twisted branches scraping against the weathered walls. I shivered. The castle looked like something I had seen in an old Dracula movie.

"This was once a popular tourist attraction," Mr. Jasher said over his shoulder. The SUV's tires ground against the gravel road as Malcolm steered through the opening. "It's been used as a prison for many centuries, even during the Napoleonic Wars, and housed some fairly famous soldiers throughout history. Just recently, I was able to acquire somewhat of a lease on the property so it only serves our specific purposes."

"And now you've got Dorothy chained up in it," I said, glaring at the back of Mr. Jasher's bald dome.

Mr. Jasher chuckled. "Don't be silly, girl. She's not chained to anything."

Malcolm pulled the vehicle to a stop in a handicapped parking stall.

"Don't do anything stupid," Malcolm whispered as he leaned over the center console to unlock my handcuffs. The manacles clicked free, and I instinctively massaged my wrists.

"Malcolm, she's not going to run away. Not now, at least," Mr. Jasher said, cynically. "There's nothing but miles of unpopulated forest in either direction, teeming with wolves and lions and all sorts of other vicious beasts. She's not a fool, are you, Amber?" He looked back at me and winked.

I wanted to stick my tongue out or offer some sort of completely rude gesture, but I opted to remain silent. Truthfully, I hadn't even thought about running away because of my eagerness to talk with Dorothy. Why would I blow that chance? Plus, I still had Trendon to think about. What would happen to him if I never returned to Istanbul?

By the light of Malcolm's flashlight, the three of us crossed the short distance from the vehicle to an employee-access stairwell on one side of the fortress, hidden behind several unused dumpsters. A couple of large rodentlike animals shot out from beneath the dumpsters and scattered away from the beam of Malcolm's flashlight. I yelped and jumped behind Mr. Jasher.

"Don't be alarmed. They're only foxes," Mr. Jasher said.

"Those are foxes?" I asked. They didn't look like the clever, bushy-tailed animals I always saw in pictures; these looked more like giant rats.

After descending the dark stairwell, we arrived at a steel door. Malcolm knocked, and a slot near the top of the door opened. A pair of eyes peered out, and a man grumbled something in Turkish. Mr. Jasher

answered back shortly, and the door opened. Down we walked over several more flights of stairs, deep into the belly of the fortress. With each passing level, the temperature dropped several degrees until we arrived at the bottom and my teeth chattered uncontrollably. The stairs poured down into a long hallway with dirty stone floors. Over every surface, I could see insects crawling and scuttling in the dim light. Directly to the right loomed another heavy steel door with a slot near the top. Flickering torches ensconced on the walls provided the only source of light. As my eyes began to adjust to the dimly lit hallway, I saw six separate recessed prison cells carved into the rock. Bulky metal rods barred their entrances, but all of the cells appeared empty except for the last one near the eastern wall. I could hear the sounds of silverware clinking against a plate and saw the slight movement of shadows bending with the sputter of firelight.

"Go now and speak with your friend," Mr. Jasher whispered, gesturing toward the furthest cell. "Cheer her up, won't you? Make her realize her foolishness so we can all return to our normal lives. If you need anything at all, I'll be in this next room, meeting with my guards." He nodded reassuringly, and after I made a few steps toward the cell, Mr. Jasher and Malcolm exited through the steel door and closed it behind them. Standing alone in the hallway, I started to freak out and considered dashing up the stairs to take my chances in the wolf-infested forests. What if this was a trick? What if there was someone else in that cell?

What if it was some criminal just waiting for me to get close to the bars so he could reach out and strangle me? I shivered at the thought and hugged my arms tightly.

"Stop it, Amber," I whispered. I hadn't come this far to chicken out now. I passed the first five cells before coming to a stop in front of the final one. Gasping, I covered my mouth and forced back a scream. At first I actually thought my worst fear had come true and they had caged someone else in the cell, someone terrible. Then I recognized Dorothy and caught my breath at the sight of my poor, withered teacher. Immediately, I started to cry.

"Dorothy?" I asked, wiping my tears with the back of my sleeve.

Dorothy looked up from her plate of food and licked her fingers. Her hair, matted with dirt and cobwebs, was plastered against her shoulders like the head of an over-used mop. Wearing jeans that no longer possessed any blue color and a shirt that was ripped beneath her neckline, the normally fair-skinned Dorothy now had a dark, sickly complexion. For a moment, she revealed no recognition of me on her face, just a blank, confused stare.

Then her eyes widened, and she dropped her plate against the stone floor, shattering it into several pieces. "It can't be!" she yelled. "What are you doing down here?" Dorothy laughed as she sprang to her feet and shot her hand through the bars. I grabbed her hand with mine, and the two of us embraced as best we could around the barricade. "I can't believe it! I simply can't believe it!"

"You look terrible!" I sobbed. "They're torturing you!"

Dorothy looked down at her emaciated body and smirked. "Nonsense! I've never felt so good in my life. I've always wanted to lose those twenty pounds, and now look." She glanced down at her broken plate and the remaining food mingled in the dirt. "But seeing you would definitely explain the sudden feast they gave me tonight. I thought they were going to execute me and this was some sort of final meal. Now I see it's something much better." She pulled back and gave me a thorough looking over. "Well, it appears you've been kept well."

I shrugged. "Never mind me, what are we going to do about you?" I asked, still sniffling but finding courage in seeing Dorothy in such good spirits.

"My dear Amber, you never should have come here. This is a dangerous place with very wicked people. Didn't you read my instructions?"

"I had no choice," I said. "Mr. Jasher gave me the opportunity to come down here and talk with you, so I took it. He's been keeping me and Trendon locked up like prisoners in his mansion. But I have no room to complain now that I've seen how they're treating you."

Dorothy's eyes narrowed. "I absolutely hate that man, don't you?" She lowered herself to the ground. I followed suit, sitting cross-legged across from her. "So you were able to convince Trendon to follow you? I'm quite impressed. What about the others? Joseph and Lisa?"

I hesitated, knowing this might not help Dorothy, and, if anything, it would ruin her mood.

"Tell me everything," she said, snatching a chunk of potato off the floor and wiping it free of dirt. "Bring me up to speed so I can figure out how to get you out of this mess."

I took a deep breath and over the next ten minutes filled Dorothy in on everything that had happened over the past few days. With every bit of bad news, Dorothy's countenance noticeably drooped. When I told her about Abraham and the poison, her eyes glazed over, and she tried fruitlessly to conceal her sadness. I felt horrible but resolved to get it all out at once. Better to rip the Band-Aid off quickly. I continued, telling Dorothy how I had followed the clues in the letter and found the stone in the hidden compartment of her safe. But I purposely withheld the information about the other items I found there, the map and the stick, knowing Mr. Jasher was most likely listening in. I told her about Lisa's tragic accident and about how Joseph had been a traitor since the very beginning. Dorothy buried her face in her hands.

"This is awful, simply awful. Joseph was such a bright and promising young man, but that does explain so much. He never quite made sense in my class. From the beginning he always seemed withdrawn, uninterested, yet there he was, week after week, year after year."

I sat looking at my shoelaces, feeling angry with myself, mostly about Joseph. I had literally wasted a couple years of my life daydreaming about him being my boyfriend.

"Listen, Amber," Dorothy drew in close and whispered in my ear. "I can't talk much on the matter because you and I both know ears are listening. I need you to continue this. Don't give up yet, no matter how difficult the road becomes. You are my arms and legs, and I need you to be sharp."

"I don't understand what I can do now," I said. "I've already failed you."

Dorothy smiled. "No, no, don't be silly. You've quite impressed me. True, you gave them the locator stone," she said in a normal voice, but then in a whisper almost inaudible, she said, "but you kept something for yourself, didn't you?" I knew she meant the map—the real map, the one hidden in my shoe. Dorothy must have sensed something because she quickly shook her head and mouthed the words, "not yet."

Then she continued, "You haven't failed at all, Amber. On the contrary, you've done wonderfully. Why do you think you're here right now, talking with me?"

I shook my head. "Mr. Jasher said he wanted me to talk some sense into you, so we could all go home." I knew he had withheld the real reason, and when I said it, it sounded ridiculous.

"First of all, be watchful. There have been instances recently that lead me to believe Mr. Jasher is not the one completely in charge."

"Who else is there?" I asked.

"I don't know, but I get the sense that whoever it is, they're much worse. For now, since we have no way of knowing who the real culprit is, we'll stick to despising Mr. Jasher." She smiled. "You're here because Kendell is frustrated. He has the map, doesn't he?" Dorothy gave a slight wink. "He has the locator stone, and I'm sure he has a team of hundreds of professionals working around the clock, and yet no discovery has been made. It should have been a walk in the park by now. Make no mistake—you're here because he needs you to find out what he's missing."

I felt an instant swell of purpose. "So what is it? Why is the ark so important?"

Dorothy giggled. "You see? This is why you've always been my most prized student in all my years of teaching. Nothing gets past you. That mind of yours is simply amazing. But, indeed, why is the ark so important? Since this is information our enemies are already well aware of, I see no need to hold back." Dorothy licked her lips. "Most legends in archaeology, as you've learned in class, are based on truths. There are numerous historical documents that back up the claims made by men and women thousands of years ago. The ark is no different. According to ancient papyrus scrolls, after the great flood, Noah's mighty ship landed in the mountains. Over time, the rock and mud walled up around it, and it has stayed hidden for millennia. That's what we believe. But why hasn't it been discovered? So many people have looked for it and are still looking for it, and with today's technology, nothing should stay hidden for that long. Yet, here they are, and when I say 'they,' I mean Jasher and his men, and they're no closer than the tens of thousands of clever souls that went in search of the ark in times past. Why?"

I considered the question. It seemed valid. Why was it so hard to find? The Bible described the ark as being absolutely massive.

"Well," I started, "I think what you're getting at is that the ark has gone undiscovered because it was never intended to be found."

"Precisely!" Dorothy beamed. "I don't know if it was Noah or his sons or his grandchildren, but somewhere along that line, specific and detailed measures were taken to ensure the ark was never found. For starters, why would you need a map? You know a little about locator stones and how they reveal secret passageways. Why would such tools be needed? This leads us to our next question."

"Yeah, what's so important about a big boat?" I asked.

"Again, precisely. Because it's not the boat itself, but rather what's hidden inside it that matters. And that's what Kendell Jasher will stop at nothing to get, and that is also why I am here right now, because he thinks I know something that will help him find it."

"So what is it?"

Dorothy peered over my shoulder, trying to see past the bars. "Is there anyone out there?"

I turned and shook my head. "No, not yet."

"Ah, peace and quiet. That's because they're waiting for me to slip, but I haven't slipped yet, have I?"
she asked, projecting her voice so her words echoed
against the stone walls. Dorothy crossed her legs and
bent over, resting her left elbow on her knee. With her
other hand she began poking her fingers in the dirt
next to her. "You have an open mind, don't you?"

"Yeah, I guess," I said, shrugging.

"Of course you do. You read the Bible from time to
time, which I'm assuming is how you figured out the
part about Noah."

I looked at her sheepishly "I don't read it as much
as I should."

Dorothy waved her hand dismissively. "Nonsense.
You're a scholar. What do you notice when you read
the Bible?"

"What do you mean?"

"I mean, what tends to be the theme intertwined
throughout, let's say, the Old Testament? Aside from
the wars and destruction."

I thought about it for a moment. "Well, most of the
stories all have some sort of supernatural tie."

Dorothy giggled once more and patted my shoulder through the bars. "You've always been the best at
picking up on my subtle hinting. You're correct. The
story of Noah is particularly amazing. Where did all
that rain and water come from? How did he know
to build the ship? And then there's always the question that I've had, how did he control all of those animals? Lions, lizards, ostriches, all the beasts under his

command and riding with him aboard the giant ark. How is that possible?"

I stared blankly at my teacher. After several seconds of silence, I realized Dorothy hadn't asked a rhetorical question. "Isn't it because of . . . God?"

"That is how it's written, and indeed I do believe a higher power was at work in that legend. I've seen too many unexplainable and miraculous things in my line of work to discount that power. But according to ancient writs, documents that are not always available to the public eye, there was something else Noah used. I've seen sketches and drawings, of course, but those are just the artist's representation of what it actually is. I believe, and unfortunately so does Mr. Jasher, that it really does exist."

"What exists?" My pulse quickened. "What are you talking about?"

"The Tebah Stick is what we call it in the circles I associate with. I'm not really sure what the appropriate name is for it, but let's just say it's some sort of staff or a scepter capable of control." Dorothy leaned back to study my expression. She seemed pleased with the result, actually starting to laugh. She watched me with interest, continuing to twirl her finger through the dirt.

After several moments, I licked my lips. "Are you saying you believe there's some sort of magic wand Noah used to control all the animals?"

Dorothy laughed even louder. "Clever. Never considered it like that before, but yes, that's exactly what I believe."

"Huh." My jaw stayed open.

I remembered dozens of stories from the Bible, all of which contained amazing tales that baffled the mind, but this seemed new. "So Kendell Jasher has launched this all-out war to try to find something that can control animals?"

"It seems almost humorous at first, doesn't it?" Dorothy asked with a nod. "So what if there was a device that could bend all creatures' wills to your bidding? Why is that so devastating? Think about it, Amber, what could be done with something like that?"

My mind raced as I thought of the worst possible scenarios. Common knowledge told me the world's wildlife outnumbered humans. If this mythical weapon really could be used to control animals, I supposed the wielder of it could force animals to migrate and completely remove themselves from an area. Control the animals, and you could control the world's main source of food. In the wrong hands, it could cause hunger and starvation. What would stop an enemy from using it as a weapon to force animals to attack? What else could happen? As I thought of more, I realized the potential dangers of the Tebah Stick.

Dorothy must have read my expression. Her face grew dim. "This is why Kendell Jasher must never find it. A man like that would not use the Tebah Stick for the benefit of mankind. No, he would be the catalyst that sparked Armageddon."

"So why haven't I heard about this in church?" I asked.

"Because people like me have worked very hard over the years to keep it a secret."

"People like you?" I asked, searching Dorothy's face carefully. "You mean, people that battle against Kendell Jasher?"

Dorothy sighed. "As I'm sure you've been told, I'm a bit of a terrorist." She winked again.

"But not a real terrorist, right?" I suddenly felt alarmed.

"Oh, I don't take hostages . . . necessarily, but to people like Jasher and his followers, I'd say they were somewhat accurate in my description." Dorothy clasped my hand. "Don't worry! I'm nothing like what society deems a terrorist to be. I would like to consider myself a protector, but in truth my real title is that of Collector."

Dorothy pulled down the sock on her right ankle and showed me a strange tattoo—an image of a scroll rolled back with Ancient Egyptian markings. I had never noticed it before. "This is the mark of the Seraphic Scroll. We are a society of followers that devote our lives to protecting artifacts and relics that have no business being discovered. I'm a Collector, which means I, and sadly only a handful others in the world, are allowed to handle the artifacts and move them when necessary."

I remained silent, but inside, my heart raced rapidly.

Dorothy continued, "There are also those called Sentries who live in areas where dangerous and protected artifacts reside. They guard the way and keep evil from getting near their locations. Then there are the Destroyers, who, as you can probably guess from their name, must go to much more drastic means to protect mankind from what some of these artifacts are capable of doing. We use whatever means are necessary to keep these relics hidden and safe, but, when required, we must remove them completely from the earth."

I felt like I had been struck by lightning. Dorothy had chosen this life. And "whatever means necessary"? What did that mean exactly? I assumed it had something to do with acts of violence.

"You're having trouble with this?" Dorothy asked quietly. "I know your mind is probably ready to explode, but I couldn't see any other way around it. Especially now, since I need you to act in my place."

I had been looking down at my knees but quickly looked up at Dorothy. "What do you mean?"

Dorothy pulled in close until her lips spoke through the bars directly into my ear. "I need you to finish what I came to do. It won't be easy—in fact, it will be near impossible—but I need you and Trendon to try." She lowered her voice to a whisper. "The Tebah Stick needs to be moved. It is no longer safe where it is hidden. I need you to move it for me."

I pulled away from the bars. "How am I supposed to do that? I have no idea how to find it, and I wouldn't even know what to do with it if I did."

Dorothy held her finger to her lips. "I know, I know," she whispered. "But you have to realize if

Kendell Jasher finds it . . ." Her voice broke off as she checked the hall behind me. "We can't let that happen."

"But I'm being held captive in Mr. Jasher's home. They have guns! We're just kids!" I didn't mean to speak so harshly. I wanted to help, but how could I escape from Mr. Jasher? And even if I did, what would I do next? I didn't know how to get to Mt. Ararat. I didn't have any money, and, even worse, I no longer had the locator stone. Dorothy had said earlier that Kendell had the stone and a map, and even with all of his help and technology, he couldn't find the entryway leading to the ark. How could Trendon and I, two kids with no experience in this field, have any more success? My chest heaved. "How am I supposed to do this?"

From down at the end of the hall, the heavy metal door opened. I looked down and saw Kendell and Malcolm enter the hallway. Dorothy yanked on my sleeve, pulling me once more against the bars to embrace me. In her quietest voice possible she whispered, "You'll get your chance soon enough. Just nod your head yes or no. Has anyone at the mansion tried to approach you yet? Any of the guards?"

I thought about it quickly and shook my head.

"Don't worry. Someone will, once they learn you've visited me."

"How will they know?" I asked. Panicking, I shot a quick look in the direction of Mr. Jasher and Malcolm. They still stood by the door discussing something with another guard, but they wouldn't be long.

"A friend of mine named Temel is employed there on the grounds. He'll have ways of finding out. He can help you escape and can provide you with everything you need. You can trust him."

"What do you mean he can help us escape?"

"Don't worry, he's very resourceful." I opened my mouth to question, but Dorothy quickly cut me off. "Look at your map closely. Study each word and look for mistakes. Most important, remember this, there are no Sentries in Turkey." She pulled me so hard it felt as though my face would be forced through the bars. From this angle I could see what Dorothy had been scribbling in the dirt. My eyes widened as I read the word "Philippines." What did that mean? Dorothy quickly wiped the word away with her foot.

"Come along now, Amber," Mr. Jasher said as he and Malcolm passed the third cell. "You have had plenty of time to catch up. We need to be going."

With one final hug, Dorothy whispered into my ear, "Good luck, Amber." Then she kissed me on the cheek.

Malcolm pulled me up from the floor and removed Dorothy's lingering hands from my shoulders.

"Ah, it's been too long, Kendell," Dorothy said, pulling her lips back in a wide, toothy grin. "I was afraid you were never going to pay me a visit."

Mr. Jasher returned the smile. "Indeed, too long. Perhaps there will be other days for us to . . . catch up, but for now, I need to get this child home to rest. You take care of yourself." He turned, putting his arm around my shoulders. I wanted to break away from his grip, but I couldn't focus. What did she mean by "there are no Sentries in Turkey?" What was important about the Philippines? Why couldn't she have told me this earlier in our conversation so I could've at least probed further? Craning my neck, I tried to look at Dorothy as Mr. Jasher pulled me out of view. I wanted to run back and stay there with her.

I was sure we would never see each other again.

14

The SUV came to an abrupt stop, startling me awake.

"My dear, I am sorry, but we have one more stop before our night is over," Mr. Jasher said, staring over the center console at me with a somewhat troubled gaze.

I rubbed my eyes with the back of my free hand and stretched my neck. Outside the world had turned completely black. No streetlights. No sign of any homes. Only a sparse gathering of trees beneath the sky covered with dense clouds. I looked over at the clock. Almost midnight. We should've been back at the mansion by now.

"Where are we?" I asked. My throat was dry.

Neither Kendell nor Malcolm spoke as they exited the vehicle. Malcolm opened my passenger door and unlatched the manacle attached to my wrist.

"You know the drill," he said in a gruff whisper. "Stick by my side."

I had no choice but to exit the vehicle. An unpaved road with coarse gravel clinging to the tires of the SUV stretched out before us. On the far side of the vehicle, the road tapered into a ditch. Why had we stopped here?

"Malcolm, let's go," Kendell said, his voice urgent, which made me all the more frightened.

They led me along the gravel road for about a quarter mile until eventually the path veered east, and I caught a glimpse of a dark structure that reminded me of a park pavilion. It stood in a flat, empty field. There were a few benches and tables beneath the awning but not much more. Shrouded in the darkness, three figures sat on one of the benches.

Kendell stopped and turned to me. "Listen carefully, Amber. I need you to follow my every command. You and I have been invited, but Malcolm has not." Kendell paused and stared at Malcolm. I followed his eyes and couldn't prevent myself from gasping as I caught sight of Malcolm's gun.

"What is this place?" I asked. Was this like some sort of cruel test? Was he trying to scare me? It was working.

"These men are very powerful and dangerous. They are not to be trifled with. I did not intend to introduce you, but lately they have grown uneasy with our situation and have insisted on a meeting."

"What does that have to do with me?" I asked.

Kendell's eyes flashed. For a second, he appeared to be on the verge of smacking me. "Your clever tongue has been amusing up to now, but I want you to mind it in front of my employer."

Kendell's employer? Dorothy had been right. I turned and tried to focus in on the three ominous figures looming beneath the pavilion. Mr. Jasher, quite possibly the wealthiest and most powerful man I had ever met, had an employer.

Mr. Jasher held out his hand toward me. "Do I make myself clear?" he asked sternly. I quickly nodded and looked toward Malcolm, who had his gun pointed directly at my back. I wouldn't run. I placed my hand in Kendell's, and the two of us walked the rest of the way to the pavilion.

As we approached, my eyes adjusted to the dark and I noticed that the three individuals sat with perfect posture on the center bench. All three wore similarly dark suits with the lapels open, revealing bare, hairless chests. They had pale white skin, and even though it was hard to see, their green eyes sparkled. Almost as if they glowed. The man seated in the center commanded Kendell's reverence as we approached. A long, wooden staff with what looked like an ivory hand piece, rested across the man's knees. His gaze pierced me, as though he could look straight through me. I felt nauseated and petrified. I wanted to look away but felt I had no choice but to hold his gaze. The man struck a match and lit a lantern on the table in front of him. He motioned toward the bench in front of theirs, and Kendell sat down.

"Sit!" Kendell said harshly, his tone declaring it was

not an option. I kept quiet as I walked around next to Kendell and sat on the edge of the seat. An awkward silence followed for several moments. The man's eyes still seemed to bore right through me. Most people looked at the eyes of a person when they spoke to them, but he directed his eyes at my throat, like some starving vampire.

"This is Amber," Kendell said, extending his hand toward me and bowing slightly. "Amber, this," he held two fingers toward the man in the center, "is Mr. Baeloc."

"Uh . . . hello," I whispered, at a loss for any type of conversation.

Mr. Baeloc's lips gave no indication whether he smiled or frowned. His daunting green eyes rested on me for a moment and then turned to Mr. Jasher. He snapped his fingers, and the man flanking him to his right handed him a pen and a piece of paper. Mr. Baeloc's pen danced between his long, pale fingers as he made several strokes on one of the pages. Once he finished, he passed the paper to Mr. Jasher.

Kendell moistened his lips and, to my amazement, began reading Mr. Baeloc's message aloud. "I want to thank you for your valuable role in obtaining the locator stone. Because of your involvement and cunning, this precious heirloom has returned to its rightful owner."

I sat still, my eyes darting rapidly between Kendell and Mr. Baeloc. What had just happened? Why didn't Mr. Baeloc speak? What was with the notes? None of it made sense, but something else lingered in the atmosphere, something cold and hollow as though the oxygen had drained from the pavilion. I felt lonely and afraid, and I didn't like being this close to Mr. Baeloc and his servants.

Still no expression appeared on Mr. Baeloc's face as he wrote another passage. His head nodded ever so slightly with each rhythmic stroke of his pen. This message took longer to complete. Mr. Baeloc filled up an entire page before handing the message back.

Kendell skimmed it and then said, "He wants you to know you will be rewarded resplendently once the mission has been accomplished. But now he requires your assistance. He needs to know what Dorothy told you. What are we missing? What secrets did you learn in your visit?"

Kendell's eyes rose from the page and rested on mine. Though it was dark, I could see the seriousness of his expression. Both he and Mr. Baeloc waited for my reply. I knew it would be best for me to remain silent and not say anything, but I could no longer help myself.

"I don't know who you are, but I'm not helping you."

Rage blazed in Kendell's eyes for a moment. Surely now he would show his true nature, but instead, Kendell waited patiently while Mr. Baeloc wrote several more lines on another piece of parchment.

"'We both want the same outcome. The artifact we seek is too dangerous, and your friend has foolishly chosen the wrong side.' " the message read.

"Wrong side?" I blurted out. "You're holding Dorothy prisoner in some awful cell. Because of you, several people have died, and I'm sure more will. Why would I ever help you? Besides, you must've heard our entire conversation. Dorothy didn't tell me anything you don't already know."

"Don't play games!" Kendell hissed, but he quickly regained control of his composure. "I apologize, Amber, but this is a serious matter. Mr. Baeloc's time is valuable, and we cannot waste another moment in vain pursuits. We need to know what you and Dorothy know."

Dorothy had been right about that as well. She knew the search wasn't going well for Kendell and his men. They had the locator stone, but it wasn't working. I couldn't help but smile, knowing their map, the one they had stolen from Abraham, wouldn't lead them anywhere.

"I don't know what you want me to tell you," I said. "I'm no archaeologist."

"And yet here you are, Amber. For reasons beyond our comprehension, Dorothy has placed her trust in you. Surely, you know something—something we don't," Kendell pressed.

A feeling of triumph quivered in my body. "I'm sorry, but you're right. Dorothy does trust me, and I will never do anything to break her trust." I folded my arms in defiance.

For the first time, I noticed a break in Mr. Baeloc's

emotions as a thin smile tugged at the corners of his lips. He wrote another message, but this time Mr. Jasher didn't read it aloud. Instead, he removed the pouch containing the blue locator stone from his suit pocket. He handed it to Mr. Baeloc, and I watched in silence as Mr. Baeloc scrutinized the stone's quality. When he appeared satisfied, he returned the item to Mr. Jasher. Then he scrawled another message on the paper. Mr. Jasher read it, and his countenance dropped.

"I assure you, all measures are being taken. If we have to tear down the mountain, we'll do just that." Mr. Jasher turned once more to me with a pleading look in his eyes. "Amber, please, you don't understand what's going on here. Dorothy is your friend, but we need to ensure the safety of an important artifact. It is for the greater good, and if you know something about why this stone is not working properly, I insist you share it with us right now!"

All eyes fell on me, and the evil sensation hovering around the pavilion thickened. I felt pressure to speak, but I knew I might mess up and reveal something I shouldn't. Instead I closed my lips and stared down at my hands in my lap. I wouldn't let them break me. If I gave in, Dorothy, Trendon, and I would no longer be important to them. A dangerous position to be in, especially for Dorothy.

In a voice barely audible to my ears, Mr. Baeloc whispered to the others in some hideous language. Guttural and deep, his voice sounded like someone choking on a chicken bone. Mr. Baeloc's voice growled and hissed. Then he clucked his tongue against his teeth. The others sitting next to him responded in the same type of language. Cold, unnatural fear filled my body. Mr. Baeloc wrote one last message and then rose to his feet. Mr. Jasher stood as well while he read. He nodded and placed the paper into his jacket pocket.

Without any sign of approval, Mr. Baeloc and his companions turned and began walking away from the pavilion. Within a few moments, the strange figures slowly shrank into the darkness.

"Amber, it would be easier for everyone if you just gave in," Kendell whispered, clutching my hand in his and leading me away from the pavilion. I remained silent. "Mr. Baeloc is not a man you want as an enemy."

"Who is he and why does he talk like that?" I had studied some languages over the course of my tenure at Roland and Tesh. As far as I knew, nothing on earth sounded like that.

Mr. Jasher studied me silently and shrugged as if to say it didn't matter anyway. "Mr. Baeloc is a descendant of a race of people that were on this earth thousands of years ago. Their history coincides with what we're trying to unearth in the mountains, and they are incredibly invested in ensuring our success at uncovering the relic. "

"What race of people?"

"In Ancient Egyptian they are called the Qedet."

I had certainly never heard that word before. "Qedet? What does that mean?"

"It means the Architects."

As we walked back to the SUV, I felt a mixture of emotions. Anger at the way they were treating Dorothy. Worry for her well-being. But I also felt proud for withstanding the urge to buckle under pressure. Kendell had grown desperate. Why else would we be meeting with his employer? And why else would he have a sudden interest in what I might be hiding? Because of the measures Dorothy had taken, they might never discover the location of the ark and more important the valuable artifact concealed within. Another emotion, however, started to take precedence in my mind. Fear of Mr. Baeloc. Who was he, really? Who were these Architects? What role did they play, and what did they want with the Tebah Stick? Trendon and I had to get to the bottom of this, and we had to escape before Mr. Jasher's dwindling hospitality completely ran out.

15

I spent the entire morning looking over the map, searching for mistakes or clues, but without a working knowledge of Ancient Hebrew, it seemed hopeless. Still, I had to do something to occupy my time, and to keep the images of the pale-skinned Mr. Baeloc and the sound of his hollow, choking voice from popping back up in my thoughts. I wanted so badly to talk with Trendon about everything, though I doubted he would know anything about the strange Architects. Just after lunch, I was about to pull the map out once more when a warning knock sounded on my door.

"Come in," I said, not sure if it mattered whether or not I gave permission. The door opened, and there stood Trendon, between three of the guards. "What's going on?" I asked, springing off my bed and racing toward the door.

"We're being forced to go on a mandatory walk for exercise," Trendon answered.

"Huh?" I almost started to laugh until I realized he wasn't joking. "Why?"

"Don't ask me. And don't ask these guys, either. Their English is awful, and when they talk, they sound like the voice off a Speak and Spell." He made his eyes peel back wide and moved his mouth like a robot while he mimicked them. "You must go outside now. Take walk. Good for health."

"All right." I smiled. "Do we get to go alone?"

Trendon scratched his chin. "Apparently so, but I doubt we'll really be alone, if you know what I mean. They'll be watching us from the roof with sniper rifles and smoke grenades and all that."

We rode with one of the guards down an elevator that opened onto a loading dock. Several motorized lifts and stacks of pallets butted up against the wall next to the locked rolling doors of four loading bays. The guard held his hand toward a door on the right. "That's backyard. You have one hour." The elevator door closed, leaving the two of us staring at each other in complete confusion.

"What do you think this is all about?" I asked, starting to walk toward the door.

"They're probably searching our rooms for stuff we may be hiding, or better yet, Mr. Jasher got smart and is having them install spy gear everywhere. I'd bet those guards are in there right now, ripping apart our beds." Trendon opened the door, and we stepped down into a neatly trimmed yard where several large hedges that had been sculpted into wild animals sprouted up from the grass. We passed under a stone archway and onto a beautiful wooden bridge across a lazy stream gurgling with giant fish.

"Not too shabby." Trendon yanked a branch off the nearest tree and stripped it clean of twigs.

"I'm worried things aren't going the way Mr. Jasher planned," I whispered.

"Worried? Isn't that a good thing?"

"Yes and no. I don't want him to win, but I'm afraid he'll start going to drastic measures to get his way. Don't forget, we're still here because we're supposed to be leverage."

Trendon rubbed his eyes. "Well, this will trip you up for sure. Guess what happened before breakfast?" I shrugged. "Malcolm returned my laptop and iPhone to me."

I froze. "What? Why did he do that?"

"Malcolm said it was always the plan to give us back our stuff. They just had to make sure it wasn't tampered with or anything."

"You didn't believe him, did you? Please tell me you didn't try to send out anything about what we know. They've bugged it for sure!" I grabbed Trendon's arm.

"Relax, will you? I played Mahjong for, like, three hours straight. That's why my eyes hurt so bad." He pulled his arm free.

I breathed a sigh of relief, but it only lasted for a moment. "That's all you did? Played games?"

"They've got some pretty advanced monitoring software uploaded in all sorts of encrypted folders. It's kind of like a shattered glass program, you know. Of course not—you don't have a clue. But it's like high-tech *Alice in Wonderland, Looking Glass* type stuff. You can't just wipe the files and start from scratch; you have to physically attack each strand. Nothing I haven't come up against before but worthy tech, nonetheless. I took the liberty of attaching some of my own personal viruses to their entry files. Should cause a little itch under their collar, if you follow me."

"I don't follow you, but I'm going to assume you know what you're doing." I knew better than to question his hacking ability. Trendon was the Leonardo Da Vinci of computer wizards.

"Yeah, well, they've blocked my access to most websites with a security firewall. Again, I could probably hack it in like five minutes, but all that would do is get my laptop taken away. The odd thing is, they've granted me access to Google and a few email accounts." He shrugged.

"They want you to mess up," I said.

"Yeah, probably."

"Not probably—definitely! They're hoping you'll get on and research something that answers one of their questions. So don't do anything just yet unless you know you can keep it completely covered."

"Oh, I can keep it covered, no doubt about that, but what would I research anyway?" he asked.

I cupped my hand over my mouth and whispered "Did you get my message?"

"Not until three o'clock this morning," Trendon

answered. "Thought it was some sort of insect nesting in my belly button."

I stuck my tongue out in disgust. "Well, what do you think?"

Trendon stopped walking and stared at me skeptically. "Noah's ark? Are we talking about the same story with the bearded guy and all the animals, two by two?"

"Yes," I said. "Don't laugh. This is for real. Dorothy confirmed it."

"That's got to be the most ridiculous thing I've ever heard!" Trendon started laughing. "You're all a bunch of nuts! Why are we looking for a big boat?"

"It's not the boat. Dorothy said she thinks there's an artifact inside, a powerful, dangerous artifact."

"I'm sure there is. It's probably unicorn droppings or something like that." Trendon flung his stick across the yard.

"Trendon, this is serious. Dorothy wants us to continue our mission. We need to find this artifact and move it to a safe location."

"Sounds like a plan," Trendon scoffed. "We'll just hail a cab from here, go hike up Mt. Ararat—"

"Stop it! I don't want to argue with you, but I need you to do something for me. I want you to take Dorothy's map and see what you can find out about it online. I'm not even sure what you should look for, but see if you can figure out if there are any mistakes on the map. I know you've got creative ways of doing research." Trendon held out his hand, and I quickly knocked it away. "Not right here! Do you want everyone to know we have it?"

"Geez, Angry, why you gotta hit me that hard?" Trendon sulked, rubbing the back of his hand where the skin had already reddened from my slap.

"You've got to promise me you'll guard it with your life. No one can know you have it. You have to be extremely careful with your research. I know you think you're hot stuff with the computer, but Mr. Jasher is growing desperate. If he gets his hands on this—"

"All right, all right! He won't. I'll be careful. But how are we supposed to make the exchange without Big Brother finding out?" He pointed to the roof, where the spotlights rotated on large turrets. Even in the daylight, the machines scanned the yard like clockwork. What a ridiculous waste of money.

I looked around, trying to think of a way it could work. "I'm going to drop it near the entrance to the loading dock. You pick up a few rocks and do what boys do." My eyes narrowed as Trendon started to grin. "You know, chuck them at a wall or whatever. I don't care. Just make sure you pick up the map and keep it hidden."

"Sounds like a fabulous plan," he said sarcastically, barely dodging out of reach of my fist.

"Can you think of a better one?" I hissed.

As we turned to head back toward the door, one of the security spotlights made a strange humming noise. I looked up as the bulb on the mechanical fixture started to flicker and smoke. Suddenly an explosion of tiny shards of glass showered down on top of us. Shielding our heads from the downpour, we dove off the cobbled path and toppled into the stream. A guard appeared on the roof, shouting in Turkish and speaking into a radio. He directed another man on the ground level wearing a blue jumpsuit and carrying a broom and dust pan over to where the glass had scattered across the path. The cleaning worker had dark brown skin, short, cropped black hair and a thin, almost nonexistent, mustache under his nose.

When the man saw us, he bowed apologetically and started sweeping up the mess, muttering to himself. I thought he seemed overly timid, acting as though he had just bumped into royalty. Not once did he look up, but instead kept his eyes on his work, timidly clearing glass from the flags. After finishing, he removed a towel from his back pocket, and, keeping his eyes on the ground, pointed at me, offering to dry me off.

"Sure," I said, picking myself up out of the stream. I approached the man, who immediately shied away from me, extending the towel out as though a bomb would go off if I touched him.

"Sorry this happened," he said.

"What exactly did happen?" Trendon asked.

"So sorry, so sorry," the man muttered.

Water soaked through my shoes from splashing in the stream, and it gave me an idea. As I undid my laces, I got Trendon's attention. It would be risky, but probably our best chance to make the switch. While I removed my shoe, Trendon looked up at the smoking spotlight and pointed.

"Did that thing blow up?" he asked, drawing the man's attention toward the roof. When he followed Trendon's gaze, I tucked the map into Trendon's wet sock.

"Ah, maybe. I don't know," The man answered. He returned his focus to me. I had already laced up my shoe and now stood next to Trendon. Taking back the towel, he shook his head and looked away as though ashamed.

"Again, sorry about this. Not my fault." Then, under his breath, he whispered. "You went to Dorothy."

At first, I thought I imagined it, but when I looked back at the man, his eyes fixed on mine, no longer appearing timid.

"What did you say?" I asked.

The man stooped down and gathered the glass into a dustpan. "Sorry about the glass. Happens sometimes." Brushing past us, he hurried toward the far wall to his parked cleaning cart.

"That dude's messed up!" Trendon said, brushing a few shards of glass off his shoulders.

Once the man had emptied the dustpan into a large trash bag, he began to push his cart toward the exit. I watched him leave, wanting to call out to him for an explanation. Was my mind playing tricks on me, or had he really said what I thought he did? He had almost passed through the gate when he stopped and realized he had left his broom back by where we stood.

Dashing across the yard, he bent down and plucked the broom from the edge of the stream.

As he turned to move away, he whispered something again. "Stay clear of the windows."

Even Trendon heard him that time. Was this Temel, Dorothy's friend?

"What's going to happen to the windows?" Trendon asked.

"I think we'd better do exactly what he says."

For the rest of the afternoon, I kept a close eye on the windows, wondering if something would actually happen. Maybe it wasn't Dorothy's friend Temel at all. Maybe the man had just offered a bit of advice to us because he spent most of his time cleaning the windows. Whatever the case, I felt anxious and on edge, partly due to spending four days imprisoned in Mr. Jasher's guest bedroom and partly because Trendon had the map now, not me. Normally, I would've taken a nap in the afternoon to pass the time, but thinking of Trendon's carelessness kept me awake. I dug my nails into my knee and returned my attention to the copy of *The Jungle Book* in my lap—the tenth book I had tried to read without any success. As I thumbed through the pages, catching only a tiny portion of the story, my eyes grew heavy, and I fell asleep on the bed.

About an hour later, as I lay on my side and faced the window, I heard the distinct click of my door latch. I rolled over to find Malcolm sitting in my desk chair with his legs crossed, twiddling a knife with his fingers. I sat up quickly and pressed myself against the headboard.

"What are you doing in here?" I asked.

Malcolm smiled, his eyes focusing on his blade. "It was bound to come to this. You had to know at some point you and I would be having this conversation."

"What are you talking about?" I had no clue what he meant.

"I admire your defiance. It's a unique quality in someone so young, but you'll forgive me if I call your bluff." Malcolm stood, continuing to twirl the knife. I tried to distance myself, but he had me cornered on the bed. The only way out was through him.

"Give me the real stone, Amber," Malcolm growled.

"You have the real stone. You took it from me!"

"Don't lie to me," he hissed.

"Your dumb friend took the stone from my backpack, remember?" I fired back. "Right after that, he was stung—" Malcolm cut me off midsentence with a fist across my mouth. Tears boiled in my eyes as my mouth filled up with blood. I had never been hit in the face before, at least not on purpose, and never that hard. My upper lip began to swell, and I spat a glob of blood onto the carpet. The sharp metallic taste burned my tongue.

"Stop! Please!" I begged, covering my mouth with my hand.

"I'm not going to stop until you give me what I'm looking for." Malcolm waved the knife in front of me.

"Do you want me to use this?"

I shook my head frantically. "Please! I'm telling the truth. I don't have the stone."

Malcolm pulled his hand back again, but before he could strike, I dove under his arm and collapsed on the floor. Scrambling to my feet, I charged toward the door and screamed for help. It was locked, and I wasn't strong enough to force it open.

Malcolm chuckled. "I had the guards lock us in here. Just you and me. I don't even have the key." Malcolm turned away from the bed. "So you had better start doing as I ask before I decide to beat the truth out of you."

I cowered against the door. "I don't have it!"

"Very well." Malcolm gripped the knife in his hand and took a step toward me.

Something sparkled in the sunlight above Malcolm's shoulder, catching my attention. I only had a second to look at it before the strange object surged through the window and the entire back wall of my bedroom exploded.

Malcolm disappeared from view under a mountain of rubble and glass. Smoke filled the room as the bed burst into flames. The explosion temporarily deafened me. An obnoxious buzz rang in my ears as I staggered to my feet. Beating away the smoke, I saw a humongous hole now looking out onto Mr. Jasher's backyard—a backyard resembling a war zone. The buzzing softened a little, and I got my hearing back just as another explosion erupted somewhere out on the grounds. The fire on my bed spread across the room. I needed to get out, but when I tried the door again, it wouldn't budge.

"Somebody help me!" I screamed at the top of my lungs. I could hear excited voices, probably the guards shouting at each other as they stormed away down the hall. "Hey, I'm in here!" I tried again, but with no luck. Machine guns went off down below in the yard and were answered with more explosions. I pulled my shirt up over my mouth to keep the smoke from filling my lungs as the fire grew hotter.

"Amber, you all right?" Trendon said from the other side of the door.

"Trendon! You have to get me out of here!" I ordered.

"It's locked!"

"I know!" I shouted.

A pause followed, and then Trendon spoke with an annoyed voice. "All right, get away from the door!"

I moved to the side by the closet, hacking into my shirt from the smoke. I jumped when a loud crack sounded and Trendon's upper body appeared through a massive hole in the door.

"Ugh! That hurt way more than I thought it would," he groaned, forcing his way through to the other side. I looked at Trendon in disbelief as I helped him to his feet, and then the two of us stepped through the door and into the hallway.

"It's like World War III out here," Trendon said, clutching his shoulder. "We need to get out of Dodge right now. We better keep our eyes open for Malcolm."

"Don't worry about him," I said, jutting my thumb behind me. "He caught the brunt of one of those missiles."

"Ah, pity," Trendon said. "Come on, one of these hallways has got to lead toward the front. I'd say we should avoid the backyard at all costs."

We ran through the mansion unnoticed. It appeared everyone had already run outside, trying to stop the mayhem. After two failed attempts to find the front foyer, Trendon growled. "Who would want to live in this stupid maze?"

"Over there!" I pointed. A gigantic chandelier had toppled over on its side, hedging up the way down the far hallway. "That leads to the stairs."

I surged ahead, sprinting as fast as I could, but not paying attention. Before I could stop myself, I tripped over someone lying prostrate on the ground. A badly injured Joseph, with cuts and burns peppering his body, moaned beneath me. He had a large, bloody hole on his thigh and a nasty gash across his forehead.

"You've got to be kidding me," Trendon said as I pulled Joseph up into a seated position. "What are you doing?"

"He's hurt! We've got to help him," I shouted, yanking a corner off Joseph's shirt and pressing it against his thigh wound. Joseph cried out in pain. I could tell Trendon was about to protest, but instead he squatted down and draped Joseph's arm over his shoulder.

"We can't stay here." Trendon nodded toward the stairs. "Let's get him out on the road, and maybe someone can give him medical attention." I followed Trendon's lead, draping Joseph's other arm over my shoulder and rising to my feet.

Joseph's dead weight slowed our escape. Trying to support him while we stepped over the chandelier nearly floored us, but somehow we managed. As we started down the staircase, Joseph groaned.

"Stop!" he ordered.

"We have to get you out of here. It's not safe," I said. Joseph looked dazed and out of it, and the gash in his forehead still bled badly.

"Take me to my uncle's office," he said. "That way." He pointed toward an adjacent hallway.

Trendon shook his head. "No way, bro. No pit stops for us!" He bulled forward, but Joseph resisted.

"We can't stop, Joseph," I pleaded. "We'll help you once we're outside, but you have to let us go."

"Please, just take me to his office. I promise it will be all right."

I glanced at Trendon. I could tell he disliked the idea, but my gut told me to follow Joseph.

"This is a bad idea," Trendon whispered as more explosions rumbled out from the eastern wing of the property. I nodded but gave in anyway.

When we reached the office, Joseph fumbled with the doorknob. He didn't have much energy to open the door, so Trendon helped. We found the office empty, and since it faced the front of the grounds, it had managed to escape the onslaught of shelling.

"What are we doing here?" I asked. Joseph motioned

toward the desk where, resting like a paperweight, was the blue locator stone. I grabbed it and shoved it in my pocket. I watched as Joseph rummaged in the drawers and produced a key.

"Use this on that closet," he instructed, pointing to a small door at the rear of the office. I inserted the key and found my backpack inside. I unzipped the pocket and saw my notebook and the stick from Dorothy's safe still resting at the bottom.

"Why are you helping us?" I asked, strapping the backpack to my shoulders.

"I made a stupid mistake." Joseph forced his grimace into a smile. "Trying to make things right, that's all." He handed me a weathered piece of paper with an image sketched on one side.

"What is this?" I asked.

"It's what you're looking for," he answered. The drawing depicted some sort of staff, with a large, rounded object at the top.

"This is the artifact?" I showed the image to Trendon, who looked at it momentarily before gesturing toward the door. Voices rang out from somewhere down the hallway. More of the guards flooded in from outside.

"Break time's over. Let's get moving." Trendon moved toward Joseph and tried to help him up.

"No," Joseph said, pushing him away. "Leave me here."

"We're not going to do that." I slipped the paper into my pocket and joined Trendon at his side. "You can't stay in here with all these explosions."

"I'll just slow you down. Besides, someone has to cover your tracks. Who better than me?" The three of us ducked as another missile struck the room right next to the office. The battle drew dangerously close.

"Where's your uncle?" Trendon asked.

"Conveniently away on business. He flew to Mt. Ararat less than two hours ago. Things aren't going well with the search." I shot a quick glance in Trendon's direction. I didn't like leaving Joseph there, but we couldn't stay any longer.

"Amber," Joseph said as Trendon and I started for the door. "I'm sorry for everything." I reached out and grabbed his hand, giving it a tight squeeze. Then Trendon yanked on my arm and forced me through the door.

16

Tears plopped from my eyes, and I didn't even care that Trendon could see me. Part of me felt vindicated, knowing I had been right about Joseph and that he could change, but I also felt like a traitor. We had left Joseph behind, bloodied and badly injured. What would happen to him? What would his uncle do once he discovered Joseph had played a role in our escape? I pawed at my eyes with the back of my hands, trying to rid my mind of those terrible thoughts. Now wasn't the time to reflect on everything that had gone wrong. Now was the time for survival, and if Temel really was trying to help, all of his explosions were making it very difficult to stay alive.

After taking a flight of stairs down to the main level, we discovered the familiar path we had taken the day before, which ended at the loading dock. Three of the loading bay doors had been torn open, the charred metal resembling gaping mouths with black, pointed teeth.

"Good night!" Trendon shouted. "Who the heck is this guy? Rambo?"

Stepping out through one of the holes, Trendon reared back at the sight of a burning tractor-trailer— the cab of the semi blazed white-hot with flames. Trendon grabbed my hand, directing me around the vehicle and up the drive. Four guards in tan uniforms with black soot covering their faces charged past, paying no attention to us sneaking around the concrete wall.

"You've got to see this!" Trendon said, pulling me up next to him. The side of the mansion crumpled inward where another semi had plowed through the wall and exploded. Trees burned everywhere, looking like gigantic torches, and numerous two-foot-deep craters pocked the ground. Just visible past the wall, several of Jasher's expensive automobiles were parked by the corner of the wrap-around driveway, miraculously still in one piece. Cowering beside the eastern wall, clutching automatic weapons, at least a dozen of Jasher's men looked as though they were deep in prayer.

"Where do we go now?" I asked. I wanted to hide in some hole and wait out the destruction, but the adrenaline pumping hard under my skin kept me going. The explosions and the gunfire and all of the obliterated property could have been the handiwork of an Academy Award–winning special effects team.

"I don't think we have much of a choice," Trendon shouted over a sudden pulse of gunfire from Jasher's men. "On the count of three, we run for that flower garden!" Trendon pointed across the lawn to where a plot of lilies and sunflowers shot up next to the driveway.

"I don't know. What if those soldiers shoot at us?" I asked, scanning the grounds for a better solution.

"They're too busy hiding," Trendon said. "It's our only option. But don't run straight toward it. You've got to kind of zigzag, left and right," he instructed, using his hands to explain. "And if you can, try to separate, just in case those guys get itchy trigger fingers."

"What good will separating do?" My eyes darted wildly between Trendon and the battalion of guards.

"Makes it harder for them to pick us off if we're not on top of each other."

"Pick us off?" I didn't like the sound of that. This had to be the worst idea ever.

"Stop freaking out. This will work. Trust me." He rolled his shoulders, trying to get loose.

Trendon always watched action and war movies, so I figured he knew best. I made sure to secure my backpack on my shoulders as I readied for the dash.

"One . . . Two . . ." Trendon started the count.

"Three!" both of us screamed in unison, darting away from the wall. I didn't dare look toward the eastern wall, for fear I would see someone aiming a machine gun at me. Instead, I followed Trendon's lead, crisscrossing the lawn, randomly ducking and side-stepping. It actually would've been hysterical to watch if we hadn't had the fear of death looming over our heads.

We made it almost to the flowerbed when the most amazing and horrifying round of explosions ignited.

Temel must have been saving his best stuff for the grand finale. In a matter of milliseconds, three of Mr. Jasher's beautiful cars launched off like rockets from the driveway. The awesome sound and the shockwave sent the two of us tumbling painfully onto the concrete. I scraped my arms and knees, and my head throbbed from where I knocked it against Trendon's large skull. Covering my face with my hands, I squeezed a peek through my spread fingers as the last of the charges erupted. One by one the rest of the vehicles—two Ferraris and a Lotus—were engulfed in flames. But the crowning jewel of the fireworks show came when the fountain centerpiece in the middle of the driveway blew up, sending the sculpted concrete remains of the giant condor statue showering down across the yard.

Trendon groaned, wiping rubble from his forehead. "I've never felt so much pain in my life! It feels like every bone in my body has—" His eyes widened with alarm as his hand shot down toward his leg. Carefully removing his iPhone from his pants pocket, he inspected the small electronic device and gave a deep sigh of relief. "Phew!" he said, smiling at me.

I rolled my eyes. Leave it to Trendon to worry more about his toys than his own well-being. "Where do we go now?" I asked, rising to my knees.

Another round of gunfire rang out from the mansion as a speeding yellow taxi shot through the gates, heading directly toward us. As the taxi pulled up, the passenger door popped open. The peculiar cleaning worker from the night before smiled down at us, only now he was dressed in camouflage fatigues with a pair of sleek black sunglasses to hide his eyes.

"Get in!" he shouted. We didn't argue. After waiting for Trendon to shut the door, the man who I could only assume was Temel slammed the cab into reverse and pressed down on the gas. The car screamed backward down the drive, but Temel steered the wheel so casually it seemed as though he was just backing into a parking spot.

"'Scuse me, please," he said in what sounded like a thick Mexican accent. He grinned as armed guards dove out of the way of the car. I buried my head under Trendon's arm as the angry guards resurfaced on the drive and started firing at the taxi. Bullets ricocheted off the hood, and a few shot through the windshield. Temel smiled, offered the guards a friendly wave, and yanked on the wheel. The taxi spun around, positioning itself perfectly on the main stretch of street. With the ease of a professional racecar driver, he shifted into drive, and the car sped off, leaving the demolished mansion in its wake.

Once we hit the road and were out of range of the machine guns, Trendon heaved a massive sigh. "What just happened?" he asked, looking cautiously over at the driver.

Temel smiled. "What? That?" He jutted his thumb behind him. "Oh, that was nothing. Just several days of planning."

"How did you do all that?" I asked, starting to breathe more normally.

Temel's lower lip curled down for a second, but then he smiled again, revealing splotchy teeth. "I can't take all the credit. My team works well under pressure."

"Who are you?" I asked.

"Oh, I'm sorry, my name's Temel Ridio. At your service." Temel extended his hand, and I clasped it in mine.

"So you work for Dorothy?" Trendon asked, already sliding his fingers nimbly over his iPhone.

"Ah, yes . . . and no. She's a friend of mine, but I don't exactly work for her little . . . group."

"Who do you work for?"

"I work for Temel," he said, looking down at me and winking. "Me." He pointed to his chest.

"Okay, what now?" I asked. It wouldn't take long for Mr. Jasher's men to spot our taxi, which was currently doing close to a hundred miles per hour down the road.

"Well, that depends," Temel said, never slowing the vehicle as he made a dangerous right turn onto an onramp of the highway.

"On what?" Trendon asked, glancing at me suspiciously.

"On where you need to go," Temel answered. "I'm no mind reader."

I looked down and noticed for the first time that despite his heavily camouflaged attire, Temel wore flip-flops. I barely stopped myself from laughing. "You mean you'll take us wherever we need to go?"

"Uh-huh."

"But we don't have any money, dude!" Trendon said.

"Is okay. You're covered, but don't call me dude!" Temel's eyes flashed dangerously, and Trendon held his hands out in defense.

I grabbed Trendon's arm as Temel steered the taxi through a narrow gap between two buses. The bus drivers slammed on their horns, and Temel giggled.

"Trendon, please tell me you brought Dorothy's map." I had forgotten all about the map until now. If Trendon had left it back at the mansion, we would be in serious trouble.

"Would you please give me some credit?" Trendon asked. "Not only do I have it, but I found something out that is way weird."

I glanced up and noticed his peculiar expression. He motioned for me to look down at his iPhone.

"What is it?" I whispered, inspecting the screen.

"I think I may have figured out why Mr. Jasher isn't having any luck locating the entryway. I looked at the map last night at least a hundred times, and I tried searching on the web for anything like it." I nearly voiced my concern, but Trendon held his hand up. "Relax, I put so many blockages on that laptop, there's no way they could've been watching."

"Where is your laptop?" I looked down at the floor of the taxi.

"Smoldering back on my bed! When those first explosions went off, my laptop practically caught on fire."

"Sorry," Temel said, whistling. "I told you to stay away from the windows."

"Anyway," Trendon continued. "At first, I didn't have much luck finding any maps or anything like that, but then I got to thinking. Remember when Abraham said he had put the map on eBay for like an hour but then pulled it back off because he felt guilty?"

I nodded. I hadn't thought much about Abraham since arriving in Istanbul.

"Yeah, well, I was able to bring up that image from the archives and blow it up on my screen."

"You're a genius, you know that?" I said, quite impressed with my friend.

"Yes, I do. So get this, there's a typo on one of the maps. I'm not sure which, but I'd be willing to bet the one Mr. Jasher is using right now has the mistake."

"What kind of typo?"

"I'm no expert in Ancient Hebrew, but I think I was able to do a pretty good job translating it. From what I could tell, the words were all written in alphabetic characters."

To most people, that would have made no sense, but to the other members of Dorothy Holcomb's archaeology class it was crystal clear. Whoever inscribed the words on that map chose to use direct alphabetic lettering instead of pictorial hieroglyphics, which made it a lot easier to translate.

"Look at this." Trendon showed the image of Mr. Jasher's map on the screen. "That word right there," he pointed to the top, "is translated to read 'Ararat'."

Pressing the button on his iPhone, Trendon brought up the image of the Ancient Egyptian alphabet in another window.

"Okay," I agreed.

"Now, look at your map." He pulled the folded material from his pocket and handed it to me. Immediately, I recognized that the images seemed slightly different, but most of the wording looked identical. Trendon must have been able to sense my confusion because he smiled and pointed to the word *Ararat*. "Look at that letter, right there." He pointed to the fourth character on the map, which should've represented the second "r" in the name *Ararat*. My eyes widened. "Completely different!" he said. "Every other letter is the same, except that one." The character on Mr. Jasher's map looked like an eye missing a pupil, but the one on Dorothy's map, the real map, resembled two flags.

"What is that letter?" I enlarged the window of the alphabet on Trendon's phone and searched the characters for a match. Trendon helped by pointing to the letter "y." An excited chill prickled in my arms. "That would make the word Arayat, right?"

"Yep," Trendon said, grinning. "I searched Google for any information about this mysterious Mt. Arayat, and guess what country I found it in?"

My heartbeat thudded in my ears. "The Philippines," I whispered.

Trendon's jaw dropped, and he sputtered incoherently. He looked down at the screen on his iPhone and shook his head in disbelief. "How in the world did you know that?" he asked, scratching his fingers through his curly black hair.

"Just a lucky guess, I suppose," I answered.

Trendon blinked his eyes in a baffled expression. "Dorothy told you that?" I nodded. "Why didn't you say something?"

"Because it didn't make any sense until just now."

Temel honked his horn at a slow-moving pickup truck and shouted something in Turkish out the window. "Where are you going?" he asked, craning his neck to look at Trendon's iPhone.

"I guess we have to go to the Philippines," I answered softly.

"Philippines?" Temel asked, looking as though trying to figure out the meaning of a strange word. "Okay, I take you."

"You're going to take us to the Philippines?" Trendon blurted out.

"No." Temel chuckled. "I take you to airport, buy you a ticket. Dorothy and I have a friend there who will help you the rest of the way."

"But we don't have passports," I said. "How can we leave the country?"

Temel sucked back on his front teeth as he swiveled the steering wheel, instantly crossing four lanes of blaring traffic and exiting off the ramp. "Um," he started to say, but lost his train of thought as he exploded with several incoherent words out the window at a slower truck trying to merge in front of his taxi. He crunched a soda can resting in the cup holder next to the emergency brake and chucked it out the window. The can skidded across the hood of the truck, causing the driver to slam on his brakes. Temel gave us a toothy smile and chuckled as he returned his focus to the wheel.

"What are we talking about?" he asked in a very calm and controlled voice.

"Passports," I said, slamming my hand against the dashboard in an attempt to brace myself for impact as Temel swerved the taxi, barely missing a motorcycle.

"Ah, yes," he said. "I take care of that."

"You can take care of our passports?" Trendon asked. Temel nodded. "How is that legal?"

Temel shrugged. "Is not."

"Oh, boy," Trendon said.

I found the idea of using a fake passport alarming, but at the moment I couldn't decide what disturbed me more—doing something illegal or riding as a passenger while Temel rocketed down the freeway with reckless abandon.

"There's no way it will ever work," Trendon said. "They'll catch us at the airport and lock us away forever in prison."

Temel's smile widened. "Temel has many friends. You won't get caught."

I didn't doubt Temel had many capable friends, but that didn't boost my confidence. Still, what other choice did we have?

"Besides, if they do catch you, you saw what I can do. Don't worry, kids." Temel nudged me with his elbow. "I can get you out of any prison."

"I like this guy," Trendon said.

"Of course you like me," Temel said, his mouth pulled wide in a toothy grin. "I blow stuff up!"

Shortly after we arrived at the airport, Temel ditched his taxi in the short-term parking but not before removing a blue ball cap from the trunk and a stack of money, three inches thick. He left the two of us by the vending machines and then went and spoke with a man at one of the ticket counters. Thirty minutes later, he led us into a tiny office where someone snapped our pictures. Temel did have many friends, and they all seemed to work at the right places.

"Here you go," Temel said. He handed us our boarding passes and our brand new fake passports. "It's not first class, but I think they feed you."

"Sweet." Trendon grinned.

"Gate B-36," Temel whispered, checking his back for any signs of trouble. "You board in one hour. Can you handle yourselves till then?"

I glanced around at the throngs of boarding passengers. It seemed safe for now. No one was looking at us from what I could tell. "Yeah, we'll be fine. How can we repay you?" I wanted to hug him.

"Pssh. Is nothing. Remember, look for my friend at the airport in Manila. He's good. He does what Dorothy does, whatever that is." Temel winked. "And don't separate from each other. Stick together and you two just take care of business, yes?"

"Oh, we'll take care of business, all right," Trendon said in his most pathetic attempt to sound macho.

Temel smiled. "You be good, Fatki." He slugged Trendon in the shoulder.

"Ouch! Did you just call me fat kid?"

"No, I said Fatki. It means 'friend.'"

"In what language?" Trendon rubbed his arm.

"Dunno. Just made it up." And with that, Temel slid away and blended in with the crowd of travelers.

I watched as the peculiar man wove his way through the airport toward the exit. He wouldn't be far. I could sense it. Temel would be watching from a close distance to make sure we made it aboard the airplane. Dorothy had some amazing connections. I allowed myself a moment to breathe, knowing I would be safe for the next thirty minutes with Temel watching.

Our flight had two scheduled connections—one in Bombay, India, and another in Seoul, South Korea. I had never seen any of these locations before. In different circumstances, this would have been a dream vacation, but standing next to the windows at the gate with my head bowed to avoid eye contact with anyone made this trip anything but.

"I don't get it," Trendon whispered. "According to legend, the ark was supposed to have landed on the top of Mt. Ararat. How can all these Biblical scholars be wrong?" He stared at the image of Mr. Jasher's map on his phone.

"From what I gathered from Dorothy, somebody

went to great lengths to keep the location of the ark hidden. The King James Version of the Bible wasn't published until the seventeenth century. Maybe it wasn't included in the original translation."

"But the Philippines? Do you know where that is on a map?" Trendon asked, his expression revealing his disbelief. "It's a bunch of islands in the middle of the ocean below Japan. It's not even part of the same continent as Turkey. That doesn't coincide with the story of Noah at all."

I gnawed on my lip. He voiced the same concerns I inwardly felt. Pressing my eyelids closed tight, I searched my memory. Something in there would help with this puzzle; I just needed to pull it up in my mind. Sometimes I imagined my brain like a card catalog at the library. All of the information was stored inside, just waiting on an able body to find it. I forced my recollection back to the day a couple of years ago when Dorothy had taught us about the ark. Although not the most important lesson she'd given in class, several pieces of important information had been ingrained in my memory during her lecture.

I opened my eyes and looked at Trendon. "Peleg!" I said, a little too loudly.

"Shush!" Trendon covered my mouth with his hand. "Don't draw any attention to us!" he scolded. "What are you shouting about?"

"In the days of Peleg, the land was divided," I whispered.

"The soccer player?" Trendon blew out his cheeks.

"No. Not Pele. Peleg. It's in Genesis. In one of the verses it says, 'during the days of Peleg, the land was divided.'"

"You really are wasting that brain of yours, you know that? Shouldn't you be like figuring out codes for the CIA?"

I giggled. "Shut up." I nudged him in his side.

"So divided? And that means?"

"Well, many biblical scholars believe this was just a way of saying that Noah's inheritance was split between his three sons, but there are a few scholars who believe it refers to something else. Dorothy told us in class that before the days of Peleg, all of the continents were one big landmass until some catastrophic event occurred right after the great flood, causing them to separate."

"Well, that's complete garbage. You're talking about Pangaea, right? One big land mass? That supposedly happened in prehistoric times."

"Not according to the Bible," I retorted. I looked at him defiantly. "And since we're dealing with biblical stuff, it's probably our best resource, don't you think?" Trendon yawned, but I ignored the gesture and continued. "If my theory is right, then the Philippines were once connected to Asia and most likely broke away during some massive earthquake. Peleg's time was right after Noah, which could've been centuries, but still, chronologically, not too many events happened in between the two periods. Noah's ark could've easily landed on that mountain in the Philippines when it was still part of Asia's landmass, but then, by some act of fate it was taken away into the ocean."

Trendon smirked and shook his head. "Well, whatever, I guess it doesn't matter. What matters is how we, a couple of dumb high school kids, are going to finish Dorothy's quest without getting ourselves killed." He thumbed the power button off on his iPhone and plugged it into his charger, which was connected to an electrical outlet below the window. At least he had his toys. Trendon didn't do so hot cooped up for hours, and we had a long flight awaiting us. I didn't mind the wait, knowing that once we landed in the Philippines, our real mission would begin. I could only hope Dorothy's contact would be there waiting for us. Otherwise we would be on our own once again.

17

Trendon ignored the flight attendant's instructions to wait and stood to remove my backpack from the overhead storage compartment. "That was a ridiculous flight! I never heard of those stupid movies before. And seriously, who eats squid on an airplane?" The waitress had offered him calamari with a tomato and caper ragout, to which Trendon erupted with a verbal tirade. "Whatever happened to Salisbury steak for crying out loud?"

"It didn't look all that bad," I said, yawning. I pulled my shoulders back and stretched, my body stiff from sitting so long. The layovers in Bombay and Seoul hadn't lasted long enough for us to really get out and stretch our legs. Altogether, we'd spent close to seventeen hours onboard an airplane.

Trendon pushed past me into the aisle, ready to weasel his way to the exit.

"Don't get ahead of yourself!" I yanked on Trendon's sleeve. He seemed on the verge of bolting for the front of the line. "Don't you remember what Temel told us? We shouldn't separate, even for a minute."

Trendon rolled his eyes. "You know, there are people born into this world that have to be surgically removed from each other. Their families pay through the nose for it. Now you want to do the opposite? With me of all people?"

"I thought you liked the extra attention I was giving you. Don't you?" I smiled up at Trendon, who hesitated.

"What? Don't go getting any weird ideas. Let's just get off this plane and find our ride. I only hope he knows a good place for grub that doesn't have tentacled creatures on the menu."

Beyond the protective, circular windows of the plane, a black Philippine sky loomed overhead, crowded with storm clouds that hedged up our view of the stars. The storm had delayed our landing by almost an hour, and the airport runway glistened with a fresh coat of rain water. I clung to Trendon's shoulder as he bullied his way through stalling passengers. I couldn't help but giggle every time he made an attempt to excuse himself in a foreign language. The hushed bustle inside the airplane transitioned to a cacophony of rushing throngs in a jam-packed airport.

"Stay close, please," I urged Trendon, who was already making a beeline for the moving walkway. Cool air conditioning came in from the overhead ventilation so strong I almost wished I had a jacket to wear.

"How are we going to find anybody in this mess,

anyway?" Trendon bellowed. He hopped back just as a motorized passenger shuttle rumbled through the main aisle, preceded by a piercing warning beep. "It's like playing Frogger out here!"

"I think that's our guy," I said, tugging on his sleeve.

"Where?"

I pointed to a Filipino man holding a cardboard sign with the message ECNCC10S written in black marker.

"And why would he be our guy?" Trendon asked.

"Because that's the code for next semester's archaeology class, Extra-Curricular Non-Credit Course October Semester."

Trendon smirked. "I'm sorry. Why do you remember junk like that?"

"Obviously it comes in handy from time to time."

The two of us approached the man.

"You must be Amber," he said, offering me a warm smile. He wore a long-sleeved button-down shirt with the sleeves rolled into cuffs, pleated dress slack, and polished black dress shoes. One piece of his attire seemed slightly out of place—his bright red Philadelphia Phillies baseball cap. "And Trendon, I presume?" he tilted his head as if examining Trendon.

"I guess that depends on who you are," Trendon said, staring back. I didn't always appreciate Trendon's lack of tact, but considering what we had been through over the past few days, I also saw it necessary to proceed cautiously. Temel had said he and Dorothy had a friend waiting for us in the airport, but until this guy convinced us of the truth, we wouldn't allow him to lure us into danger.

"Ah yes, my apologies. I am Cabarles Godoy. Our friend, Temel, wanted me to assist you on your . . . um . . . quest, I guess would be the proper term. If it makes you feel any better, I am also very close with Dorothy."

Relief began setting in, but I needed to make sure of a few things before trusting Cabarles. He had a warm, almost jovial façade, but was it real?

"How do you know Dorothy?" I asked.

"Unfortunately, I have never met her in person. I found her quite lovely from our online conversations. Allow me," he reached for my backpack, but I resisted.

"I'm fine." I gave the straps draped over my shoulders a secure tug.

"You've never physically met her?" Trendon asked. He shared an incredulous stare with me.

"No, I'm afraid not. Up until recent events, there hasn't been a demand for personal interaction here in the Philippines. A shame, though, that only trying times merit such an opportunity."

"So, Cabarles, was it?" Trendon continued. "Let's cut right to the chase. How are we supposed to trust you? For all we know, you've been sent here by someone else."

Cabarles bowed slightly as if admitting a mistake. "That does place us in a bit of quandary." He drummed his fingers against his chin, appearing deep in thought. "What sort of proof do you prefer? I could provide you with identification, which would give you my legal name and proof of residency, or perhaps we could call your friend Temel in Istanbul to authenticate me as a reliable source. But I don't think either one of those options would leave you satisfied. Am I correct?"

Trendon shrugged his shoulders. "Yeah, anyone could conjure that stuff up—fake IDs, fake phone calls. We need something more solid."

"I could show you this." Cabarles undid the top three buttons of his shirt, revealing a bluish tattoo of a scroll slightly rolled back, with Ancient Egyptian markings written upon it. It was an identical match to the one on Dorothy's ankle.

"Whoa, pal, we don't need to see your scars and stuff," Trendon said, taking a step back from Cabarles.

"It's the mark," I whispered.

"The what?" Trendon asked.

"The mark of the Seraphic Scroll. Back in Turkey, Dorothy showed me hers. It was on her ankle."

Cabarles nodded. "Did she tell you what it meant?"

I shook my head. "Not exactly, just that there's a society of men and women trying to protect powerful artifacts. Their goal is to prevent evil men like Kendell Jasher from taking them and using them as weapons."

"She told you plenty," Cabarles said, puckering his lips in veneration. His eyes twinkled as he pointed to his chest. "My symbol's location indicates I am a Sentry, someone who is entrusted with guarding artifacts. The mark on the ankle or the wrist means the wearer of such is a Collector. Did she tell you any more?"

"She said something briefly about the Destroyers." I looked over my shoulder to see who else might be eavesdropping.

"Those bearing the mark beneath the ear." Cabarles leaned in and lowered his voice. "Let us hope our troubles do not require their expertise."

"When did she tell you all of that?" Trendon asked, looking at me in disbelief.

I felt my throat starting to tighten again as I recalled Dorothy's thin frame, trembling from lack of food. I shook my head, choking back the urge to cry. "You speak very good English," I said, changing the subject. The flight attendants had stumbled over simple phrases. Cabarles spoke with almost no trace of an accent.

"Yes, I speak it well, along with Spanish, Latin, German, Egyptian, and a few other languages."

"That's impressive," Trendon said.

"Oh, not quite. I am a linguist. It is expedient I learn the various phonetics of all significant languages, but many of my colleagues have truly mastered the art."

"So you are going to take us to Arayat?" I asked.

Cabarles held his finger to his lips. "Let's not engage in this conversation out in the open. Temel wanted me to follow strict security measures in order to ensure your safety. This way, please." Cabarles pointed toward the far end of the terminal. "You'll draw too much attention if we stand here long. There's a jeep outside that will take us out of the airport to a main hub. From there we can ride another shuttle all the way to Malolos."

"What's in Malolos?" I asked, removing the straps of my backpack from my shoulders. I opened the zipper and plucked out a folded, laminated map of the Philippines I had purchased from a travel store in the Seoul airport.

"I'm afraid we have quite the voyage in store this evening. Malolos is on the outskirts of Manila. We'll need to board another vehicle there and take three more jeeps in Calumpit, Apalit, and Santa Ana before we reach the city of Arayat."

I gave Trendon a worried look. "Won't that be expensive?"

"Not really," Cabarles answered, never slowing his pace. "A nonstop trip in a taxi would cost you at least ten times as much, but don't worry, your expenses are covered. Besides, we'll be better off avoiding the traffic on the National Highway. Who needs air conditioning, anyway?"

Trendon began to raise his hand, but I pulled down on his sleeve. Although I'd been hesitant at first, I felt we could trust Cabarles. He was a member of the Seraphic Scroll society, Dorothy's secret organization. He also had the title of Sentry, which according to Dorothy, meant someone trustworthy enough to know the locations of ancient, powerful artifacts. I felt confident Cabarles would do all he could to assist us with our mission.

As he escorted us through the crowded airport, I instinctively clutched my backpack. Several uniformed security guards, armed with machine guns, wove in and out of the current of travelers. I had seen enough guns during the past week to last me my entire life-time. We attracted several curious gazes from passing children, and we paused once at the vending machines to allow Trendon an opportunity to stock up, but for the most part, our journey through the airport went uninterrupted.

Trendon handed me a small, slender bottle of brown liquid. "What's this Sarsi stuff?" he asked, twisting off the metal bottle cap and downing a big gulp.

Cabarles glanced over his shoulder while quickly sidestepping a convoy of Filipino businessmen decked out in expensive-looking suits. "Ah, you'll like it. It's very similar to your—"

"Tastes like root beer, or close to it," Trendon said, cutting him off. He belched and licked his lips.

I sipped my bottle timidly before surrendering to my thirst and guzzling the drink.

"Watch your step." Cabarles approached the down escalator, which led to the main level. Beneath the descending steps, literally thousands of people moved in between the rotating baggage claims, departure and arrival monitors, and the check-in terminals. *How do so many people fit in there?* I wondered. Surely the airport had long since surpassed its maximum capacity.

"What's the weather like out there?" Trendon asked before taking a huge gulp from his second bottle of Sarsi.

"I'm afraid it's very hot and humid," Cabarles said. He could've saved his breath. Within seconds a wall of heat coming from the open automatic doors hit us. Trendon gasped, tugging on his collar. It felt as though someone had opened an oven door. The smell of smog, garbage, and exhaust burned my eyes as we briskly passed through the exit, leaving us craving the air conditioned hubbub of the airport. More people than I had ever seen in one place shoved past us, carting luggage on rollers behind them. Dozens of buses chock-full of passengers sped by alongside red and yellow taxis. Occasionally, one of the taxis would stall in front of our group, and the driver would motion for us to get in. But Cabarles waved each of them on their way.

"What are we waiting for?" Trendon covered his mouth and nose with his shirt and wiped away the sweat on his forehead.

Cabarles pointed to a rapidly approaching vehicle with blaring lights and what appeared to be a bullhorn attached to the roof. "Here we go."

Expecting a taxi, I found myself speechless at the sight of the unusual mode of transportation.

Trendon seemed to be losing the struggle to control his laughter. "What is that?" he snorted.

"We call them jeepneys. They can be a little loud, but it will be our least expensive ride."

The jeepney, a long rectangular vehicle resembling a miniature bus, had an entrance directly in the rear. Graffiti covered the chrome exterior, and rows of blinking neon lights stretched beneath the windows and lit up the interior. Instead of the usual chairs, there were two rows of padded benches beneath the windows, with aluminum handrails bolted to the ceiling above them. These benches provided the only place to sit. The three of us entered through the rear, followed by two teenagers wearing Chicago Bulls T-shirts. I clung to the handrail as the jeep swerved away from the curb and into the stream of fast-moving traffic.

Trendon leaned in close to me. "I thought we didn't want to draw attention to ourselves. This thing looks like a twisted clown sculpture."

"I assure you, if you are looking to blend in, there's no better way," Cabarles said, apparently overhearing him.

It took only twenty minutes for the jeepney to travel the distance between the airport and a central hub of jeeps at the crossing of the South Super Highway and Ayala Avenue. We exited our ride into a haven of street vendors. Nauseating smells of bizarre foods wafted through the crowd, forcing me to pinch my nose closed. Small glass kiosks, illuminated by halogen lights, housed a peculiar array of items including boiled peanuts, zigzagged chicken intestines on barbecue skewers, and tiny bananas deep frying in golden oil. Men wearing nothing but shorts and flip-flops walked past, baskets brimming with eggs on their shoulders.

"You want a Balut, Joe? Masarap!" one of the vendors asked Trendon, who shook his head. He rubbed his stomach, indicating he was quite full, which brought on a burst of laughter from several vendors, who pointed at his round belly.

"I think they're making fun of my weight," Trendon said, glaring at a man who had puffed out his cheeks.

Cabarles frowned and shrugged. "Ah, yes, maybe they are." He wasted no time flagging down our next shuttle. Clasping my hand, he led us to yet another jeepney. Crammed in almost every available spot, Filipino men, women, and children all directed their attention to the new American passengers.

Trendon glared at me. "If I end up sitting on some dude's lap . . ." He ascended the three chrome steps into the belly of the jeepney. Loud thumping music droned inside. Trendon pointed at a mini disco ball dangling from the ceiling. I nodded and forced a smile. After several people politely shifted sideways, Trendon and I crammed ourselves in between the entry and a woman toting a large wicker basket full of strange purple objects.

"Comfy?" Cabarles asked, ducking his head through the opening.

"It's a little snug," Trendon said, his narrowed eyes announcing his discomfort.

"We're good." I smiled politely. "What about you? Where are you going to sit?"

"Oh, I'll be fine hanging off the back," Cabarles answered. He grasped another handrail that lined the opening of the jeepney.

"Now that's what I'm talking about!" Trendon began shimmying out from his seat in order to snag the available space next to Cabarles on the exit steps, but another Filipino man carrying a green cloth satchel full of mangos hopped on before he made it. Trendon sighed, plopping back against the window. "What were those eggs that guy back there was trying to sell me?" he asked as several other vendors carrying similar baskets of the strange eggs passed by the opening of the jeepney.

"They're called Balut," Cabarles said, smiling. "They're a delicacy here, but I suppose aborted baby ducklings might be a bit much for your first sample of Filipino cuisine."

Trendon mimicked vomiting into his hand. "Whatever happened to good ole hardboiled?"

Cabarles laughed.

"How long will our trip take?" I asked, glancing down at my watch for the first time since our arrival. It was already nearing eight o'clock.

"Two hours, maybe three," Cabarles shouted. The driver of the jeepney must have found his favorite song on the radio because the volume increased to an almost deafening level.

"What did he say?" Trendon bellowed, cupping his hands over his ears to shield the noise. "I know he didn't say two hours!"

"It's about sixty miles to our stop," Cabarles continued, unfazed by the rise in decibels. "Throw in traffic and stopping for passengers, and we'll be lucky if it's less than three."

"Why would we stop for passengers?" Trendon asked. "We're already squished like a can of kipper snacks."

"Oh, believe me, there's still plenty of room."

Our mouths dropped open as yet another commuter boarded the jeepney and a ripple shifted through the passengers as they made room. Trendon hugged his knees in his lap. With a blaring announcement from the bullhorn, the jeepney launched onto the main road.

I sucked in my stomach and attempted to squish back against the wall. "Maybe we should do some more research on Arayat before we get there," I said, literally shouting in Trendon's ear.

"Yeah, right. You think I'm going to pull out my phone here? I don't want it swiped."

"So what do we do for the next three hours?"

"You could start by telling that lady next to you her potatoes are going bad," Trendon said, glancing down at the basket of purple tubers.

I giggled. "Can you believe this?" I asked. "We're actually here in the Philippines and on the path to one of the greatest discoveries of all time."

"Forgive me if I don't share in your enthusiasm." Trendon closed his eyes and allowed his head to thud heavily against the window.

18

The three hours it took to cover the distance from the airport to the tiny city of Arayat whisked by surprisingly quickly. It rained most of the way, peppering the metallic roof of the jeepney and making conversation impossible. I tried to sleep but found myself continually drifting over onto the shoulder of the lady sitting next to me. At almost midnight, we exited our jeep onto the quiet streets. Thunder rumbled overhead, and a few scattered raindrops began to fall sporadically.

"The storm has subdued the mountain. Now she sleeps quietly," Cabarles said, pointing at the outline of Mt. Arayat that loomed in the distance. I hadn't seen the mountain when I first descended the jeep. Now the sight of the ominous mass jutting up in front of us caused a shudder to tingle in my shoulders.

"What do you mean by the storm has subdued her?" Trendon asked.

"Come, let us not linger. It can be a trifle dangerous after dark," Cabarles said, ignoring Trendon's question.

"I live in the barangay of Lacquios, which is a five-minute walk from here. I have made up two beds with clean sheets, and we have running water. I'm willing to wager my wife has a hot meal waiting for the three of us if we hurry."

"Nothing too weird, I hope?" Trendon asked.

Cabarles offered a polite smile. "You'll sleep tonight, and in the morning we shall head into the market for supplies. Mt. Arayat is somewhat of a tourist attraction. It can get crowded during the day, so we won't be able to embark until tomorrow evening."

The humble surroundings of the neighboring houses made Cabarles's home a pleasant surprise. A gate surrounded the stone house, which had a shingled roof. Two tall coconut trees sprouted up in one corner of the yard. Melodious wind chimes dangled from an overhanging awning, and a wicker rocking chair moved slightly from the breeze on the porch. A carport, housing a motorized tricycle, stood directly off the house.

A light shone from the kitchen, where we found Cabarles's wife just removing a large boiling pot of water from a camp stove. "I'm taking this to the restroom, so you'll have warm water to wash with after you eat," she said, leaning in to kiss Cabarles on his cheek. Short and skinny with graying hair and strong, muscular arms, Mrs. Godoy wore an apron over what appeared to be a nightgown and house slippers. "Cabarles, take them into the kitchen while the food is still hot." She too spoke English almost flawlessly.

Place settings had been laid around the kitchen table, where a pitcher of mango juice, a plate of vegetables, and a steaming wok of cubed meat and potatoes awaited us. Trendon inhaled the aroma and smiled, giving Cabarles an approving thumbs up.

"This will do," he said.

The three of us sat and ate in undisturbed silence. I hadn't expected to truly enjoy the foreign cuisine, but my meal in the Godoys' home quickly rose to the top of my list of favorites.

"Your wife is very nice to do this for us," I said. "Do you have children?"

Cabarles's eyes lit up. "Yes, I have four. My two oldest sons are studying abroad in Japan, and my oldest daughter is on campus at the university in Manila. We live here with my youngest, Marley. She's seven."

"You don't look old enough to have college-aged kids," I said.

"Oh, I assure you, I am quite old."

Trendon belched and helped himself to yet another glass of the juice. "Well, that was awesome!" he announced, leaning back in his chair and appearing very content.

"I trust it wasn't too bizarre for you?" Cabarles collected the empty plates from the table and carried them over to the sink.

"The meat wasn't anything weird like puppy dog, was it?" Trendon asked, picking his teeth with his finger.

"Trendon!" I blushed with embarrassment from his rude comment.

Cabarles shook his head but humored Trendon's brazenness. "I'm afraid you watch too much television."

After our meal, Cabarles showed us to our rooms. "The bathroom is across the hall, and if you need anything, our room is three doors down." He pulled a chain on a table lamp, and my bedroom lit up with a dull glow. After dropping his stuff in his room, Trendon joined us, sitting in the chair by the open bedroom window. A warm, gentle breeze drifted through the curtains.

"We won't have much time in the morning to discuss what it is you're up against with this mountain, so we will have to talk softly now," Cabarles said.

"What do you mean? Are we going to need climbing gear or something?" Trendon glanced up from his phone's screen.

"No, it isn't a strenuous hike. In fact, it is almost one-fifth the size of Mt. Ararat in Turkey, so it won't take you too long to reach the summit," Cabarles answered. "What do you know of our mountain?" He looked over at me.

I shrugged my shoulders. "Nothing. Before this trip, I had never even heard of it."

Outside, the wind picked up, carrying with it a haunting sound of something moaning in the distance. The noise caught everyone in the room off guard, and Trendon pulled at the curtains, poking his head out the window.

"That sounded like some lady crying. Did you guys hear that?"

Goose bumps formed on my arms. Cabarles's face grew stern as he stared at the window. Again the faint sound of howling broke the silence, and Trendon quickly pulled his head back in. No one spoke as more voices joined the first in the distance. Though the wind masked most of it, all three of us could hear what sounded to be many women crying in anguish.

"Something's going on out there," Trendon whispered. "It sounds like they're hurt."

I strained to listen, looking at Cabarles, whose disturbed expression remained unchanged. The voices sounded unnatural, as if the wind was creating the disturbance in the distance.

"They are more vocal than usual," Cabarles said. "Perhaps it is a sign."

"What are you talking about? Who are more vocal than usual?" Trendon asked.

"Have either of you heard of the legend of Mariang Sinukuan?"

"Who?" Trendon asked abruptly.

Cabarles offered an awkward smile. "I suppose if you hadn't before heard of our mountain, then it is doubtful you would have heard of her." He hesitated. "I'm afraid you'll discover the people of the Philippines are very . . . superstitious. It is not uncommon to hear high-ranking government officials make mention of dwarfs or fairies."

Trendon chuckled, and Cabarles joined him momentarily before taking a more serious tone. "It does seem humorous, doesn't it, my friend? Having studied in the United States, I know how believing in the paranormal is frowned upon by your society. I try not to find myself too involved in such beliefs, but perhaps you'll have an open mind for just a moment." Cabarles no longer smiled as he spoke directly at Trendon. Outside, another gust of wind carried with it the sound of the moaning voices.

"Are you talking about that sound outside?" Trendon asked sarcastically. Cabarles looked fleetingly at the window and nodded.

I pulled the sheet up close to my neck. "Maybe you should close the window," I suggested.

"It's quite all right," Cabarles said. "She doesn't come out of the mountain."

"Who doesn't come out of the mountain?" Trendon distanced himself from the open window.

"The people of the Philippines believe that several thousand years ago, a *diwang,* or fairy, named Mariang Sinukuan came to dwell on our mountain. Because she had great love for this people, she blessed the land with an abundance of fruit and wildlife. The forests of Arayat were filled with the most amazing creatures— animals never before seen in the Philippines."

I perked my head at the mention of animals. Perhaps this legend could solidify the possibility the ark had landed on Mt. Arayat.

"The people prospered because of her bounty, but as is always the case, their greed grew. They began to take more than what was needed. They hunted the animals for sport. This angered Mariang Sinukuan, and she cursed the people. Their food turned to stone, and the animals disappeared." Cabarles walked over to the window as another chilling howl erupted in the distance. Thunder followed it, and a heavy rain began to fall upon the house. He pulled the window closed and latched it, snuffing out the chilling sounds from the mountain.

"Mt. Arayat is visited by several hundred people every day, yet no one has discovered the source of that sound." Cabarles stared down at Trendon. "And every night, we are haunted by her lament."

Trendon swallowed. "Okay, so what are you saying, there's a chance we're going to run into some ghost tomorrow night?"

Cabarles tried to offer an encouraging smile but ended up grimacing. "It's a possibility. Access to the mountain is restricted after dusk, but unfortunately we will need the cover of darkness if you intend to locate the hidden entrance unobserved by anyone else. I feel Mr. Jasher and his followers have not arrived here yet, but one can never be too sure."

"I'm a little freaked out right now," I said, pulling the sheet up even tighter.

"I apologize if I have frightened you. I wanted to make sure you were both aware of what might lie in wait." Cabarles's penetrating gaze softened as it rested upon me. "If it is indeed a ghost, then according to superstition, it cannot physically harm you. But I don't know for sure."

"This is a bad idea!" Trendon announced. "This whole situation just keeps getting weirder and weirder.

I say we head back to the States, alert the authorities about what we found out in Turkey, and just forget the ark. Kendell Jasher has no idea the thing is anywhere near the Philippines."

I stayed quiet, inwardly trying to process Cabarles's words. "Will you be going with us into the mountain?" I asked.

Cabarles frowned. "Unfortunately, it is not my place to do so."

"What? That's a load of bull!" Trendon shouted. "You mean you're gonna make us do all the work?"

"It is not that simple. I am a Sentry. I must only guard the location. It's forbidden for me to do any more. I can take you there and help you with any supplies you may need, but after that, my stewardship ends. Only a Collector may go forward."

"But we're not Collectors," Trendon said, almost laughing. "So we're not supposed to do this either, right?" He looked at me. I had brought my backpack up from off the floor and had unzipped the pocket.

"Dorothy told me we had to go in her place. We need to continue what she started." I pulled out the blue stone and held the map in my hands, running my fingers over the worn inscriptions.

Cabarles rested his hand on Trendon's shoulder. "She's right. That is the only way. I must not break code, no matter what."

"What's that junk going to do if we run into Mary-Jo-what's-her-face?" Trendon asked, pointing to the items in my hands.

"I do know this, my young friends: what you are about to do is very dangerous. Dorothy must have a lot of trust in both of you to send you on her errand. There are things that can't be explained by simple logic, and you will undoubtedly witness those things tomorrow evening. What you should know is that this is ultimately a conflict between those who are righteous and those who are not. I'd suspect there will be evidence of both forces as you draw closer to the discovery." Cabarles walked to the door. "Now, I have kept you up longer than intended. You will need plenty of rest tonight."

"How are we supposed to sleep with all that racket going on outside?" Trendon asked. "Especially after the little ghost story you told us?"

"I'm sorry I did not sugarcoat it for the both of you. After a while you will get used to it." Having said that, Cabarles excused himself from the room.

I stared down at the peculiar objects on my bedsheets, occasionally shooting glances toward the window with every hint of a sound from beyond the closed glass. Trendon joined me on the bed, plucking the stone up with his hand and holding it like a baseball.

"Do you really think that mountain's haunted?" I asked quietly.

Trendon tossed the stone in his hand for a moment before sighing. "I don't know. Probably not, but I'm definitely spooked now. That Cabarles is a peach."

"I like him," I said, placing the items back into

my pack. "I think he really wants to help us. He's just trying to warn us, that's all."

"Sure." Trendon rose to his feet.

"What about what he said about the animals in the forest?"

Trendon nodded. "Yeah, I thought about that too. Most legends have some truth to them, and that one's probably no different. If Noah's ark really did land on Mt. Arayat, there definitely would've been a crud-load of animals."

"What have we gotten ourselves into?"

"Hey, let's make something perfectly clear—*you* got *me* into this. Now if you're done spooking me out, I'm going to go browse the Internet from my bed. I don't think I'll be sleeping much."

"Me either," I said. "Keep your window closed."

Trendon scoffed. "Easy for you to say. This place is like a sauna. And, by the way, if you see any white ladies bounding around outside, I really don't need to know."

19

Cabarles's car idled in a parking area beneath several coconut trees. Flipping off the headlights, he popped the trunk and got out. I peered out the window at the jungle. Strange growths of vegetation with thick, elephant-ear leaves covered the jungle floor. I opened my door and sighed from the immense heat. It really hadn't cooled with the setting sun, and I dreaded leaving the air conditioning of the car.

"Your packs are heavy, but they're full of much-needed provisions," Cabarles said, handing both of us a separate backpack, bulging with supplies. Earlier that day we had gone into an open-air market called a *pelengke*, where crowds of street vendors were crammed beneath bright cloth canopies and awnings, selling everything from slices of sour mangoes served with mashed fish parts, to handguns. I had never seen anything so incredible or smelled anything so rancid. Flies sputtered through the tight, crowded walkways, alighting on dangling pig and cow carcasses. Under the canopies, some of the toughest women I had ever seen wielded razor-sharp bolo knives as they removed the innards of coconuts. Had Trendon and I been traveling alone, it would have been easy to get completely overwhelmed by all the noise and bustle of vendors. Fortunately Cabarles proved to be a seasoned guide.

At the market we'd purchased new backpacks as well as two heavy flashlights, a first-aid kit, matches, extra batteries, a small bottle of kerosene, several big bags of trail mix, and lots of bottled water. Trendon also selected a pocket knife from an array of weapons spread out on a tarp, and Cabarles added a small ten-pack of road flares. Both of us bought new clothes: jeans, T-shirts, jackets, and hiking boots. We forced all of our provisions, aside from our clothing, into the two backpacks, and I added the items from Dorothy's safe into one of the pockets on my pack.

"The hike should take you less than two hours to get to the top. You'll find a cave there in the rock that will lead you into the mountain. The caverns can be a bit tricky for someone not familiar with the territory. There are switchbacks and drop-offs that will sneak up on you if you're not careful." Cabarles offered me a faint smile. "Follow your map. If you get confused, retrace your steps back to the mouth of the cave and start over. You should be undisturbed by anyone until 10:00 a.m. tomorrow morning."

"Yeah right. That is if we don't consider Marty-Beth-skunk-bomb to be anyone," Trendon said.

Cabarles chuckled, but his eyes showed his concern.

"When you get an opportunity, and if you can find any sort of kindling, build a fire. If anything, it will buoy up your spirits and keep you warm. The caves get colder as you travel inward, so you'll need the jackets."

"What do we do once we find the opening?" Trendon asked, clicking his flashlight on to test the batteries. "Is there even an opening?"

Cabarles patted him on the shoulder. "I've been in the caves before, and I don't recall any opening. According to legend, your stone," he pointed to my backpack pocket, "will glow bright if it nears the correct point."

"How does it do it?" I asked.

"The stone is like a magnet that repels a mineral in the rock door. I'm sure the method is mostly scientific."

"Do you really think we'll find it?" My eyes wandered to a beaten path cut into the jungle.

"Oh yes, I definitely do." He put his arm around the two of us and gave us a tight squeeze. "I'll be waiting for you here tomorrow. Good luck!" I waved as his vehicle lurched out of the parking area and slowly descended the hill.

Several moments passed with neither of us making any step toward the tree line. I thought back to the night before when the howling and screaming had started. Would I be able to continue once the voices returned? Closing my eyes, I thought about Dorothy trapped in her cell. Then I thought about Lisa and Abraham. But I found courage when I thought of Joseph.

Trendon crunched a mouthful of trail mix in his

mouth, dropping crumbs and whole peanuts on the gravel beneath him. He had already munched through a quarter of the first bag.

"Hey," I whispered. Trendon glanced up, a handful of mix inches from his open lips. "You ready for this?"

He crammed the food in his mouth and dusted his hands together. "Let's do what we do," he answered.

The hike to the top took slightly longer than two hours. We walked along a well-worn path, easy enough to follow, but the variety of wildlife rustling the fallen branches beneath the dark cover of the jungle disrupted our progress. We constantly beamed our flashlights into the thick vegetation, trying to catch a glimpse of some animal scampering off. At almost ten o'clock, we arrived at the cave. Trendon took a swig from his bottle of water and pointed his flashlight toward the mouth of the cave.

"What now?" he whispered.

I removed the folded map as well as a page of notes we had made earlier that day with our best attempt at a complete translation of the markings on the map. Most of the characters had been alphabetic, but there were a few symbols we couldn't figure out.

"According to this—" I started to speak, but a sharp gust of wind whipped out from within the mountain, blowing us back a step from the cave and silencing me.

Then the howling started, quietly at first, starting deep within the mountain. We froze as we listened to the voices grow in strength until they bellowed out of the cave. Sometimes it sounded like laughter; other times it sounded tortured. I turned away from the cave and hid my face, expecting something hideous to scramble out. The howling continued for another minute and then as quickly as it started, the voices vanished on the wind, leaving the two of us in complete silence.

Trendon's chest rose and fell rapidly. I could feel his body shaking. "Where do you think that's coming from?" he whispered.

I swallowed and forced myself to look toward the dark and foreboding cave. Was this what it was like for Dorothy whenever she ventured into mysterious parts unknown? Was I ready to follow suit?

"I have a bad feeling about it," I said.

"Don't tell me, it's waiting for us next to the ark."

I nodded. I had no doubts. Whatever made those hideous sounds awaited us deep within. I tried not to think of some ghastly woman floating across the stone, but the image was burned in my mind. What would it do to us if we came across it? Was there really a phantom haunting the mountain?

"Okay," Trendon said abruptly. He gripped his flashlight tighter and stared at me. "If we're really going to do this, we'd better get going. I'm close to changing my mind."

"We have to do it, Trendon," I said. "I'm just glad you're here with me." I squeezed his arm, and he grunted.

"Yeah, whatever,"

One hour later, grumbling, frustrated, and forced to retrace our steps, our search brought us back to the beginning of the cave.

"We're never going to find the opening!" Trendon bellowed for the fourth time.

I couldn't concentrate, and since I was the one holding the map and navigating our course through the cave, we kept backtracking or stopping to get our bearings. Trendon stared down at the blue locator stone in his palm. He had tried rubbing it against several walls to see if it would glow, only to be disappointed when the color never brightened.

"Maybe this doesn't even work," he said, tossing the stone in the air and catching it again in his hand.

"Be careful with that!" I snapped, losing my patience. "I think we just started off wrong." I pulled the map close to my eyes and shined the flashlight over it. Upon entering the cave, two paths veered off in opposite directions. From what I could see, we needed to take the path trailing to the left, but I couldn't be certain. The inscriptions were so tiny, and the directions we had translated didn't make any sense. "Proceed down" was one of them and "Descend out" was another— both of which seemed terribly vague. Why were those terms used instead of something easier to understand like "go left" or "step right"? That would've been ideal. I tugged on my hair in frustration.

"Let's try that way," I said, pointing to the right.

Trendon joined me at my side and shook his head,

looking at the map. "I don't think so. Unless you're holding that thing upside down, it definitely points to the left."

I blew out a breath, trying to get the hair off my face, and growled. "We just came from that way! It ends at a wall, and the wall's not the opening."

"Wait a second," Trendon said. "Look, it says to proceed down somewhere near that wall we bumped into. I don't think it means we keep going until we hit the wall. I think it means we proceed down. Like into the ground."

I gripped the map tighter and studied it for a moment, forcing my eyes to focus and my head to ignore the fear creeping its way in.

I took a deep breath. "I think you're right." Why hadn't I thought of that? "Proceed down" could easily mean into the ground.

The second attempt down the left path went faster, and after twenty minutes, we approached the dead end we'd seen earlier. About six yards from the wall, we discovered a narrow passageway we hadn't noticed before. Trendon pointed his flashlight into the darkness of an eight- to ten-foot drop that would take us down into another room. We looked at each other, sharing a silent realization. Something could be waiting for us at the bottom. Trendon continued to scan the darkness below with his flashlight. After a minute of searching, he stood up.

"Seems safe enough," he said, beaming his light in my eyes.

I shielded my face. "It won't be, though. You know it won't." With the way our luck had been going, it would be anything but safe.

Trendon chewed on his lower lip, and a hint of a smile broke across his face. "Yeah, well . . . told you I was right. Let's never forget who deciphered the first code." He jabbed his thumb at this chest. "Me, not the great Amber Rawson. Boy, does that feel awesome."

I laughed, breaking the gloom of the cave. For a fleeting moment I felt reassured, almost confident that we could do this.

"Rock, paper, scissors to see who goes first?" Trendon asked, making a fist with his hand.

I licked my lips, nodded, and held up my fist, but Trendon only smiled.

"Nah, I won't make you go first." He attached his flashlight to his wrist and raised his foot toward the crack in the wall.

"Are you sure?" I asked, honestly surprised by the offer.

"No, I'm not, but oh well." He shimmied his body further into the wall until I could only see the top of his head and his hands gripping the rock.

"Be careful," I said, shining the flashlight into the hole. Then he dropped. I waited less than ten seconds before I called his name. I couldn't stand being alone in the darkness. Trendon didn't respond, and I grew desperate.

"Trendon, you better answer—" my voice broke off as the sound of crumbling rocks caught my attention. I yelped and spun around, pointing my flashlight in the direction of the sound and catching a glimpse of something small and furry scuttling away. Only a gigantic rat. "Trendon!"

A light clicked on from down in the crack, and I could hear Trendon's sputtering cough.

"I'm fine. I just couldn't get my flashlight to work," he said in between choking.

I breathed a sigh of relief. "Is it safe down there?"

There was a pause and then Trendon chuckled. "Would I be having a casual conversation with you if it wasn't?"

After I dropped down into the room, the two of us scanned the walls for any sign of danger. The temperature felt colder here than above, and I removed my jacket from the backpack. We took a short break to eat some of the trail mix and remove anything else we thought we might need on short notice. Trendon whipped out his pocket knife, and I laughed.

"You're like Peter Pan with that little sword," I said, nibbling on a raisin. "Too bad you can't fly."

"Yeah, but I'd love to be wearing some green tights right about now," he said. "And that stylish cap with the feather."

I snorted, spewing water out of my mouth. We laughed for more than a minute. It felt really good, but it didn't last. I wondered when the howling would return. We hadn't heard it since we entered the cave. Why was it so quiet? I wondered if something lay in wait to ambush us.

"Do you think you can scale that and pull yourself back up through the crack?" Trendon asked, pointing to the craggy surface of the wall.

"Why? That's not the way we need to go."

"Yeah, but that's our only way out once we're finished, and we may need to hurry."

I chewed my trail mix and studied the wall. I could do it. I would have no choice.

From the newly discovered room, the directions led us to the right, through an opening in the far wall. Stalactites, dripping with cave water, towered above our heads like the incisors of a giant beast. I followed the map as best I could and, with Trendon's help, we found more than one area where we needed to squeeze through uncomfortable cracks in the stone floor. Rocks and deep puddles of water constantly appeared in our way, delaying our advance.

Over four hours had passed since we started down at the trailhead by Cabarles's car, but from the moment we had entered into the cave, the howling had not returned. Finally, we followed the last instruction and arrived at a solid, impassable rock wall.

"Is this it?" Trendon whispered.

I examined the map, rereading each of the instructions carefully before concurring. "Yes, I believe so," I whispered back.

Trendon pulled the locator stone from his pocket and gave me a wary look as if to say "this had better work." Holding it against the center of the wall, we waited for something phenomenal to happen.

A full minute passed with no result. Trendon tried rubbing it at different points on the wall, but nothing happened.

"Try it near the floor," I instructed. Maybe we needed to go under the wall. Trendon tried it and growled in anger.

"Stupid rock!" he shouted, squeezing the stone tightly so as to smash it. "It doesn't work! Probably never did!" He kicked at the wall with his boot and yelled.

"Give it to me!" I said, reaching for the stone. I mimicked Trendon, rubbing the stone across every possible inch of wall, hoping and praying something would happen. After several tries, I gave up. I groaned in defeat, physically drained from our journey through the caves and dreading the trip back. What if I had made a mistake on one of the directions? Did we both have enough energy to retrace our steps and try again?

A large albino cave cricket scuttled past my boot, and I screamed out in shock. I sprang to my feet, losing my grip on my flashlight. The bulb shattered against the floor, and my light went out, engulfing us in darkness.

"Hang on," Trendon said. He had turned his flash-light off to conserve the batteries, but now I could hear him frantically scrambling for it.

"Wait!" I said excitedly. "Don't turn it on!"

"Are you crazy?" Trendon asked, still fumbling with his flashlight. "I'm not going to stand here in the dark while those bugs crawl over me."

"Look at the stone!" I held the stone out in my hand toward the wall. It glowed with a soft bluish hue. As I brought it closer to the wall, the color got brighter. The locator stone did work, and it had been working the entire time. We'd been expecting something so powerfully bright, we didn't realize the light from our flashlights had prevented us from seeing it glow.

"That's it!" Trendon said, his voice growing with enthusiasm. "We've found it!"

"Yes! We did." I reached over and hugged him around his neck. "We found it."

We hugged for a moment, dancing around and kicking stray stones with our boots. Even thinking about all the problems ahead couldn't bring us down.

Trendon turned his flashlight back on and pushed against the wall, trying to move it. It didn't budge. "So now that we've found this wall, how do we get through it?"

We searched for an opening or some sort of crack that could give way and expand, but there didn't seem to be anything like that. I put my ear against the wall and listened.

"Find something to smash against it," I said, scanning the ground for any sort of blunt object.

Trendon picked up a large stone and hammered it against the wall. A deep fissure spread out from where he had struck. He pounded over and over again with his rock, and more pieces of the wall crumbled away. I helped too, pulling away the debris and widening the hole. Soon we'd made quite an opening. We would have to climb because the hole stood above our waists, but we had expanded it enough for both of us to get through.

I peered in, grasping Trendon's jacket for support. Beyond the opening in the wall, a dark, narrow corridor stretched for several hundred yards with the walls and ceiling forming a tunnel. I couldn't see the end of it. The smooth ground on the other side glimmered like volcanic glass.

"The path continues straight forever!" I said. "It's like a massive—"

My words cut off as the howling roared from within the opening. I toppled back into Trendon's arms, but not before I caught sight of a large creature darting down the path toward us.

20

"What did you see?" Trendon hovered over me, shaking my arms. "Snap out of it!"

I exhaled sharply through my nostrils and got to my knees. "There's some kind of animal in there," I whispered.

"Animal? What kind of—" The sound of heavy breathing a few feet beyond the hole cut off his words. Both of us jumped back, yelling at the top of our lungs. In the darkness, behind where we'd punctured the wall, two lidless eyes, sickly white without pupils, hovered at least six feet from the floor.

Trendon pulled me behind him, my whole body trembling with fear. The deep, guttural breathing persisted, sounding more like the raspy exhaust from a dilapidated automobile. Suddenly a hand shot through the opening, grabbing at Trendon's shirt but just barely missing the fabric. I tugged on Trendon's arms, trying to pull him to safety, but in the process, he dropped his flashlight. The light went out, plunging us into darkness, except for the faint glow of the locator stone. Trendon yanked a road flare from his backpack and ignited the fuse. A red glow emitted from the end, illuminating the opening, and the eyes reared back in alarm. I tried to catch a glimpse of the thing beyond the hole, but it retreated just out of range of the flare's light.

"Back!" Trendon shouted, swinging the flare like a weapon. "Get back!"

The creature shrieked, which sounded like the noise of a dying woman. I clamped my hands over my ears. This must be what made the sounds the villagers heard every night. I felt like I was on the edge of passing out.

"I said get back!" Trendon ordered, heaving the flare through the opening. A hissing sound erupted as the end of the flare struck the creature. The eyes vanished from the hole, and the cave was filled with howls and the sound of the creatures' claws clacking against the stone floor as it fled.

Several moments passed with me cowering behind Trendon in the darkness, not daring to take another step in any direction. I knew the creature would return.

"Okay, genius," Trendon said quietly. "What was that? I've never seen anything like that before!"

"I don't know," I muttered. "I couldn't see what it looked like. It was taller than you, and its eyes were unnatural—hollow and cold, like white marbles.

"Did you see that it had five fingers on its hand? What is it, some kind of ape?"

"I got the feeling it was intelligent. Like it was studying us, debating how to attack."

"We're getting out of here!" Trendon searched for the flashlight with his hands. When he found it, it wouldn't turn on. "Worthless piece of junk! I knew they were too cheap to be any good." Removing another flare from his backpack, he lit it and then started heading back the way we came.

I shook my head adamantly. "No, we can't!" I squeezed his arm.

"Uh, yes we can," Trendon fired back. "No one said anything about having to play monster squad. That thing wanted to tear us apart."

From deep within the room beyond the hole, the creature bellowed, and we held our breath. It sounded softer, distant, indicating the creature had fled farther down the corridor. I opened my mouth to speak when suddenly more terrifying voices joined in chorus with the first.

"That thing's not alone," Trendon whispered. "We don't stand a chance."

I gritted my teeth together and snatched the lit flare from Trendon's hand. "We can't just leave. We've made a big hole in the wall. The artifact won't be safe anymore. If we leave now, someone else could find it. Maybe even Jasher." I took a cautious step toward the hole and stretched my neck forward to peek through. The flare Trendon had thrown had fallen a few yards down the path, illuminating the room with a dull pink light.

"Then we'll go tell Cabarles what happened. Even if he's not supposed to come in here, he can call some of his buddies to take care of this mess. I'm not going to get eaten today." Trendon backed away from the opening.

"Those things will come out of the hole we made. Someone went to great measures to hide the artifact. Whoever it was walled those hideous things up with it to protect it. Now we've let them loose."

"So?"

"I'm not leaving until I've finished this!" My voice was firm and commanding. I was *not* going to let everyone down.

"Amber, think about this," Trendon tried to reason with me.

"I *have* thought about it." I looked toward the hole and then back at Trendon. "I don't want to go in there either, but I can't quit." Trendon rolled his eyes in frustration. "And I need your help," I said softly. "I know you don't want to do this, but deep down inside, I also know you're not going to give up on me."

He gnawed his lower lip and gave one last look to the path leading back to the cave's entrance. "Oh, brother." Folding his arms, he glared at me. "Sure, play the guilt card, that's fair." Dropping his backpack on the floor, he opened the zipper. "My guess is the flares will keep them at bay until they get smart, and then we're dead. These flares have a life span of about twenty minutes, give or take, so that gives us three hours tops to find whatever this thing is we're looking for and get out." He handed two more flares to me and kept the others for himself. Then he shoved the bottle of kerosene in his front pocket.

We slipped through the opening down onto the empty path without incident. Trendon picked up the still-burning flare and held it above his head to look around.

"Come on, let's go," he said. "Keep your voice down and your eyes peeled. We don't want any of those things to sneak up behind us."

Our boots created hollow footfalls, and our images reflected back from the black, shiny walkway. I clung to Trendon's arm, my eyes anxiously darting back and forth, waiting for the monsters to leap from out of nowhere. But for the moment, the flares seemed to be working. Although we heard the clatter of paws against stone from somewhere up ahead, nothing attacked. The path stretched for quite a distance. Along the walls, thousands of icky, white cave crickets zipped in and out of burrows.

Up ahead the corridor narrowed, with the walls tightening to a thin walkway that forced us to proceed sideways, our stomachs pressed against the wall. Trendon sucked in his gut as best he could. I gagged as cave crickets scurried out of our path and then returned, their antennae brushing against my neck.

"I'm going to scream. I'm going to scream!" My voice teetered on erupting into a high-pitched squeal.

"Don't!" Trendon ordered. "Just think about hand sanitizer or wet wipes. That's the only way I'm going to survive this." He trudged forward, creating a wake of cave crickets with his body.

More of the crickets gathered around us as we shimmied through the narrow passage. I knew there must have been at least a hundred of the repulsive insects scurrying across my back. It took all of my self-control to stop me from screaming out or vomiting. One tickled my ear, and I bit my lip so hard it drew blood. Trendon started whimpering like a homesick puppy. He used the flare as a weapon, but the crickets wouldn't scatter away from it. Instead, several of them sizzled to death when they curiously got too close to the tip.

Finally the path ended at a doorway carved neatly in the rock. The square doorway stood slightly wider than the corridor we'd passed through. The assemblage of crickets stopped along the edge of the opening and, for some reason, none of the insects ventured farther.

"I'm not going back through there unless I'm armed with a giant can of Raid. We're going to have to find an alternate route out!" Trendon said, stepping through the doorway and swatting at his body to remove any straggling crickets. Grunting, he stomped down on any he could reach as they scurried back into the corridor.

I did the same, almost retching when I smashed one of the bugs with my hand. Flipping my hair to make sure I'd cleared it of crickets, I surveyed the unusual, oval-shaped room. Its smooth walls encircled a bowl-shaped floor. In fact, aside from the two openings, the room resembled a giant stone cup. I could tell its shape had not been carved out by nature. Above our heads, strange stone faces etched into the walls stared blankly down at us, the mouths opened wide, forming circular holes sinking deep within the wall.

"What do you think those are for?" Trendon asked, staring up at a total of six cherubs with their cheeks puffed out. Each one had a similar opening for a mouth.

I had no idea what their purpose was. Across the room on the far wall, a doorway led to yet another corridor. "I guess we continue that way," I said, gesturing toward the opening.

"There had better not be any stinking bugs in there or I'll just . . . break something." Trendon lashed out angrily at a straggling cricket, rendering it into a goopy mess beneath his foot.

"I wonder why there aren't any in here." I gave the walls a quick perusal. Oddly, it seemed the insects couldn't enter the bowl-shaped room. Was there some invisible barrier keeping them at bay? I didn't care. Fishing a bottle of water from my backpack, I took a long drink. Then, assuming I would need to be ready for anything, I snatched out the blue locator stone and held it tightly in my hand.

As we neared the next doorway, Trendon stumbled over a large square-shaped stone jutting up from the floor. His weight pressed down on the rock, and the stone shrank, disappearing beneath our feet. Before we could react, massive stone blocks fell from above, barricading both openings.

"What in the world?" I said, my forehead wrinkling at the absurdity of the sudden obstructions.

From deep within the walls, a gurgling noise arose. It sounded like old, quivering pipes unable to handle the flow of water. I searched the room for the source of the noise and noticed that black sludge had begun to dribble out from the strange carved faces. The sludge smelled like sewage, and it poured out from each one of the holes, splattering against the floor. Trendon hopped back from the splashing filth that instantly started filling up the floor with muck.

"It's like those faces are the ends of some kind of plumbing," he said, pinching his nose closed with his fingers. "Please don't tell me this mud is what I think it is," he gagged.

Murky water replaced the flow of black gunk, tumbling faster until a steady stream blasted out from each of the stone cherubs.

"This isn't good," I said. Already, the water was rising up to my knees.

"Yeah, where's the drain at?" Trendon asked. Both of us realized the urgency of our situation and began desperately searching the walls for a way out.

The level rose higher and higher, but we couldn't find an opening. It reached above our waists and kept rising. The liquid was cold and heavy, like the two of us were floating in a mud bath at a local spa, only this mud smelled foul.

"Any bright ideas?" Trendon clung to the wall as the sludge rose above his chest.

"There has to be a way out!" I shouted.

"I'm not seeing anything!" he shouted back. The rising pool forced us to tread water, an almost impossible task in our clothing and with our heavy backpacks. The dark, thick water started pulling us down like a vacuum.

Breathing hard and kicking my legs to try to stay afloat, I looked everywhere for the exit. I lost my grip on the side of the wall, momentarily submerging in the muck and losing grip on my flare. Flailing about, I caught hold of Trendon's outstretched hand as he pulled my body up, allowing me to catch my breath. Drowning had to be one of my darkest nightmares. It seemed to be the worst way to go— feeling your lungs fill up with water and trying to breathe, only to be denied the air. This would be so much worse, drowning in the thick mud. The water still poured from the mouths, and the two of us began rising toward the ceiling.

"This isn't supposed to be happening!" Trendon gasped for air but took in a mouthful of sludge. He gagged and spat out the liquid.

I shot my hand up out of the rising water and pressed it against the ceiling. This felt like being in a swimming pool, but underneath a tarp.

Black slop now covered Trendon's face. "What do archaeologists do in situations like this?" he asked. "They don't just drown! You've got to think of something!"

"I can't! We've searched everywhere! There's

nothing but walls . . ." my voice broke off. "Oh no!" I screamed. "I dropped the locator stone!" I scanned the surface of the water, pleading with myself to find it. I frantically shot my hand into the muck, fishing around in the darkness. How could I have been so careless?

"I think that's the least of our worries right now!" Trendon shouted.

Our heads bobbed almost to the ceiling. Only a matter of moments remained before all the air in the room would be replaced with water. Trendon gasped, his backpack heavier than mine, and he struggled to stay afloat and hold the flare above the water.

"Here, let me take that." I grabbed the flare from him.

I needed to focus. There had to be a solution to this mess.

"What do we do?" Trendon pleaded.

"Quiet!" I ordered. "I need to think!"

"There's no time!"

But I couldn't hear him anymore. I cleared my mind and began scanning through the memories of Dorothy's class. But as the ceiling came within a foot of the top of my head, my mind drew a blank. I could think of nothing. I looked at Trendon, who bore an expression of sheer horror. How could I have failed him? My persistence to not turn back when we still could had brought us to this end. Because of me, Trendon and I would never make it out alive.

"I'm so sorry!" I sobbed, turning away from Trendon's face.

"Amber," he whispered.

His voice cut me to the core. I had failed everyone. Now we had nothing left to do but consign ourselves and surrender to the rising murk. If only I had paid closer attention to Dorothy's lessons. If only I—

Something pulsated against my chest. Not my heartbeat, because I could feel that thudding in my ears, but something else, warm and vibrating. Like some strange insect buzzing against my skin. My eyes widened in alarm, and I tore at my shirt with my hands. Trendon watched, unable to talk, since it took all his concentration to stay above water.

I pulled my hand up out of my shirt and produced the small blue stone from the necklace Dorothy had given me weeks ago—the night we had snuck into the museum. The stone glowed bright blue, illuminating the darkness and instantly filling me with hope.

"It's a locator stone!" I screamed. I looked up and nodded toward the ceiling. "Trendon! The ceiling is a false wall! We need to somehow break through."

Trendon stared at me for a moment, trying to catch his breath, and then his head went completely under.

"No!" I cried.

I nearly dove in after him, when Trendon's foot suddenly shot up out of the sludge, bursting through the thin layer of ceiling. Rocks broke away from his kick and collapsed into the water. Trendon resurfaced, panting, his face no longer recognizable because of its thick casing of mud.

I lunged for the hole and snagged hold of the edge.

More rocks gave way from my weight, and I yanked at the pieces violently. Trendon smacked at the ceiling as well, and soon most of the rock broke away. The water continued to rise, but fortunately the ceiling no longer blocked us. Up and up we went until finally the water level slowed its swell and stopped completely.

Paddling to the edge, I helped Trendon pull himself out of the muck and onto solid floor. After taking a deep breath of air, he grabbed my hand and pulled me up next to him. The two of us lay side by side next to the pool of dark water, trying to make the painful aching in our lungs go away.

"My necklace . . ." I gasped. "Dorothy gave it to me a while ago." I showed the silver chain to Trendon, who plucked it from my hands and cradled it in his own before kissing it. The necklace had saved our lives. I thought back to the night Dorothy and I had shared hamburgers on the park bench, and I remembered Dorothy's explanation about the necklace. It had been Asian, but not from China. No doubt, it came from the Philippines.

21

As I wiped gunk from the corners of my eyes, Trendon grumbled to himself, holding his now worthless iPhone. After grunting a few choice words under his breath, he tossed the thing into the muck and watched it sink out of sight.

I cleared the mud from my mouth. "You should've kept that in your backpack."

Trendon glared at me. "You think?" he spat.

The backpacks were proving their value. All the provisions we'd sealed within the zippered pockets, including the remaining flares and Dorothy's artifacts, came out dry and clean. Sadly I had failed to zip up one of the pockets containing my trail mix and bottles of water. I hoped we wouldn't need them that badly. I had lost one locator stone, but luckily Dorothy had provided me with a spare. After cleaning off the necklace, I returned it to its spot around my neck and allowed it to sink beneath my collar.

"Come on, grumpy. I'm sure your mother will buy

you another one," I said, nudging Trendon with my foot.

"That iPhone contained a life's work of notes, hacks, and cheat codes for every video game I've ever played, owned, or illegally downloaded. I can't even begin to explain how long it will take me to recover it all."

"It's not important right now."

"No, you're right, it's not important. Being chased by monsters, getting kidnapped by criminals, and breast stroking through poop is important."

"We're so close. Can't you feel it?"

He looked up at me and smirked. "All I feel is the void where my iPhone used to be in my pocket."

I helped my friend to his feet and feebly attempted to clear the back of his neck of sludge. Even if Trendon couldn't feel it, I did. It was like the feeling I got right before opening a mysterious Christmas package. If we could survive the next few hours and somehow find and save the dangerous artifact, all of our troubles would be worth it.

Down more corridors we trudged, leaving brown footprints behind us on the floor. The path continued straight, with very few bends and turns, but sloped downward. After using up two more flares, I felt my throat tighten. We were being forced to ration the only water bottle not ruined from our recent swim, and my small sips failed to quench my thirst. We took another break on a couple of small boulders to rejuvenate.

"We have to be getting close to the belly of this mountain, don't you think?" Trendon asked, tipping the bottle to his lips.

"It feels like it, but we've made quite a few detours."

"Detours? Yeah, that's what I'd call them," Trendon said sarcastically.

A thunderous howl echoed through the corridor, louder than we had ever heard. I sprang to my feet and strapped the backpack to my shoulders.

"Where are you going in such a hurry?" Trendon asked.

"Trendon, whatever that thing is, it must know we're here for the artifact. The only way we're going to find the right path is if we follow the howling."

Trendon reluctantly rose from his boulder.

To be safe, we both held lit flares as we passed through another room similar to the booby-trapped one from before with six stone faces peering down from above. This time, however, we avoided stepping on any triggers.

Upon exiting the room, I noticed a difference in the walls and ceiling surrounding the corridor. I ran my hand across the cold surface.

"This is petrified wood," I said, digging my fingers in what looked like a knot in the wall. Weathered lines splintered the rock like the bark of an ancient tree. It appeared giant slabs of the unusual wood made up the mountain stone itself. At the end of the corridor, the ceiling expanded into a massive room at least three times the size of a football stadium, with the ceiling towering so high above us, I couldn't see to the top. The flare lit up the room with an eerie glow, faintly revealing our surroundings.

"Are we still in the same mountain?" Trendon asked, glancing around.

My lungs ached as I took in the breathtaking view. The floor in the room changed from black, volcanic glass to something similar to the petrified wood I'd seen in the last room. Wide and beveled in the middle, the stone stuck up like partitions from the floor, creating what could only be described as cubicles. At either side, stone staircases ascended, connecting to multiple levels with walkways and more rooms. Everything was fashioned out of stone but crumbling from corrosion. I looked at Trendon, his eyes wide with amazement. We had walked right into the belly of Noah's ark.

"Oh my," I whispered, smiling in spite of the fear.

"This is so bizarre," Trendon said. "I mean, I guess I figured it'd be big and all, you know? It would have to be to hold all those animals, but I never imagined it to be like this. I can't believe this is real. I always thought it was just a made up story."

I couldn't help but feel overjoyed with our discovery. How long had the ark stayed hidden? Six thousand years or more? Did this prove the great flood actually happened? We walked several yards, gaping at the gigantic structure. From all of the pictures and illustrations I had seen in Bible school and in books, the artist had always portrayed the ark resting upon the top of the mountain. We had ventured deep within the bowels of Mt. Arayat. It truly appeared as though the mountain had grown up around the ark.

The sound of several creatures scampering across

the floor yanked us from our marveling. We spun around, just in time to see the creatures vanishing behind one of the partitions on the main level.

"Those things run like humans!" Trendon shouted.

What kind of creature are they? There weren't too many beasts in the animal kingdom that walked on two legs. I had a feeling we had discovered a species of animal not listed in any encyclopedia.

Trendon's flare sputtered as it died out, and he quickly lit another. "I don't think we're getting our full twenty minutes out of these flares. We bought them from the same guy who sold us those crummy flashlights."

"Try to keep one lit at all times," I said. "At the moment those things seem more curious than anything else. Maybe they're just as surprised as we are."

"Yeah, 'curious.' That's what I'd call it. Quit kidding yourself! The only thing that's been on their menu for thousands of years is cave cricket. We must look like a couple of walking meat loaves." Trendon waved the flare as a warning.

I forced my eyes to look away from the wall where the creatures hid, waiting. The ark wasn't our most important discovery. We needed to find the Tebah Stick, and fast. "The artifact has to be around here somewhere. Can you see anything?"

"I don't even know what to look for."

I removed the drawing from my backpack. "It looks like some sort of staff or a scepter." I held the image up as a visual for Trendon.

"Got it," he said.

"I think we're going to have to climb one of those staircases up to the next level."

"Yeah, I was afraid you'd say that."

With our eyes fixed on the looming partitions, we backed toward the closest staircase and ascended slowly to the next level. Once we reached the top and stepped off the stairs, we heard the creatures slide out from behind the partitions and scurry over to the bottom step.

I chanced looking down below. Six pairs of ghastly red eyes watched me like floating spectral orbs in the darkness. Shadows gathered around their long thin bodies, making it impossible to see their true form. "Do you think they'll follow us?" I asked. He didn't need to answer my question as one of the creatures stepped up onto the stairs and began to climb, the shadows still clinging to it like a hazy fog.

"No more questions." Trendon tested his weight on the level. Once he was confident it would hold, he inched along the edge nearest the wall with me clinging to his backpack. With no banisters or guardrails to prevent us from tumbling to certain death, our safety depended on the support of a petrified wooden walkway, several thousand years old.

"Look over there!" I said, pointing to an opening in the wall that looked like a doorway into another spacious room with more partitions. I took a few steps forward and gasped at the sight of a man standing motionless in the center of the room with his hands outstretched in front of him.

Trendon practically dropped the flare in shock. "Who's that?" He fumbled with the flare, trying to push past me back onto the walkway.

"It's okay," I said. "It's just a statue."

We held still and listened as the creatures reached the top of the staircase and their claws clacked against the stone of the walkway.

I tugged Trendon's sleeve. "We need to do something to keep those things out of here," I said, my tone urgent. "They'll block our only escape."

"Good point," Trendon said. He grabbed his bottle of kerosene and drenched the floor just beneath the opening of the door with the transparent liquid. Then he extended the flare away from him, and the flames sparked the puddle into a bright blaze. The result came instantly. From somewhere beyond the room and terribly close to the opening, the creatures roared in surprise. Clutching my flare like a gun, I listened as they fled from the fire back down the stone steps. The distraction would buy us a little time, but we would have to hurry.

The statue had a beard and wide, friendly eyes. Every detail in the stone—the wrinkles in his skin, the veins in his feet, even his robe, which flowed down around his body as though a breeze had ruffled the fabric, had been intricately sculpted.

"Do you think that's supposed to be Noah?" Trendon asked.

"I hope so," I said. It seemed logical, though the

statue didn't look exactly like any of the pictures I had seen back home. Of course, how would any of those artists have a clue what Noah looked like?

The howling rose several decibels, vibrating the walls like a tuning fork.

"They don't want us near this!" Trendon shouted over their ear-splitting cries as the blaze of kerosene at the opening petered out.

I immediately discovered the reason for their growing anxiousness. The statue of Noah grasped in its left hand a wooden scepter with glittering red jewels and a smooth stone the size of a softball at its crown.

"That's it! That's the Tebah Stick!" I shouted.

Trendon started for the door to relight the fire but stopped a few feet from the statue. "Um, I think you'd better hurry," he said.

Out of the corner of my eye, I could see the outline of a creature standing in the doorway. Several more crowded next to it. I spun around as a total of six monsters stepped into the room, completely blocking the exit. Some of the animals crawled on all fours while others walked nimbly on two legs with their front claws stretched out, ready to attack. Why couldn't we see their faces? Though I was standing in a dark room, my eyes had adjusted to the dim light of the flare. I could see Trendon easily, so why not these abominations?

Trendon slashed out with the flare, managing to stall their pursuit momentarily. But the creatures no longer turned and fled from the presence of the flame. "Amber!" Trendon's voice rose with alarm.

I leapt onto the statue's arm and grappled for the scepter, trying with all of my strength to pry it out from the solid stone hands, but it wouldn't budge. "It's stuck!" I shouted.

"No! It can't be!" Trendon shouted back.

With two hands, I grasped the top of the scepter and leaned back with my weight. It was no use. Neither I nor Trendon would be strong enough to pull it free.

I panicked. "I can't do it!"

"What do you mean you can't do it?"

"I mean, it won't come free. The hand is stuck to it!"

The creatures closed in. I could smell them—like wet dogs that had rolled in garbage. Their white eyes narrowed, and I sensed their eagerness to attack.

"What do we do?" I pleaded.

Trendon looked at me. "Keep trying. I've got an idea." He unscrewed the bottle of kerosene. "But it very well may be the dumbest idea ever." Winding up, he flung the bottle toward the creature nearest to us. The bottle passed through the shroud of mist and doused one of the monster's chests completely with kerosene. The creatures howled collectively, but Trendon didn't give them time to flee as he tossed the burning flare in their direction. The room lit up with a blinding purple light as three of the monsters caught on fire. Squealing with pain, they writhed on the ground, clawing at their burning skin. Even with the illumination, I couldn't see their faces. Somehow, the injured creatures managed to beat out the flames with their hands, and they, along with the others, scattered away out of the room, leaving us, once again, in darkness.

I lit up my last flare. Trendon still had one more left, but with nothing else to use as a weapon, our chances of escape were dwindling.

"Did you get it?" Trendon asked, joining me on the statue. He tried tugging on the scepter for a couple of minutes, wrenching with all of his strength, but it wouldn't come loose from the statue's death grip.

"Why can't we move it?" I asked.

Trendon shrugged. "Maybe we're not supposed to move it. Maybe Dorothy was wrong."

I yanked out the map and studied the instructions, but nothing on the map explained what we should do once we found the statue. In fact, the map didn't even mention the existence of a statue.

"There has to be a way." I ran my fingers through my hair.

"Those things are going to come back any minute now, and I don't have any more firebombs left to chuck at them. If we don't get out of here soon, we're both dead."

I didn't want to think about getting gnawed on by those creatures. My lips quivered with anger. We had come so far, escaped impossible odds, and here, right at the finish line, we ended at the edge of a bottomless pit.

"Why didn't Dorothy tell us about this?" I asked. "Why do we have to solve every riddle by ourselves?"

Trendon scrunched his nose. "I don't know why, and frankly I don't care so long as I can live to eat another bag of corn nuts."

"This is not possible!" I growled in aggravation. "We have no choice but to give up!" I looked at Trendon in defeat. We had failed. Now all we could do was try and escape with our lives.

Trendon scanned the room. There was still no sign of the creatures, but that would change soon enough. He licked his lips and closed his eyes. "Yeah, you're right. We have no choice but to give up, but you haven't let me do that from the beginning. Nothing would tick me off more than for you to roll over and quit now. Seriously, even though you're a girl, I will dropkick you in the teeth if you walk away without that stupid stick!"

I started to laugh. It wasn't exactly the best time for humor, but I couldn't help myself.

"You can do this, Amber. You were born to do this crazy stuff." Trendon fired up the last flare, giving me enough light to fully see the statue.

I stared up at the scepter and then closed my eyes tightly. I thought for several moments about Noah's story in the Bible, but the answer still eluded me. Opening my eyes, I examined every feature of the statue. Noah's eyes looked up. Why? What would he be looking at? My thoughts swirled. I looked at his right hand, which also extended skyward, but not as a gesture—rather, it looked like he held his hand out to accept something. I considered this for a moment.

"You keep thinking, but kick it in high gear," Trendon said.

I looked around. The creatures had returned, ready

to kill. "How much time do you think we have left with the flares?"

"Maybe fifteen minutes. Just figure it out!"

I groaned. It would take at least ten minutes to get back to the hole in the wall, and then we'd be forced to walk in darkness. I pushed the worry from my mind and focused. Noah held his hand out as if trying to reach for some object, but what?

"They were on the ark for a long time because it rained forty days and nights," I spoke aloud. "When the rain stopped, they searched many days for land."

"Yeah, yeah, I remember," Trendon chimed in urgently. "And then a dove fluttered down and they knew land was close by."

I caught my breath. "The dove! That's it! That's what he's holding his hand out for." I looked around the room.

"A dove?" Trendon asked, shaking his head in confusion. "Where are we going to find a dove?"

"I'm not sure, but that's definitely what happened." I had heard that story at least a hundred times growing up.

"Are you sure a dove landed in his hand? That doesn't make any sense at all."

My eyes dropped to the floor, staring at my backpack next to the base of the statue. Smacking my forehead with my hand, I dove toward it and tore at the zipper.

"What are you doing?" Trendon shouted.

I pulled the strange stick I had found in Dorothy's

safe out of the bag and held it up for him to see. "It's an olive branch. We had it with us all along, and none of us realized it. I don't even think Dorothy knew what this stick was for because she would have mentioned it."

"What does an olive branch have anything to do with Noah's ark?"

"When the dove landed on the ark, it dropped an olive branch in Noah's hand. That's how he knew there was land nearby. That's the answer!" Not wasting any time, I stood next to the statue. "Please work," I whispered. Closing my eyes, I placed the olive branch into Noah's outstretched hand.

The scepter dropped free and toppled to the floor. It happened so suddenly, neither of us had any time to react. Before we could stop it, the scepter rolled clumsily away from the statue, right toward the gathering mob of creatures.

"Get it!" Trendon screamed. I watched in shock as he charged toward the creatures, waving the flare wildly and shouting at the top of his lungs.

"Trendon, stop! Those things will tear you apart!" Amazingly, Trendon's distraction worked. The creatures didn't attack right away but instead shuffled back a few paces, staring at each other, probably wondering what the crazy kid was doing.

"Just get it!" Trendon ordered.

I trained my eyes on the scepter, which wobbled back and forth on the floor, and raced toward it as fast as my body would allow. One of the creatures swung out at Trendon, raking his chest with its claws and knocking the flare onto the floor. Trendon screamed in agony. I wanted to run to him, to help him, but I knew I had to get to the Tebah Stick.

"Trendon!" I watched him topple to the floor, a dark red gash oozing from the tear in his sweater. The rest of the creatures filled the room with their howls and lunged toward me just as I fell upon the stick and closed my fingers around the handle.

22

Cowering on the floor, I clung to the Tebah Stick, tears streaming down my cheeks. A strange humming sound vibrated from the artifact. It felt warm and alive, like mechanical cogs were operating within the wood. I opened an eye, expecting to be gobbled up by a monster at any second, but the room was empty. Only Trendon, who lay on his back, moaning and pressing his hand against his chest, remained with me. There was no sign of the monsters anywhere. I couldn't even hear their hideous howling.

"Are you all right?" I whispered.

Trendon moaned even louder. "No, I'm not all right! I've been filleted!" Slowly, he rose to a sitting position. "What happened?"

"Uh . . . to be honest, I haven't the slightest idea. One second they were here, and now they're not," I said, positive the Tebah Stick had something to do with it. I rushed over to Trendon's side and examined his wound. The skin across his left pectoral flapped sickeningly. There was a lot of blood, and the disgusting muck from our earlier swim was mixing into the gash. Trendon needed medicine and stitches, and he needed them fast. I dumped the contents of my backpack out onto the floor. Turning the material of the backpack inside out to the cleanest spot, I pressed it firmly against his chest.

"Ouch!" he shouted. Tears streamed from his eyes.

"Can you hold that there?" I asked, placing his hand against the pack. "You've got to keep pressure on that cut, and we have a long trip out of here."

"What's it matter? Those things are just going to pick us off once we leave this room."

I looked through the entryway. Still vacant. I listened for a moment, but nothing other than Trendon's labored breathing filled the room. "I think we'll be okay," I whispered. "I don't think they'll attack us while we're holding this." I extended the scepter toward Trendon.

"Don't give it to me," he said, rearing back like I'd just handed him a baby wearing a soggy diaper. "I don't want to hold it."

"It's really quite remarkable." I rolled the handle in my hand to examine it further.

"Why hasn't it turned to stone like everything else in this cave?"

I shook my head. I knew the artifact resonated with unearthly power. Holding it next to me, I felt reckless. I figured it would be safest to hide the staff in our stuff somehow, in case we ran into anyone else in the cave, but something told me it would be a foolish mistake to take my hands off it.

The final flare sputtered out on the floor, but the room stayed lit. The Tebah Stick glowed with a vibrant blue light. We still had a long, frightening trip back through the mountain ahead of us, but at least we would have the companionship of the scepter's light protecting us.

"We'll take it slow," I said, supporting Trendon with my shoulder.

The first part of the trek went quietly. In too much pain to make conversation, Trendon added only grunts of consciousness whenever I asked him questions. When we arrived at the room with the black, festering pool of water, I thought we'd hit a serious roadblock. My thoughts, however, came clear and collected. I never panicked. Even with Trendon nearly collapsing from dread, my mind stayed focused. Removing Dorothy's locator stone from around my neck, I felt guided by some unseen force to a spot on the far wall. The stone glowed bright, and I discovered a heavy rock by my foot to hammer against the wall.

"Watch out for those monsters!" Trendon warned as I opened a hole into the wall.

"They're not going to hurt us," I said with confidence.

"What makes you so sure?" he asked.

"I just know it." Again, I didn't want to tell him the truth—the Tebah Stick was keeping them at bay.

We stopped periodically to let Trendon rest. The

blood ceased to flow, but when I checked his wound, I could feel clumpy, black ooze forming a clot. How much longer could he go on? I didn't want to think about it. We would make it out, and he would live.

Our hardest obstacle came once we returned to the room where we had been forced to drop through the ceiling. I would have few difficulties climbing out, but I worried about Trendon, who was too weak and miserable to move.

"Trendon, Trendon!" I shouted, snapping my fingers in front of his face. "You've got to hold out just a little longer. I know you're sick and in pain, but we've got to climb out."

Trendon's breathing came in shallow puffs, and his whole body shook. "I can't . . . climb." He coughed and groaned from the pain it caused.

"You have to!" I ordered.

"Just go out there and call for help. Need to sleep . . ." he coughed again, "for a moment."

"Absolutely not!" I snapped. I knew if he stopped to sleep, he might not wake up. Using all of my remaining strength, I shoved Trendon up into a standing position and guided him toward the hole in the ceiling. Too weak to verbally protest, he instead grunted his dissatisfaction as I forced him to climb. Twice he nearly stumbled, but miraculously, he made it, and, after catching my breath, I joined him at the top of the hole.

By the time we finally arrived at the point where the path first branched off in opposite directions, about one hundred yards from the mouth of the cave, I was literally carrying Trendon on my back. My adrenaline propelled me forward, and I knew barring some sort of medical wonder, I wouldn't be walking for several days after this. I bent over and propped a delusional Trendon, who was mumbling about food and monsters and a bunch of other odd topics, up against a rock.

"Hang in there, pal. Help is on the way." Carefully peeling back the backpack, I flinched. Trendon's wound looked seriously infected, and it was starting to puss. I only hoped I could get him to a hospital close enough that had the proper medications to administer to his injuries.

"Am I hallucinating?" Trendon mumbled.

I laughed, relieved to hear him finish a coherent sentence. "You've been losing it for over an hour, but we made it."

"What is that, though?" he asked, nodding his head toward the direction of the cave opening. It broke my heart to hear my normally quick-witted friend slurring his speech.

"That's our exit," I said, patting him on the shoulders. "We made it back to the mouth of the cave."

"Amber?" he asked, his head bobbing. "Who are those guys?" Trendon's legs gave out, and he collapsed to the ground.

"Don't, please! You can't rest yet!" I shouted.

"Oh, my dear, what have you done to your poor friend?" a voice droned from behind me.

I swallowed and spun around to face Kendell Jasher, who was standing several feet away in the cave. I wanted to scream. We had done all of the work, and now Jasher would reap the benefits. I felt an instant tinge of sorrow as I noticed Dorothy at his right, bound tightly in cords. Malcolm stood behind her, holding his gun to her head. Dorothy's eyes showed mixed emotions. She looked proud of me for all I had done, but also defeated.

Standing to the left of Kendell, the strange Mr. Baeloc honed his hungry eyes in on the Tebah Stick.

"Mr. Baeloc says he is very pleased you've brought him that." Mr. Jasher gestured toward my hand.

"He can't have it!" I snapped.

Mr. Jasher laughed. "You're so defiant! I am deeply impressed. How you could've ever made it back with that powerful weapon in your hand is truly remarkable."

"It was a piece of cake." I looked at Dorothy and grinned.

"A piece of cake, hmmm? I believe your friend would think differently."

Though unconscious, Trendon was still alive. But his breathing sounded raspy.

"Amber, give us the artifact so we can take you and your friend to the hospital and have you treated." Mr. Jasher took a step closer but stopped as I reared back against the wall.

"Don't come any closer!" I shouted.

"Girl, don't be reckless. It's not only your life that hangs in the balance. Think of Trendon, or, if you don't care about him, think of Dorothy here. You wouldn't want to see her . . . hurt, now, would you? Wouldn't that be awful to witness?" he hissed. "I have taken care of all of your flight arrangements back home. You, Trendon, and Dorothy are free to go. You'll never be bothered by anyone. Just give us the Tebah Stick so we can end this quickly."

As if sensing my surrender, Dorothy piped up. "Don't give in to him, Amber," she said. "You know he's lying. Remember, our lives are not as important as preventing the destruction he would cause."

"Malcolm," Mr. Jasher said. He looked down at the ground and smiled as Malcolm slugged Dorothy in the gut with his fist. Dorothy groaned in pain and would've toppled to the floor had she not been forced to remain on her feet.

"Don't you touch her!" I shouted.

"As you can see, we are not able to keep up cordial appearances anymore. Dorothy doesn't know what she's talking about. She has a radical way of thinking, but I'm much more practical. The world won't be destroyed by me and that valuable artifact; rather it will prosper and flourish."

I needed to buy some time to think through this, but with Trendon fading at my feet and Dorothy's life in the hands of a murderer, my mind couldn't function.

"How did you find us?" I asked, trying to stall.

"Like I said, I'm very impressed with how you solved this age-old puzzle, but don't get arrogant, Amber. We are the professionals here. I have limitless resources at my beck and call. And your talented friend, Trendon, filled in all the gaps once I was able to rescue and preserve his laptop from the rubble of my mansion. We pieced it all together and came here to the Philippines, where we bumped into one of Dorothy's old friends."

Cabarles! What had they done to him and his family? My skin felt hot. I glared at Jasher. "Did you kill him too?"

Kendell chuckled, but Dorothy spoke first. "Cabarles and his family aren't hurt. Don't worry about us, Amber. The artifact is what's important now!" She gasped for air but managed to right herself on wobbly legs.

I glanced back down the path leading into the mountain. Dorothy was right. This weapon was too dangerous to fall into Jasher's evil hands. I needed to be willing to lose my life in order to protect it.

As if reading my mind, Mr. Baeloc opened his mouth and spoke in his awful language. His eyes stayed glued on the artifact, but I realized a little too late what his choking noises meant. Two men with pale skin stepped out of the shadows on either side of the path, blocking my chance of escape. They had been hiding there, waiting for the signal to move out and end the conversation.

"As you can see, it would be foolish to resist any longer." Mr. Jasher tightened the knot of his necktie. "This is my last offer of assistance for your friend. You either give us the artifact willingly, or we shall take it by force, and the three of you will die."

I knew he meant every word. He would murder us all without a second's remorse. The artifact hummed beneath my fingers. My eyes lowered onto the beautiful jewels engrained in the wood. For a second, I thought I saw a flicker of light pulse from the round stone at its crown. Something moved beyond the line of my vision, something down the left path behind the man standing guard. I calmly looked above his shoulder and exhaled a deep breath. With a sudden flash of movement, the man vanished; snatched off into the darkness. The action came so quickly, I didn't even flinch, but I knew exactly what had happened. The glowing white eyes had warned me. Slowly I turned and looked to my right and saw the other man disappear from view—leaving both paths now clear. My heart pounded. I should've been terrified, but even with the knowledge that those beasts had undoubtedly killed two men just a few yards from where I stood, I didn't feel like I was in any danger. My chest heaved as the Tebah Stick's vibrations grew stronger. I returned my attention to Mr. Jasher. The attack had been so perfect and silent, neither he nor anyone else in the cave could have any idea of what had happened.

"No more games, Amber," Mr. Jasher spoke, oblivious that Mr. Baeloc's men no longer hedged up my escape. I could run for it now. With thousands of places to hide in the mountain, I could find safety. But I had no intention of running.

Mr. Jasher looked to his left and nodded. Mr. Baeloc opened his mouth, and more of the hideous, choking sounds emitted from his lips. He paused, and a confused expression appeared on his features. Again, he spoke, sounding as though the words strangled his throat. Nothing happened, and I smiled.

"Are you calling for your friends?" I asked, innocently. "Because they're no longer with us." The humming from the Tebah Stick now coursed through my veins. I felt so much power.

Alarm flashed on Mr. Jasher's face. He looked to Mr. Baeloc, who bore a similar expression. Holding his hand out cautiously, Kendell spoke. "Amber, you don't know what you're doing." He stared wide-eyed at the artifact in my hand. "You cannot possibly control that."

From behind him, I caught flashes of shadows. The eyes were all around now, hovering, glowing, awaiting the command to pounce on their next victim. "Let Dorothy go!" I said, my voice callous and dominant.

"Shoot her!" Mr. Jasher ordered Malcolm.

Malcolm pointed the gun in my direction, but he never fired a shot. Something exploded from the darkness, taking Malcolm, and then retreated from view just as quickly, leaving behind only the echoes of Malcolm's one last horrendous scream.

"Amber, stop!" Mr. Jasher pleaded. "Its power is too dangerous." He and Mr. Baeloc retreated carefully toward the cave entrance. My eyes narrowed as they honed in on my next targets. I stepped back, and my foot nudged Trendon, who was still lying there, his breathing shallow. Suddenly, I felt different. What had just happened? My eyes darted around the room, and I trembled at the sight of the terrifying, white eyes staring at me, waiting for their next command. Had I commanded them? The artifact felt as though it had a pulse. I stared down at it and started bawling uncontrollably.

Tears flooded down my face and splashed against my hands. What had I done? Was I the one responsible? I looked up from my sobbing. Mr. Jasher and Mr. Baeloc were fleeing from the cave, but if I wanted to, I could stop them. All I had to do was think it, and those creatures would follow my command. My eyes dropped again to the Tebah Stick, and I sniffed. *Should I do it? Should I . . . ?*

A warm hand grazed my shoulder, startling me from my trance. Dorothy stood next to me. "Amber, let's go home," she whispered.

I sobbed even harder and fell into Dorothy's embrace. "I'm so sorry!" I cried.

"Don't be sorry," Dorothy said. "You've saved us all."

I felt the artifact go slack in my hands. I wanted to drop it, to distance myself from its overwhelming power, but Dorothy caught my hand. The creatures still loomed in the shadows, peering at me with their inquisitive eyes.

"Not yet, Amber," she warned. "Don't drop it yet. I'm not sure what will happen to us if you're no longer in possession of the artifact."

My body, already weakened by the treacherous journey through the mountain, also felt physically drained from the strange power tingling in my fingertips. "I don't want to hold it anymore," I muttered.

"Just a little longer. Let's get Trendon to a hospital," Dorothy said, keeping her hand closed around my wrist.

I nodded. I could hold out a little longer for Trendon.

23

"That looks awful!" I said, instinctively clutching my side.

Trendon looked away from the photographs and stuck his tongue out in disgust. "Yeah, Lisa, I'd say that looks like a ruptured spleen," he said, jabbing a tiny headphone in his ear and returning his attention to his brand new iPhone. Despite his headphones, everyone in the room could distinctly hear the sounds of elves and goblins fighting epic battles in one of Trendon's online, role playing games.

Lisa grinned. "I guess it's somewhat common in automobile accidents. Who knew?"

Lisa had woken from her coma four days ago and showed vast improvements in her health. After several scheduled surgeries, she had perked up so impressively the doctors agreed to grant her visitors other than her parents. Trendon and I had just shared lunch with her and taken turns filling her in on our adventure.

"I can't believe it's true," Lisa whispered. "I mean,

you know, the whole bit about Noah's ark. You actually saw it?"

I nodded. "It wasn't like I expected, but it definitely was magnificent. Too bad we didn't really get a
chance to enjoy the view." I looked over at Trendon.
As if on cue, he held his hands up like bear claws and
made a pitiful howling noise.

Lisa shuddered. "I can't picture them."

"Picture what?" I asked.

"Those things. Those . . . animals you said attacked
you in the caves. What did they really look like?"

Trendon tugged a headphone bud from his ear. "It
was like a bunch of wolf men running around."

"That's not true," I said. "We don't know what they
really looked like. For all we know, they weren't scary
at all."

Trendon rolled his eyes and patted his chest where,
still visible beneath his T-shirt, we could see the outline of a thick white bandage. His gash had required
sixty-two stitches. "Yeah, not scary. You're probably
right." He glanced sideways at Lisa and mouthed the
words "wolf men" before returning the bud to his ear.

Lisa giggled. "Well, I'm really glad I wasn't there
to mess things up,"

"Don't say that. We could've used your help." I
glanced over to the many different bouquets of flowers
crowded together on the table next to the wall. Lisa's
parents had given her an arrangement of light blue
roses, lilies, and snapdragons that must have cost close
to a thousand dollars. Lisa shook her head and yawned.

"So what do your parents know?" I asked, lowering my voice.

"That I was hit by a truck," Lisa answered.

"And?"

"And that's it." Lisa rested the photographs of her surgery on her meal tray and rolled it away with her hand. "I haven't had time to really go into detail about anything. Besides, I'm not stupid. I know there needs to be some discretion."

Discretion. That was a good way to put it. I had been very selective about the information I had told my parents. It was too dangerous to reveal everything. Someone could have been listening. Luckily, my parents bought the whole study abroad program nonsense and really didn't ask too many more questions. Neither one of them had any clue their beloved daughter had been on the verge of death on multiple occasions during the past two weeks. And that suited me just fine.

We heard a knock on the door, and then Dorothy entered, carrying three bulging paper sacks.

"Hey, kids," she said. "I brought lunch," her eyes fell on the empty fast food cartons, "but it looks like you're not hungry."

Trendon yanked both ear buds out and snagged one of the bags in Dorothy's hand. When everyone in the room stared at him in disbelief, he merely shrugged. "What? I shared half my fries with Lisa."

Dorothy sat on the edge of the bed and patted Lisa's foot. "You feeling any better?"

Lisa smiled. "Yeah, Amber was just about to tell me more of the juicy details about those monsters in the cave." She looked at me grinning mischievously. "Come on, Amber. Quit holding out on me."

I hesitated and looked at Dorothy. "I don't know if I should. I mean, I don't even know that much. Maybe you could describe them."

Dorothy sighed and studied the monitor blipping all of Lisa's vitals in dull green numbers. "Amber's right. It's best we don't discuss them. I've never heard of an artifact being protected by guardians, and I honestly have no idea what kind of animal they were. They weren't supposed to be seen by anyone. It was as though our eyes were being prevented from seeing them." I shivered as I recalled the mysterious shroud blocking everything but the creatures' glowing eyes from our view. "Their sole purpose was to prevent anyone from coming in contact with the artifact."

I shifted uncomfortably in my chair. "But where are they now? I mean, we left that cave and those things had broken free from their prison. What will happen?"

"You shouldn't concern yourself about it, Amber. You've worried enough. And yes, Trendon, you may have another burger." Dorothy tossed one of the remaining bags to Trendon, who had been craning his neck and staring at the food longingly.

"You're the best," Trendon said through a mouthful of fries.

"What about Cabarles and his family?" I asked.

"They're fine—a little battered and frightened, but fine. The local authorities found Cabarles, his wife, and their daughter tied up and gagged in the walk-in closet of their master bedroom."

"So what happens next?" I asked. I was so curious to know the workings of Dorothy's secret society that it occupied most of my thinking. Sure, we had secured the Tebah Stick, and the Society of the Seraphic Scroll had locked it away in some super secure vault, but that meant nothing. Not with people as dangerous and powerful as Mr. Jasher still around, scheming a terrible new plan.

"What do you mean, what's next? You go home, enjoy the short summer break, and come back ready for an incredibly difficult semester in my class." Dorothy clapped her hands together in excitement. "I've reworked the curriculum. I think you'll be surprised at what I have in store for you."

"Come on, Ms. Holcomb, you know what I mean. What's next on the real agenda?" I cast a sideways glance toward Lisa, trying to lean forward and listen, despite the mess of tubes and receptors attached to her body.

Dorothy's eyes twinkled. "The artifact is the most powerful relic anyone in my society has ever come in contact with, and we have guarded many things over the years. Something this powerful is too danger-ous to leave alone, yet we're not really sure it can be destroyed, which would typically be our next option. It holds too much energy, and we may not have the necessary means to see to its complete destruction. You experienced first-hand the powerful effects the item can have on the one grasping it. How did it make you feel?"

I swallowed. "It's hard to describe. It was like I was invincible. I knew I couldn't be hurt and that whatever I wanted done would be carried out."

Dorothy watched me carefully, studying my eyes. "You will agree then that people like Kendell Jasher should never be allowed to handle it?"

"Absolutely not!" I said. "We have to protect it at all costs."

"We?" Dorothy smiled and crossed her arms. "Well, what would you suggest *we* do?"

I ran my tongue across the inside of my teeth. "Really? You want to know what I think?" She nodded. "Well, first you have to figure out the most efficient way to destroy the artifact. Like you said, it's too dangerous. And you also definitely have to keep tabs on Mr. Jasher. You know he's plotting something right now and trying to figure out how he was bested by a couple of fourteen-year-olds. But he's not the real threat."

"He's not?" Lisa asked. From his chair, Trendon halted his munching for a moment to listen.

I leaned in close and hushed my voice as best I could. "No, he's just a pawn. You need to solve the mystery of who his employer is. I got the feeling he's much more dangerous."

Dorothy giggled. "Spoken like a pro," she said.

"You're absolutely right on all of those suggestions. But to answer the last one, we've got somewhat of an idea of who he is."

My eyes widened. "Who is he?" I whispered. Lisa and Trendon waited for the answer as well.

Dorothy's eyes narrowed. She looked over her shoulder to check the door and smiled. "Oh, come on, you don't think you're going to get off that easily do you? After all the puzzles you've solved all by yourself, I wouldn't dream of insulting your intelligence by merely telling you something like that."

"Figures," Trendon said, not even attempting to muffle a burp. "What would summer vacation be like without an extra-credit assignment hanging over our heads?" He swatted his hand at Dorothy dismissively and unpaused his video game.

"That's not fair," Lisa whined. "How am I supposed to solve it? I missed half the show."

Dorothy sighed and checked her watch. "Now, now, if there's one thing you've learned from me it's that I don't shortchange your experience. Remember, riddles, though difficult, have already been answered at least once. Nothing towers out of the reach of your ability."

"You sound like a greeting card," Trendon said, wiping his nose with a greasy hand.

I began piecing clues together in my mind.

Dorothy must have recognized my look. "Atta girl!" she said. "Everything you need is in that amazing brain of yours." She got to her feet.

"I have one more question for you before you go," I said.

"Fire away."

"Did you have any idea what you were doing when you gave me this necklace a couple months ago?" I lifted the necklace with the locator stone out from under my shirt and showed it to Dorothy. Knowing now what it represented, I refused to remove the item of jewelry from around my neck.

Dorothy reached across and clasped the stone with her fingers, smiling. "I had a hunch you'd know what to do with this when the time came."

"Yeah, well, the time almost came too late. We were bobbing like a couple of turds in a toilet about to be flushed," Trendon said, licking grease from his fingers. Dorothy frowned at Trendon, who shrugged innocently. "What? All I'm saying is, you're a little too trusting."

"You're wrong, pal. I have full faith in Amber's abilities. You were always in safe hands." Dorothy winked at me.

"Still, you could've offered *me* something. I was the one that ended up nearly skewered."

"You're right. What would you say is a fair gift to give you for your devotion to the cause?" Dorothy asked, her eyes narrowing.

Trendon grunted. "Give me that last sack of food and we'll call it square."

"Deal." Dorothy gave each of us a hug and tousled Trendon's hair. "Good-bye, kiddos! See you in a few weeks."

"She's a strange woman," Trendon said as Dorothy exited the hospital room. He popped the last bite of his burger into his mouth.

"Watch it, Trendon. That's Dorothy Holcomb you're talking about," I warned. I continued to look at the locator stone strung around my neck.

"So who does Kendell Jasher really work for? And what connection does he have to the artifact?" Lisa asked.

I dropped the stone down my shirt and tapped my finger against my lips. "Well, his name is Mr. Baeloc, and he has some Biblical tie."

"Yeah, but don't we all descend from someone in the Bible?" Lisa asked.

"True. But that just makes the fact he's linked to a race of people in the Bible all the more interesting. Why is that important? And more significantly, what else can that fact tell us?" I chewed on my lower lip. "They're called the Qedet, which in Ancient Egyptian means Architect."

"Architect of what?"

"I wish I knew. I assume if you can figure that out, then you'd be able to figure out who he is."

Lisa yawned again and rubbed her temples. "I don't want to solve a mystery right now. My head's still throbbing. But I do have another question for you."

"What's that?"

Lisa fidgeted with her blanket. "Do you think Joseph will come back? Do you think we can ever really be friends again?"

I looked away. The questions caught me by surprise. I thought back to our last conversation and how Joseph helped us escape.

"I don't think he wants to," I said, my voice almost choking up.

"Are you sure about that?"

"Why do you ask?" I scratched at the skin below my eyes and fought back the urge to cry.

"Do you see that small bouquet of tulips over there on the table?" Lisa pointed, and I searched for the flowers she was referring to. In between two enormous baskets sat a tiny bucket with three yellow tulips barely budding. "That one's not for me." Lisa grinned.

I walked across the room and opened the card attached to the bucket. Inside I found a short message.

Amber, thanks for literally saving my life. —J

Something fluttered in my chest, and a salty tear plopped down onto the card. Could there still be hope? Maybe he'd be all right. Maybe, just maybe, our friendship could be like it had been before.

"Are you going to be okay?" Lisa asked.

I sniffed and wiped my eyes. "Yeah, I'll be fine."

"You see, there may just be a happy ending for him after all. His uncle just brainwashed him, that's all. It could've happened to anyone. When someone that powerful sets you up in an ivory tower and promises you heaven, you'd be surprised at how low you'd stoop to please him."

I nodded, slightly dazed. "Yeah, you're probably—"

I stopped, snapping back into reality. "What did you just say?"

"I said he was brainwashed."

"No, you said something about an ivory tower." I sprang off the bed and made my way around the chairs toward the desk under the window.

"Oh, it's just an expression," Lisa said.

I ignored her, too busy fumbling around in the drawers of the desk to listen.

"What's she looking for?" Trendon asked, noticing the commotion from across the room.

Lisa shook her head. "I don't know. Amber, what's wrong?"

I didn't answer, my mind too busy spinning with an idea. Lisa's expression was the second time someone had mentioned the word "tower" in the past few minutes, and now I felt positive Dorothy had meant to say it. Was it a clue?

"Yes!" I shouted, finding a copy of a Gideon's Bible in the bottom drawer. My fingers whipped through the pages excitedly, searching for the right verse.

"Yep, she's lost it," Trendon mumbled under his breath.

But I hadn't. My thoughts had never been so clear. I skimmed the verses containing the account of Noah's ark and stopped a few chapters later. Genesis 11:4:

> *And they said, Go to, let us build us a city and a tower, whose top may reach unto heaven; and let us make us a name, lest we be scattered abroad upon the face of the whole earth.*

I looked up from the passage, trying to smile, but a sudden icicle of fear burrowed in my heart. The Architects had built the Tower of Babel.

Acknowledgments

There are so many people to thank who helped make this dream a reality. First off, I have to thank my wife and most dedicated supporter, Heidi. Without her . . . forget about it. Thanks to my three children for always loving my stories and placing me on a pedestal. Thank you to my mom and dad for believing this could happen. And to my brother, Michael, and my sister, Jennifer, for their constant excitement and enthusiasm.

I'm grateful for an amazing publisher who believes in my writing. Lyle, Lee, Liz, and Jennifer: You truly are awesome! For my editor, Heidi Doxey, who pushed me harder than I thought possible with this book. It turned out great! For my illustrator, Mark McKenna. You drew my characters spot on and made them come to life. Thank you!

I'm thankful for so many friends who listened to me drone on and on with storytelling and still invited me back for dinner parties.

To my friends at all the Barnes & Noble bookstores and Deseret Book stores. Your words matter, so please continue to spread the word! To the thousands of students, teachers, and librarians I've met along the way: Thank you for being such avid readers and supporters. You're the reason I'm able to do this, and I hope to continue for many years.